THE MAN-EATER OF MALGUDI

R. K. NARAYAN

The
Man-Eater
of
Malgudi

1961

THE VIKING PRESS

NEW YORK

Published in 1961 by The Viking Press, Inc.
625 Madison Avenue, New York 22, N.Y.

Library of Congress catalog card number: 61-5919

Printed in the U.S.A. by Vail-Ballou Press

THE MAN-EATER OF MALGUDI

Chapter One

I could have profitably rented out the little room in front of my press. On Market Road, with a view of the fountain, it was coveted by every would-be shopkeeper in our town; I was considered a fool for not getting my money's worth out of it, while all the space I needed for my press and its personnel was at the back, beyond the blue curtain. I could not explain myself to sordid calculating folk. I hung a framed picture of Goddess Laxmi poised on her lotus and holding aloft the bounties of earth in her four hands, and through her grace I did not do too badly. My son, little Babu, went to Albert Mission School and felt adequately supplied with toys, books, sweets, and other odds and ends that he fancied from time to time. My wife gave herself a new silk sari, glittering with lace, every Deepavali, not to mention the ones acquired for no particular reason at other times. She kept the pantry well stocked and our kitchen fire aglow, continuing the traditions of our ancient home in Kabir Street.

I had furnished my parlor with a high-backed chair made of teakwood, Queen Anne style as claimed by the auctioneer who had sold it to my grandfather, a roll-top desk supported on bow legs with ivy vine carved on them, and four other seats of varying heights and shapes.

Anyone whose feet ached while passing Market Road was welcome to rest in my parlor, filling any seat that happened to be vacant at the time. Resting there, people got ideas and allowed me to print their bill forms, visiting cards, or wedding invitations. But there also came in a lot of others whose visit did not mean a paisa to me. Among my constant companions was a poet who was writing the life of God Krishna in monosyllabic verse. His ambition was to compose a grand epic, and he came almost every day to recite to me his latest lines. My admiration for him was unbounded. I felt thrilled to hear clear lines such as "Girls with girls did dance in trance," and I felt equally thrilled when I had to infer the meaning of certain lines, as when he totally failed to find a monosyllable but achieved his end by ruthlessly carving up a polysyllabic word. On such occasions even the most familiar term took on the mysterious quality of a private code language. Invariably, in deference to his literary attainments, I let him occupy the Queen Anne chair. I sat perched on the edge of my roll-top desk. In the other best seat, a deep basket in cane, you would find Sen the journalist, who came to read the newspaper on my table and held forth on the mistakes Nehru was making. These two men and a few others remained in their seats even at six in the evening when the press was silenced. It was not necessary that I should be present or attend to them in any manner. They were also good enough, without being told, to vacate their chairs and disappear when anyone came to discuss business.

Between my parlor and the press hung a blue curtain. No one tried to peer through it. When I shouted for the foreman, compositor, office boy, binder, or accountant, people imagined a lot of men on the other side, although if it came to a challenge I should have had to go in and play the ventriloquist. But my neighbor, the Star Press, had all the staff one might dream of, and if any customer of mine insisted on seeing machinery, I led him not past my curtain but right next door to Star, whose original Heidelberg I displayed to everyone with pride, and whose double cylinder I made out to be a real acquisition (although in my personal view that man made a mistake in buying it, as its groans could be heard beyond the railway yard when forms were being printed).

The owner of the Star was a nice man, a good friend, but he hardly ever got customers. How could he, when all the time they were crowding my parlor, even though I could offer them nothing more than an assortment of chairs and a word of welcome? But few ever having stepped beyond the blue curtain, everyone imagined me equipped for big tasks, which I certainly attempted with the help of my well-wisher (I dare not call him staff) Sastri, the old man who set up type, printed the forms four pages at a time on the treadle, sewed the sheets, and carried them for ruling or binding to Kandan four streets off. I lent him a hand in all departments whenever he demanded my help and my visitors left me alone. On the whole I was a busy man, and such business as I could not take up I passed on next door to be done on original Heidelberg. I was so free with the Star that no one knew whether I owned it or whether it owned me.

I lived in Kabir Street, which ran behind Market Road. My day started before four in the morning. The streets would be dark when I set out for the river for my ablutions, with the municipal lamps flickering (if they had not run out of oil) here and there in our street. I went down Kabir Street, cut through a flagged alley at the end of it, trespassed into the compound of the Taluk Office through a gap in its bramble fence, and there I was by the river.

I had well-defined encounters all along the way. The milk man, starting on his rounds, driving ahead a puny white cow, greeted me respectfully and asked, "What is the time, master?"—a question that I allowed to die without a reply as I carried no watch. I simpered and let him pass, suppressing the question, Tell me the secret of your magic: how you manage to extract milk-like product out of that miserable cow-like creature to supply thirty families as you do every morning? . . . What exactly are you, conjurer or milk-vender? The old asthmatic at the end of our street sat up on the *pyol* of his house and gurgled through his choking throat, "Didn't get a wink of sleep all night, and already it's morning and you are out! That's life, I suppose!" The watchman at Taluk Office called from beneath his rug, "Is that you?"—the only question deserving a reply. "Yes, it's me," I always said and passed on.

I had my own spot at the riverside, immediately behind the Taluk Office. I shunned the long flight of steps farther down: they were always crowded; if I went there I was racked with the feeling of dipping into other people's baths; but this point upstream was exclusive, in my view. Over the bank of the river loomed a palmyra tree, from which dangled mud pots. Toddy dripped into them through a gash in the bark of the tree, fermented, stank to the skies, and was gathered in barrels and sold to the patrons congregated at the eighteen taverns scattered in the four corners of the city, where any evening one could see revelers fighting or rolling in gutters. So much for the potency of the fluid dripping into the pots. I never looked up the palmyra without a shudder. "With this monopoly of tavern-running Sankunni builds his mansions in New Extension and rides his four American cars driven by uniformed chauffeurs." But I was unable to get away from the palmyra myself.

At the foot of the tree was a slab of stone on which I washed by dhoti and towel, the dark hour resounding with the tremendous beating of wet cloth on granite. I stood in waist-deep water, and at the touch of cold water around my body I felt elated. The trees on the bank stood like shadows in the dusk. When the east glowed I sat for a moment on the sand, reciting a prayer to the Sun to illumine my mind. The signal for breaking off contemplation was the jingle of ox-bells as country carts forded Nallappa's grove, bringing loads of vegetables, corn, and fuel from nearby villages to the market. I rose and retraced my steps, rolling up my washing into a tight pack.

I had some more encounters on my way back. My cousin from the fourth street gave me a cold look and passed. She hated me for staying in our ancestral home, my father having got it as his share after the division of property among his brothers. She never forgave us, although it had all happened in my father's time. Most of the citizens of this area were now moving sleepily toward the river, and everyone had a word for me. One was the lawyer known as the adjournment lawyer for his ability to prolong a case beyond the wildest dream of a litigant, a sparse, hungry-looking man who shaved his chin once a fortnight. He cried the moment he saw me, "Where is your bed? Unless you have slept on the river how can you be *returning* at this unearthly hour?" When I saw him at a distance I cried to myself, "I am undone. Mr. Adjournment will get me now."

There was one whom I did not really mind meeting, the septuagenarian living in a dilapidated outhouse in Adam's Lane, who owned a dozen houses in our locality, lived on rent, and sent off postal money orders to distant corners of the Indian subcontinent, where his progeny was spread out. He always stopped to give me news of his relations. He looked like a newborn infant when he bared his gums in a smile. "You are late today," I always said, and waited for his explanation; "I sat up late writing letters, you know how it is with all one's children scattered far and wide." I did not mind tarrying to listen to the old man, although my fingers felt cramped with encircling the wad of wet clothes I was carrying home to dry. The old man referred to four sons and their doings, and five daughters, and countless grandchildren. He was always busy, on one hand attending to the repairs of his dozen houses, about which one or the other of his tenants always pursued him; on the other, writing innumerable letters on postcards, guiding, blessing, admonishing, or spoiling with a re-mittance of cash, one or the other of his wards.

I was content to live in our house as it had been left by my father. I was a youth, studying in Albert Mission, when the legal division of ancestral property occurred be-tween my father and his brothers. I well remember the day when his four brothers marched out with their wives and children, trundling away their shares of heirlooms, knickknacks, and household articles. Everything that could be divided into five was cut up into equal parts and one was given to each. Such things as could not be split up were given to those that clamored the loudest. A rattan easy chair on which my grandfather used to lie in the courtyard, always watching the sky, was claimed by my second uncle, whose wife had started all the furore over the property. She also claimed a pair of rosewood benches which shone with a natural polish, and a timber chair that used to be known as a bug-proof chair. My father's third brother claimed, as compensation for letting these items go, a wooden almirah and a "leg" harmonium operated by a pedal, which was also being claimed by another uncle whose daughter was supposed to possess musical talent. This harmonium had gathered dust in a corner for decades without anyone noticing it. No one had even asked how it had come to find a place in our home, although a little family research would have yielded the information that our grandfather had lent a hundred rupees to a local dramatic troupe and attached their harmonium, as their only movable property, after a court decree, lugged it home, and kept it in a corner of our hall, but had died before he could sell it and realize its value. His successors took the presence of the harmonium in that corner of the hall for granted until this moment of separation.

All of the four brothers of my father, with their wives and children, numbering fifteen, had lived under the same roof for many years. It was my father's old mother who had kept them together, acting as a cohesive element among the members of the family. Between my grandmother, who laid down the policy, and a person called Grand-Auntie, who actually executed it, the family administration ran smoothly. When my grandmother died the unity of the family was also gone. The trouble started with my father's second brother's wife, who complained loudly one day, standing in the passage of the house, that her children had been ill-treated. She made out that she was steadily hated by everyone, and her cause was upheld by her husband. Soon other differences appeared among the brothers and their wives, although all the children continued to play in the open courtyard, unmindful of the attitude of the elders to one another. Before the year was out, actually on a festival day, they had the biggest open quarrel, provoked by a minor incident in which an eight-year-old boy knocked down another and snatched a biscuit from his mouth. The mother of the injured child slapped the offender on his bare seat, and a severe family crisis developed.

My father and his brothers were sitting around, eating their midday meal. My father muttered mildly, "If Mother were alive she would have handled everyone and prevented such scenes." Two of the brothers, incensed at the event, got up without touching their food. My father commented, without looking at anyone in particular, "You need not abandon your food. This is a sacred day. Such things should not be allowed to happen."

My mother, who was bending over his leaf serving ghee, whispered, "Why don't you mind your business? They are not babies to be taught how to conduct themselves on a festive day." My father accepted her advice without a word and resolved at that moment to break up the joint family in the interests of peace.

The next few days saw our family lawyers, assisted by the adjournment expert, walking in and out with papers to be signed, and within a few weeks the house had become empty. It had been a crowded house since the day it was built by my father's grandfather, with numerous children, womenfolk, cousins, relations, and guests milling in and out, and now it became suddenly bare and empty.

The household then consisted of my parents, Grand-Auntie, me, and my two sisters. My brother was away in Madras in a college hostel. As my father grew older he began to spend all his time sitting on the *pyol*, on a mat, reading *Ramayana* or just watching the street. Even at night he never went beyond the *pyol*. He placed a small pillow under his head and stretched himself there. He hardly ever visited the other parts of this immense house. Occasionally he wandered off to the back yard to pluck the withered leaves off a citrus tree which had been his favorite plant. It had been growing for years; no one knew whether it was an orange or a lime tree. It kept people guessing, never displaying on its branches anything more than a few white flowers now and then. This plant was my father's only concern. He hardly ever looked up at the six tall coconut trees that waved in the sky. They were my mother's responsibility and Grand-Auntie's, who regularly had their tops cleared of beetles and withered shoots, sent up a climber once a month, and filled the granary with large ripe coconuts. There were also pumpkins growing in the back yard, and large creepers covered the entire thatched roof of a cowshed which once, years before, used to house four of Malgudi's best-bred cows.

After my father's death my mother lived with me until Babu was a year old, and then she decided to go and live with my brother at Madras, taking away with her her life-companion, Grand-Auntie. And I, with my wife and little Babu, became the sole occupant of our house in Kabir Street.

Chapter Two

Sastri had to go a little earlier than usual since he had to perform a *puja* at home. I hesitated to let him go. The three-color labels (I prided myself on the excellence of my color printing) for K.J.'s aerated drinks had to be readied. It was a piece of very serious work for me, although my personal view was that the colored ink I used on the label was safer for a drink than the tints that K.J. let into his water-filled bottles. We had already printed the basic color on the labels, and the second was to be imposed today. This was generally a crucial stage of work, and I wanted Sastri to stay on and finish the job.

He said, "Perhaps I can stay up late tonight and finish it. Not now. Meanwhile will you . . ." He allotted me work until he should be back at two o'clock. I had been engrossed in a talk with the usual company. Nehru's third Five-Year Plan was on the agenda today, and my friend Sen was seeing nothing but ruin in it for the country. "Three hundred crores—actually are we counting heads or money?" His audience consisted of myself and the poet and someone else who had come to ask for quotations for a business card. The discussion was warming up, as the visiting-card client was a Congress man

who had gone to prison fourteen times since the day
Mahatma Gandhi arrived in India from South Africa. He
ignored for the time being the business that had brought
him here and plunged into a debate, settling himself in-
exorably in a corner. "What's wrong with the people is
you have got into the habit of blaming everything on the
government. You think that democracy means that if
there is no sugar in the shop, government is responsible
for it. What if there is no sugar? You won't die if you do
not have sugar for your morning coffee some days." Sen
disputed every word of the patriot's speech.

I listened to the debate until I noticed Sastri's silhouette
beyond the curtain. Sastri, when there was any emergency,
treated me as a handy boy; I had no alternative but to
accept the role. Now my duty would be to fix the block
on the machine and put the second impression on all the
labels and spread them out to dry—and then he would
come and give the third impression and put out the labels
to dry again. He explained some of the finer points: "The
blocks are rather worn; you'll have to let in more ink."

"Yes, Mr. Sastri."

He looked at me through his silver-rimmed small glasses
and said firmly, "Unless the labels are second-printed and
dry by three o'clock today, it's going to be impossible to
deliver them tomorrow. You know what kind of a man
K.J. is. . . ."

What about my lunch? This man did not care whether
I had time for food or not—a tyrant when it came to
printing labels, no consideration of working conditions.
But there was no way of protesting to him. He would
brush everything aside. As if reading my mind, he explained, "I'd not trouble you but for the fact that this

satyanarayana puja must be performed today in my house. My children and wife will be looking for me at the door. . . ." He'd have to trot all the way to Vinayak Street if his family was not to starve too long. Wife, children. Absurd, I felt; such encumbrances were not necessary for Sastri. They were for lesser men like me. His place was at the type board and the treadle. He produced an incongruous, unconvincing picture as a family man. But I dared not express myself aloud. The relationship of employer and employee was getting reversed now and then, whenever there was an emergency. I accepted it without any fuss.

According to house custom, my friends would not step beyond the curtain, so I was safe to go ahead with the second impression. Sastri had fixed everything. I had only to press the pedal and push the paper onto the pad. On a pale orange ground I was now to impose a sort of violet. I grew hypnotized by the sound of the wheel and the machine that was set in motion by the pressure I put on the pedal. I could hear, whenever I paused, Sen's voice: "If Nehru were practical, let him disown the Congress. . . . Why should you undertake projects which you can't afford? Anyway, in ten years what are we going to do with all the steel?"

There was a lull. I wondered if they were suddenly struck dumb. I heard the shuffling of feet. I felt relieved that the Third Plan was done with. Now an unusual thing happened. The curtain stirred, an edge of it lifted, and the monosyllablist's head peeped in. There must be some extraordinary situation to make him do that. His eyes bulged. "Someone to see you," he whispered.

"Who is he? What does he want?"

"I don't know."

Whispered conversation was becoming a strain. I shook my head and winked and grimaced to indicate to the poet that he should take himself out and say that I was not available. The poet, ever a dense fellow, did not understand but kept blinking unintelligently. Then his head suddenly vanished, and at the same moment a new head appeared in its place—a tanned face, large powerful eyes under thick eyebrows, large forehead and a shock of unkempt hair over it, like a black halo. My first impulse was to cry out, Whoever you may be, why don't you brush your hair down?

The new visitor had evidently pushed or pulled aside the poet before showing himself to me. Before I could open my mouth, he asked, "You be Nataraj?"

I nodded, and he came forward, practically tearing aside the curtain, an act that violated the sacred traditions of my press. I said, "Why don't you kindly take a seat in the next room, I'll be with you in a moment?"

He paid no attention. He stepped forward, extending his hand. I hastily wiped my fingers on a rag, muttering, "Sorry, discolored, been working . . ."

He gave me a hard grip. My entire hand disappeared into his fist—he was a large man, about six feet tall and quite slim proportionately, but his bull neck and hammer fist revealed his true stature.

"Shan't we move to the other room?" I asked again.

"Not necessary. It's all the same to me," he said. "You are doing something; why don't you go on? It won't bother me." He eyed my colored labels. "What are they?"

I didn't want any eyes to watch my special color effects and how I achieved them. I moved to the curtain and parted it courteously for him. He followed me. I showed him the Queen Anne chair. I sat in my usual place, on the edge of my desk, and now regained the feeling of being master of the situation. I adopted my best smile and asked, "Well, what can I do for you, Mr. . . . ?"

"Vasu," he said, and added, "I knew you didn't catch my name. You were saying something at the same time as I was mentioning my name."

I felt abashed to hear it, and covered it, I suppose, with another of those silly smiles. I checked myself suddenly, feeling angry with this man for creating so much un-easiness in my mind, asked myself, Nataraj, are you afraid of this muscular fellow? and said authoritatively, "Yes?"—as much as to indicate, You have wasted my time sufficiently; now say whatever you may want to say.

He took from his inner pocket a wad of paper, searched for a handwritten sheet, and held it out to me. "Five hundred copies of notepaper, the finest, and five hundred visiting cards."

I spread out the sheet without a word and read, "H. Vasu, M.A., Taxidermist." I grew interested. My irrita-tion left me. This was the first time I had set eyes on a taxidermist. I said, assuming the friendliest tone, "Five hundred! Are you sure you need five hundred visiting cards? Could you not print them one hundred at a time? They'll be fresh."

"Why do you try to advise me?" he asked pugnaciously. "I know how many I need. I'm not printing my visiting cards in order to preserve them in a glass case."

"All right, I can print ten thousand if you want."

He softened at my show of aggressiveness. "Fine, fine, that's the right spirit."

"If you'd like to have it done on original Heidelberg—"

"Look. I don't care what you do it on. I don't know what you are talking about."

I understood the situation; every other sentence was likely to bristle and prove provocative. I began to feel intrigued by this man. I didn't want to lose him. Even if I wanted to be rid of him, I had no means of getting rid of him. He had sought me out, and I'd have to have him until he decided to leave. I might as well be friendly. "Surely, whatever you like. It's my duty to ask, that's all. Some people prefer it."

"What is it, anyway?" he asked, suddenly interested.

I explained the greatness of Heidelberg and where it was. He thought it over and suddenly called, "Nataraj, I trust you to do your best for me. I have come to you as a friend."

I was surprised and flattered.

He explained, "I'm new to this place, but I heard about you within an hour of coming." He mentioned some obscure source of information. "Well, I never give a second thought to these things," he said. "When I like a man, I like him, that's all."

I wanted to ask about taxidermy. So I said, looking at his card, "Taxidermist? Must be an interesting job. Where is your er . . . office, or . . ."

"Right here I hope to make a start. I was in Junagadh —you know the place—and there I grew interested in this art. I came across a master there, one Suleiman. When he stuffed a lion—you know, Junagadh is one place where we have lions—he could make it look more terrifying than it would be in the jungle. His stuffings go all over the world. He was a master, and he taught me the art. After all, we are civilized human beings, educated and cultured, and it is up to us to prove our superiority to nature. Science conquers nature in a new way each day; why not in creation also? That's my philosophy, sir. I challenge any man to contradict me." He became maudlin at the thought of Suleiman, his master, and sighed. "He was a saint. He taught me his art sincerely."

"Where did you get your M.A.?"

"At Madras, of course. You want to know about me?"

I wonder what he would have done if I had said, "No, I prefer to go home and eat my food." He would probably have held me down and said, "You'll damn well listen."

"I was educated in the Presidency College. I took my master's degree in history, economics, and literature." That was in the year 1931. Then he had joined the civil disobedience movement against British Rule, broken the laws, marched, demonstrated, and ended in jail. He went repeatedly to prison and once when he was released found himself in the streets of Nagpur. There he met a *phaelwan* at a show. "That man could have a half-ton stone slab on his cheek and have it split by hammer strokes, he could snap steel chains, and he would hit a block of hard granite with his fist and pulverize it. I was young then; his strength appealed to me. I was prepared to become his disciple at any cost. I introduced myself to the *phaelwan*."

He remained thoughtful for a while and then went on, "I learned everything from this master. The training was unsparing. He woke me up at three o'clock every morning and put me through exercises. And he provided me with the right diet. I had to eat a hundred almonds every morning and wash them down with half a *seer* of milk; two hours later six eggs with honey; at lunch chicken and rice, at night vegetables and fruit. Not everyone can hope to have this diet, but I was lucky in finding a man who enjoyed stuffing me like that.

"In six months I could understudy for him. The first time I banged my fist on the century-old door of a house in Lucknow, the three-inch panel of seasoned teak splintered. My master patted me on my back and cried with tears of joy in his eyes, 'You are growing on the right lines, my boy.'

"In a few months I could also snap chains, twist iron bars, and pulverize granite. We traveled all over the country and gave our shows at every market fair in the villages and town halls in the cities, and *he* made a lot of money. Gradually he grew flabby and lazy and let me do everything. They announced his name on the notice, but actually I did all the twisting and smashing of stone, iron, and whatnot. When I spoke to him about it, he called me an ungrateful dog and other names and tried to push me out. I resisted, and"— Vasu laughed at the recollection of this incident— "I knew his weak spot and hit him there with the edge of my palm with a chopping movement, and he fell down and squirmed on the floor. I knew he could perform no more. I left him there and walked out and gave up the strong man's life once for all."

"You didn't stop to help him?" I asked.

"I helped him by leaving him alone, instead of holding him upside down and rattling the teeth out of his head."

"Oh, no," I cried, horrified. "You couldn't do that!"

"Why not? I was a different man now, not the boy who went to him for charity. I was stronger than he."

"After all, he taught you how to be strong—he was your guru," I said, enjoying the thrill of provoking him.

"Damn it all!" he cried. "He made money out of me, don't you see?"

"But he also gave you six eggs a day and how much milk and almond was it?"

He threw up his arms in vexation. "Oh, you will never understand these things, Nataraj. Don't talk of all that. You know nothing, you have not seen the world. You know only what happens in this miserable little place."

"If you think this place miserable, why do you choose to come here?" I was nearer the inner door; I could dash away if he attempted to grab me. Within this brief time familiarity was making me rash and headstrong. I enjoyed taunting him.

"You think I have come here out of admiration for this miserable city. Know this, I'm here because of Mempi Forest and the jungles in those hills. I'm a taxidermist. I have to be where wild animals live."

"And die," I added.

He appreciated my joke and laughed. "You are a wise guy," he said admiringly.

"You haven't told me yet why or how you became a taxidermist," I reminded him.

"Hm!" he said. "Don't get too curious. Let us do business first. When are you giving me the visiting cards?" he asked. "Tomorrow?"

He might pulverize granite, smash up his guru with a slicing stroke, but where printing work was concerned I was not going to be pushed. I got up and turned the sheets of a tear-off calendar on the wall. "You could come tomorrow and ask me. I'll be able to discuss this matter only tomorrow. My staff is out today."

At this moment my little son Babu came running in,

crying, "Appa!" and halted his steps abruptly on seeing a stranger. He bit his nails, grinned, and tried to turn and run. I shot out my hand and held him. He was friendly with the usual crowd at my press, but this stranger's presence somehow embarrassed him. I knew why he had come; it must be either to ask for a favor such as permission to go out with his friends or to deliver a message from his mother.

"What is it?" I asked.

"Mother says, aren't you coming home for food? She is hungry."

"So am I," I said, "and if I were Mother I wouldn't wait for Father. Understand me? Here is a gentleman with whom I am engaged on some important business. You know what he can do?" My tone interested Babu, and he looked up expectantly.

Vasu made a weary gesture, frowned, and said, "Oh, stop that, Mr. Nataraj. Don't start it all. I don't want to be introduced to anyone. Now, you go away, boy," he said authoritatively.

"He is my son—" I began.

"I see that," Vasu said indifferently, and Babu wriggled himself free and ran off.

Vasu did not come next day, but appeared again fifteen days later. He arrived in a jeep.

"Long time you have been away," I said.

"You thought you were rid of me?" he asked; and, thumping his chest, "I never forget."

"And I never remember," I said. Somehow this man's presence roused in me a sort of pugnacity.

He stepped in, saw the Queen Anne chair occupied by

the poet, and remarked half-jokingly, "That's my chair, I suppose." The poet scrambled to his feet and moved to another seat. "Hm, that's better," Vasu said, sitting down. He smiled patronizingly at the poet and said, "I haven't been told who you are."

"I'm—I'm—a teacher in that school."

"What do you teach?" he asked relentlessly.

"Well, history, geography, science, English—well, anything the boys must know."

"Hm, an all-rounder," Vasu said. I could see the poet squirming. He was a mild, inoffensive man who was unused to such rough contacts. But Vasu seemed to enjoy bothering a mild man like that. I rushed in to his rescue. I wanted to add to his stature by saying, "He is a poet. He is nominally a teacher, but actually—"

"I never read poetry; no time," said Vasu promptly and dismissed the man from his thoughts. He turned to me and asked, "Where are my cards?"

I had a seasoned answer for such a question. "Where were you this whole fortnight?"

"Away, busy."

"So was I," I said.

"You promised to give me the cards—"

"When?" I asked.

"Next day," he said.

I told him that there had been no such promise.

He raised his voice and I raised mine. He asked finally, "Are we here on business or for a fight? If it's a fight, tell me. I like a fight. Can't you see, man, why I am asking for my cards?"

"But don't you see that we have our own business

practice?" I always adopted "we" whenever I had to speak
for the press.

"What do you mean by that?" he asked aggressively.

"We never choose the type and stationery for a customer. It must always be the customer's responsibility."

"You never told me that," he cried.

"You remember I asked you to come next day. That was
my purpose. I never say anything without a purpose."

"Why couldn't you have mentioned it on the same day?"

"You have a right to ask," I said, feeling it was time to
concede him something. The poet was looking scared by
these exchanges. He was essaying to get out. But I
motioned him to stay. Why should this poor man be frightened out?

"You have not answered my question," said Vasu. "Why
couldn't you have shown me samples of type on the first
day itself?"

I said curtly, "Because my staff was out."

"Oh!" he said, opening his eyes wide. "I didn't know
you had a staff."

I ignored his remark and shouted, "Sastri! Please bring
those ivory card samples and also the ten-point copper-
plate." I told Vasu grandly, "Now you can indicate your
preferences, and we will try to give you the utmost satisfaction."

Sastri, with his silver-rimmed glasses on his nose,
entered, bearing a couple of blank cards and a specimen
type-book. He paused just for a second, studying the
visitor, placed them on the table, turned, and disappeared
into the curtain.

"How many are employed in this press?" Vasu asked.

This man's curiosity was limitless and recognized no proprieties. I felt enraged. Was he a labor commissioner or something of that kind? I replied, "As many as I need. But, you know, the present-day labor conditions are not very encouraging. But Mr. Sastri is very dependable; he has been with me for years." I handed him the cards and said, "You will have to choose. These are the best cards available now." I handed him the type-book. "Tell me what type you like."

That paralyzed him. He turned the cards between his fingers, he turned the leaves of the type-book, and cried, "I'm damned if I know what I want. They all look alike to me. What is the difference, anyway?"

This was a triumph for me. "Vasu, the printing business is an intricate one. That's why we don't take the responsibility in these matters."

"Oh, please do something and print me my cards," he cried, exasperated.

"All right," I said grandly. "I'll do it for you, if you trust me . . ."

"I trust you as a friend; otherwise I would not have come to you."

"Actually," I said, "I welcome friends, not customers. I'm not a fellow who cares for money. If anyone comes to me for pure business, I send them over to my neighbor and they are welcome to get their work done cheaper and on a better machine—original Heidelberg."

"Oh, stop that original Heidel," he cried impatiently. "I want to hear no more of it. Give me my cards. My business arrangements are waiting on that, and remember also five hundred letterheads."

Chapter Three

An attic above my press was full of discarded papers, stacks of old newspaper, files of dead correspondence and accounts, manuscripts, and, above all, a thousand copies of a school magazine which I used to print and display as my masterpiece and which I froze in the attic when the school could not pay the printing charges. I called up a old-paper buyer who was crying for custom in the streets. I sent him up the rickety staircase to make a survey and tell me his offer. This was an old Moslem who carried a sack on his back and cried, "Old paper, empty bottles," tramping the streets all afternoon.

"Be careful," I told him, sending him up the stairs to estimate. "There may be snakes and scorpions in that place. No human being has set foot there for years." Later, when I heard his steps come down, I prepared myself for the haggling phase by stiffening my countenance and assuming a grave voice. He parted the curtain, entered my parlor, and stood respectfully pressing his back close to the wall and waiting to be asked.

"Well, have you examined?"

"Yes, sir, most of the paper is too old and is completely brown."

"Surely you did not expect me to buy the latest editions for your benefit; or did you expect me to buy white paper in reams and sell it to you by weight?" I said with heavy sarcasm, and it softened him sufficiently to say, "I didn't say so. . . ." And then he made his offer. I ignored it completely as not being worth a man's notice.

At this point, if he really found my attitude unacceptable, he should have gone away, but he stayed, and that was a good sign. I was looking through the proofs of a cinema program, and I suddenly went in to attend to some item of work inside the press. When I came out nearly an hour later, he was still there, sitting on the doorstep.

"Still here!" I cried, feigning astonishment. "By all means rest here if you like, but don't expect me to waste any more time talking to you. I don't have to sell all that paper at all. I can keep it as I have kept it for years."

He fidgeted uneasily and said, "The paper is brown and cracks. Please have consideration for me, sir, I have to make one or two rupees every day in order to bring up my family of . . ." He went into details of his domestic budget: how he had to find the money for his children's schoolbooks, food and medicine, and rent, by collecting junk from every house and selling it to dealers in junk for a small margin of profit, often borrowing money at the start of a day. After hearing him out, I relented enough to mention a figure, at which he picked up his sack and pretended to go. Then I mitigated my demand, he raised his offer, and this market fluctuation went on till three o'clock. Sastri came at three with a frown on his face, understood in a moment what was going on, and muttered, "Sometimes it's better to throw away all old

paper under a boiler to save firewood than sell it to these
fellows. They always try to cheat"—thus lending support
to my position.

Presently Vasu arrived in his jeep and opened his valise,
mumbling, "Let me note something before I forget." He
sat in the Queen Anne chair, took out a sheet of paper,
and wrote something. Both of us, the parties to the old-
paper transaction, watched him silently. A truck was
passing down the road, raising a blanket of cloud; a couple
of *jutkas* were rattling along on their wooden wheels; a
couple of vagrants had stretched themselves upon the
parapet of the fountain to enjoy a siesta; a little boy was
watching his lamb graze a sort of lawn that the municipality was struggling to cultivate on the fringe of the
fountain; a crow sat on the jet of the fountain, hopefully
looking for a drop of water—an ideal hour for a transaction in junk. Vasu stopped writing and asked, "What's
going on?"

I turned to the old-paper man and said, "You know who
he is? I'll have to explain to him if I give away too cheap."

Vasu raised his eyes from the paper, glared at the
Moslem, and asked, "What are you supposed to be doing?
Have a care!"

The trader grew nervous and said, "My final offer, sir.
It's getting late; if I get nothing here I must at least find
another place for my business today."

"All right, go," I said. "I'm not stopping you."

"Twenty-five rupees, sir."

"If this gentleman approves," I said. Vasu seemed
pleased at this involvement. He tapped the table and
hummed and hawed.

The ragman appealed to him. "I'm a poor man. Don't squeeze me. If I invest it—"

Vasu suddenly got up, saying, "Let's have a look at your loot, anyway," and, led by the Moslem, passed beyond the curtain and clambered upstairs. I was surprised to see Vasu enter the spirit of the game so completely.

Presently the Moslem came down with a pile of paper and took it to the front step. He came up to me, holding twenty-five rupees in currency, his face beaming: "That master has agreed." He made three more trips upstairs and barricaded my entrance with old paper. He beckoned to a *jutka* passing and loaded all the bundles in it.

I asked, "Where is that man?"

"He is up there."

"What's he doing there?"

"I don't know. He was trying to open the windows."

Presently Vasu called me. "Nataraj, come up."

"Why?" I cried. I was busy with the cinema program.

He repeated his command, and I went up. I had not gone upstairs for years. The wooden stairs creaked and groaned, unused to the passage of feet. There was a small landing and a green door, and you stepped into the attic. Vasu was standing in the middle of it like a giant. He had opened a little wooden window giving on a view of the fountain, over the market road. Beyond it was a small door opening on a very narrow terrace southward, which looked on to the neighboring roof tiles. The floor was littered with paper; age-old dust covered everything.

Vasu was fanning around his ears with a cover page of the school magazine. "That man has done you a service in carrying away all that old paper, but he has dehoused a thousand mosquitoes—one thing I can't stand." He was vigorously fanning them off as they tried to buzz about his ears. "Night or day, I run when mosquito is mentioned."

"Let us go down," I said, flourishing my arms, unable to stand their attack around my head.

"Wait a minute," he said. "What do you propose to do with this place?"

I ruminated for a moment; I had no plans for it, but before I could say so he said, "I'll clean it all up and stay here for a while. I like a place where I can throw my things and stay. The important thing will be to get a mosquito net for sleeping in, a bed, and one or two chairs. The roof comes down too low," he said, looking up. He swung his arms up and down and said, "Still a couple of feet above my arms, not bad."

I gave him no reply. I had never viewed it as a habitable place. He asked, "Why are you silent?"

"Nothing, nothing," I said. "I shall have to . . ."

"What?" he asked mercilessly. "Don't tell me you want to consult your seniors or partners, the usual dodge. I will stay here till a bungalow is vacated for me in New Extension. I couldn't dream of settling here. So don't be afraid. After all you are going to put junk into it again." For a fortnight or more he'd been house-hunting.

I gave him no reply and went down to my office. He followed me down, drove away in his jeep, returned an hour later with four workmen, carrying brooms and buckets. He led them past the curtain, up the stairs. I heard him shouting and bullying them and I heard the mops and brooms at work. He discovered the water closet below the staircase and made them carry buckets of water and scrub the floor. Next day he brought in a building worker and spent the whole day washing the walls of the attic with lime. He passed in and out and hardly found the time for a word with me. I watched him come and go. Two days later he brought a bedstead and a few odd pieces of furniture.

As I found it a nuisance to have Vasu and his minions pass up and down through the press, I opened a side-gate in the compound, which admitted his jeep from Kabir lane into a little yard and gave him direct access to the wooden stairs. It took me another week to realize that, without a word from me, Vasu had established himself in the attic. "After all," I philosophized to myself, "it's a junkroom, likely to get filled again with rubbish. Why not let him stay there until he finds a house?"

He disappeared for long periods—I had no idea where he went—and then suddenly dropped in. Sometimes he just came and lounged in my parlor. My other visitors found it difficult to cope with his bullying talk. If the poet noticed his arrival, he slipped out. Sen, the journalist, had been unwittingly caught on the very first day, while he was expanding on Nehru's Five-Year Plan. Vasu, who had just come in to collect some stationery, listened to his talk for a moment and, turning to me, asked, "Who's he? You have not told me his name."

"A good friend," I said, and explained something about him.

Vasu shook his head patronizingly. "If he is so much wiser than Nehru, why don't he try and become the Prime Minister of India?"

This brought forth a fitting reply from the journalist, who drew himself up haughtily and cried, "Who is this man? Why does he interfere with me when I am talking to someone? Is there no freedom of speech?"

Vasu said, "If you feel superior to Nehru, why don't you go to Delhi and take charge of the cabinet?" and laughed contemptuously.

Words followed, the journalist got up in anger, and Vasu advanced threateningly. I came between them with a show of bravery, dreading lest someone should hit me. I cried, "All are friends here. I won't allow a fight. Not here, not here."

"Then where?" asked Vasu.

I replied, "Nowhere."

"I don't want to be insulted, that's all," said the bully.

"I am not going to be frightened by anyone's muscle or size. Do you threaten to hit me?" Sen cried. I was in a panic. He pushed me away and stepped up to Vasu.

"No, sir," said Vasu, recoiling. "Not unless I'm hit first." He raised his fist and flourished it. "I could settle many problems with this. But I don't—if I hit you with it, it will be the end of you. But it doesn't mean I may not kick."

Vasu often sat in my parlor and expanded on his philosophy of human conduct. "Nataraj!" he would suddenly say. "Life is too short to have a word with everyone in this land of three-hundred-odd millions. One has to ignore most people." I knew it was just a fancy speech and nothing more, because his nature would not let him leave anyone in peace. He'd wilt if he could not find some poor man to bully all day. There was no stopping him from interesting himself in others. If he found someone known to him, he taunted him. If he met a stranger, he bluntly

demanded, "Who is he? You have not told me his name!"
No maharaja finding a ragged commoner wandering in
the halls of his *durbar* would have adopted a more au-
thoritative tone in asking, "Who is this?"

Vasu's habit of using my front room as an extension of
his attic was irksome, as I had my own visitors, not to
speak of the permanent pair, the poet and the journalist.
For a few days Sen and the poet cleared out the moment
they heard the jeep arrive, but gradually their views
underwent a change. When Vasu came in, Sen stuck to his
seat with an air of defiance, as if saying, "I'm not going to
let a beefy fellow . . ." The poet transferred himself
without fuss from the high-backed Queen Anne chair to
a poorer seat and developed the art of surviving Vasu's
presence; he maintained a great silence but, if forced to
speak, he confined himself to monosyllables (at which he
was an adept in any case), and I was glad to note that
Vasu had a lot of things on his mind and had no time for
more than a couple of nasty personal remarks, which the
poet pretended not to hear. Sen suppressed the expression of his political opinions when Vasu was there
(which was a good thing again). But it did not save him,
as Vasu, the moment he remembered his presence, said,
"What are the views of our wise friend on this?" To which
Sen gave a fitting reply, such as, "If people are dense
enough not to know what is happening around, I'm not
prepared to . . ." et cetera, et cetera. This would act as
a starting point for a battle of words, but it never came,
as on the first day, to near-blows—it just fizzled out. I left
them all alone. If they wrangled and lost their heads and
lost control of their voices, it was purely their business and
not mine. Even if heads got broken, I don't think I'd have

interfered. I had resigned myself to anything. If I had wanted a peaceful existence, I should have rejected Vasu on the very first day. Now it was like having a middle-aged man-eater in your office and home, with the same uncertainties and the same potentialities.

This man-eater softened, sniveled and purred, and tried to be agreeable only in official presence. One day he brought in a khaki-clad, cadaverous man, a forestry official, seated him, and introduced me to him. "This is my best friend on earth—Mr. Nataraj. He and I are more like brothers than a printer and customer or landlord and tenant."

"Actually, I am not a landlord, don't want to be one," I said, remembering how much more at peace I used to be when my attic was tenanted by junk. Woe unto the day I got the idea of cleaning it up.

Vasu said, "Even among brothers, business should be business."

"True, truc," said the forester.

Now Vasu turned to the art of flattery. I never could have guessed his potentialities in this direction. He declaimed, "I have brought Mr. . . . because I want you to know him. He is a very busy man, but he came here with me today."

"Do you stay in the forest?"

Before the forester could speak, Vasu answered, "He *is* Mempi Forest. He is everything there. He knows and has numbered every beast that's there; and he has no fear. If he was a coward he'd not have been in this department, you know what I mean?"

The forester felt that it was time for him to put in a word about himself. "I have put in thirty years in the department. They gave me a third extension in my service only two weeks ago."

"See how he looks? Can you guess his age?" (I wanted to say I could do it unerringly.) "He is like a teak tree—thousands of those trees in Mempi range are in his charge, isn't it so, sir?"

"Yes, yes, that's a big responsibility," he said.

"And you know, he looks wiry, but he must be like a teak log in strength. I am a strong man, as you know, but I'd hesitate to challenge him. Ha, ha, ha!" He stopped laughing and said, "Seriously, he is one of the best forest officers in India. How many times has he been charged by a rogue elephant?"

"Eighteen times in my service," said the man statistically.

"And you just gave it a four-nought-five charge at point-blank range?"

"Yes, what else could one do?" said the hero.

"How many tigers has he tracked on foot?"

"An average of at least one every half-year," he said.

"And in thirty years you may guess how much he must have seen and done," Vasu said, and asked the hero, "What did you do with all those skins?"

"Oh, gave them away here and there," said the man. "I don't fancy keeping these trophies."

"Ah, you shouldn't say so, you must let me stuff at least one animal for you, and you will know the difference," said Vasu. "Nataraj," he said suddenly, "the main reason why I have brought him to you is, he wants a small book to be printed." My heart sank. It was terrible enough to have Vasu for a customer, and now to have to work for someone he was championing! The three-color labels were still undelivered. "Nataraj, you will have to clear your desk and do this."

I held out my hand mechanically. The forester took out of his bag a roll of manuscript, saying, "I have made it a habit to collect Golden Thoughts, and I have arranged them alphabetically. I wish to bring them out in book form and distribute them to schoolchildren, free of cost. That is how I want to serve our country," he said.

I turned over the manuscript. Virtues were listed alphabetically. "My Tamil types are not good. My neighbor has the best Tamil types available, and his original Heidelberg—"

"Oh!" Vasu groaned. "The original again?"

I looked at him compassionately. "As a man of education, Vasu," I began, "you should not shut your mind to new ideas."

"But why on earth should I know anything about the original what's-its-name?" he cried with mild irritation; it was evident that he was struggling to be on his best behavior before the man in khaki.

"It's because," I replied with the patience of a saint explaining to an erring soul, "it's the machine on which fast printing is done. For instance the kind of work like our friend's here—Golden Thoughts—the right place for it would be the original Heidelberg—lovely machine. What do you say, sir?" I said, turning to the man. Having spent a lifetime with would-be authors I knew their vanities from A to Z.

The forester said, "Yes, I want the best service possible. The book should look very nice: I want to send a specially bound copy to our chief conservator at Delhi through our chief at Madras."

"So you want two special copies?" I asked.

"Yes, yes," he agreed readily.

I looked through the pages of the manuscript. He had culled epigrammatic sentiments and moralizings from all sources—*Bhagavad-Gita, Upanishads*, Shakespeare, Mahatma Gandhi, Bible, Emerson, Lord Avebury, and Confucius—and had translated them into Tamil. It was meant to elevate young minds, no doubt, but I'd have felt a resentment if I had been told every hour of the day what I should do, say, or think: it'd be boring to be steadfastly good, night and day. I thought the book had in it most of the sentiments that Vasu had missed in life and that it might do him good to pick up a few for his own use. I told him, "I'm sure you will enjoy going over this manuscript, in case our friend does not find the time to give it a final look-over."

"Oh, yes, yes, of course," Vasu said faintly.

I was confident now that I could dodge, at least for the time being, the responsibility of printing the golden book, but I couldn't judge how long. If I took it on, with Vasu literally living overhead, he'd storm the press night and day—less mildly, with the man in khaki out of sight. There was going to be no money in it; I was positive about that. The whole transaction, it was patent to me, was going to be a sort of exchange between the two: Vasu wanted to win the other's favor through my help. So far I had done regular printing of stationery for Vasu, and he had shown no signs of paying for the work.

I told the man, handing back the manuscript, "Please go through it again and make all the final revisions and additions; that'll help. And if you are satisfied with the final form, we'll do something with it. I don't want you to

incur any unnecessary expense later—corrections are
rather expensive, you know. All the time you can give for
revisions in manuscript will be worth while . . ." Once
again my experience of would-be authors saved me: authors liked to think that they took infinite pains and
labored to attain perfection.

I could see Vasu's bewilderment: he could not understand whether it was a good thing or a bad thing that had
happened; the manuscript had changed hands too swiftly.
He looked at my face and then at the other's. I was a
seasoned printer. I knew the importance of shuffling off
a manuscript without loss of time. Once the manuscript
got lodged with you, you lost your freedom, and authority
passed on to the writer of the manuscript. Vasu ventured
to say, "How can you make him come again? Do you know
where he has to come from? From Peak House, where he is
camping." Very encouraging! Sixty miles away; it was
not often that this man was going to find the time and conveyance to come downhill.

"He won't have to come! You can fetch the manuscript,"
I said, and Vasu agreed with alacrity. "Yes, yes, that's a
good idea. I'll always be around you, you know."

A week later a brown envelope from the Forest Department arrived for Vasu. His face lit up at the sight of it.
"Must be my game license. It was embarrassing to go into
the jungle without it. Now you will see what I do. . . .
The swine!" he cried when he had read the contents. "They
think I want to go sightseeing in the forests, and permit
me to shoot duck and deer—as if I cared!" He remained in
thought for a while. "Now they will find out what I can
do." He carelessly thrust the paper into his pocket.

Chapter Four

A month later Vasu stopped his jeep in front of my office and sounded the horn, sitting at the wheel with the engine running. I looked up from a proof of a wedding invitation I was correcting. The adjournment lawyer was sitting in front of me; his daughter was to be married in two weeks, and he was printing a thousand invitation cards. This was a piece of work I was obliged to deliver in time. I didn't want to be interrupted today. I shouted back to Vasu, "Anything urgent?"

"Yeah," he said—he seemed to have picked up his American style from crime books and films.

"I am busy now," I said.

"Come on," he said aggressively; I placed a weight on the proof and went out. "Jump in," he said when I approached him.

"I really can't," I said. "That man is waiting for me."

"Don't be silly, jump in."

"Where are you going?"

"I'll bring you back in ten minutes," he said. "Can't you spare for my sake just ten minutes?"

"I said, "No, I can't spare ten minutes."

"All right, five minutes then." I climbed into the jeep, and he drove off.

I found that he was driving on and on. We had crossed Nallappa's Grove and were actually ten miles on the trunk road; he drove recklessly. I asked him where he was going.

"I thought you might enjoy a visit to Mempi."

"What—what's the meaning of this?" I asked angrily.

"So you don't like to be with me! All right. Shall I stop? You may get down and go back."

I knew it would be futile to exhibit my temper. It would only amuse him. I concealed my chagrin and said, "I certainly should enjoy walking back ten miles, but I wish I had had the time to pick up my shirt buttons at least before leaving." I had mislaid my buttons at home. My shirt was open at the chest.

He cast a look at me. "No one will mind it in the jungle," he said and rocked with laughter.

Now that I was at his mercy, I thought I might as well abandon myself to the situation. I only wished I had not left the adjournment lawyer sitting in my chair. How long was he going to be there, and what was to happen to the marriage of his daughter without invitation cards? I said, assuming the most casual tone possible, "It was a matter of an urgent marriage invitation."

"How urgent is the marriage?" he asked.

"Coming off in fifteen days, and they must have time to post the invitation cards. A printer has his own responsibility," I said.

"If man is willing and the woman is willing—there is marriage. What has a printer to do with it? It's none of a printer's business. Why should you worry?"

I gave up all attempts to explain; he was not prepared to pay any attention to my words. He was the lord of the universe; he had no use for other people's words. "Why should you worry?" he asked again and again. It was so unreasonable and unseasonable that I didn't think it fit to find an answer for him.

I noticed that the speedometer needle was showing a steady 60. "Mind the road," I said, as I saw villagers walking in a file, stepping off as the jeep grazed their sides. Truck traffic and buses swerved away, the drivers muttering imprecations. Vasu enjoyed their discomfiture and laughed uproariously. Then he became suddenly serious and said, "More people should die on the roads, if our nation is to develop any road sense at all!" A peasant woman was sitting on the roadside with a girl whose hair she was searching for lice. He saw them ahead and set himself to run into them, and swerved away after seeing them tumble over each other in fright.

"Oh, poor creatures," I said, "I hope they aren't hurt."

"Oh, no, they won't be hurt. These women are hardy and enjoy all such fun. Didn't you see how they were laughing?"

I felt it would be best to leave his words without a comment. Even that seemed to annoy him. We went up a couple of miles, and he said, "Why are you silent? What are you thinking about? Still worrying about that invitation?"

"Yes," I said to be on the safer side.

"Only fools marry, and they deserve all the trouble they get. I really do not know why people should marry at all. If you like a woman, have her by all means. You don't really have to own a coffee estate because you like to have a cup of coffee now and then." And he smiled, more and more pleased with his own witty observations.

I had never known him to be so wild. He had seemed to practice a few restraints of tongue when he visited me at my press. But now, as we rode in his jeep on the highway, his behavior was breath-taking. I wondered for a moment whether he might be drunk. I asked testily, "What do you think of prohibition, which they are talking about nowadays?"

"Why?" he asked.

I had no answer ready for the question. As I was wondering what to say, he said, "Drink is like marriage, as far as I can see. If people like it, it's their business and nobody else's. I tried to drink whisky once, but gave it up. It tastes bad," he said. He sat brooding at the wheel for a moment and said, "Wonder why anyone should want to drink."

My last hope that this man might be drunk was now gone. One who could conduct himself in this manner in dead sobriety! I shuddered to contemplate. I was glad to jump out of the jeep when we arrived at Mempi village. Riding in the jeep over all those bumps, with one leg dangling out, had been painful, and my head reeled slightly with the speed of his driving.

Mempi village, at the foot of the hills, consisted of a single street, which wound along and half a mile away climbed a steep hill and disappeared into the ranges of Mempi. The road was flanked by a few cottages built of bamboo and coconut thatch; a tea-shop with bananas in bunches dangling from a nail on the ceiling, which was a rallying point for buses and trucks; and a touring open-air cinema plastered over with the picture of a wide-eyed heroine watching the landscape. One saw the jungle studding the sides of the hill. A small shrine stood at the con-

fluence of the mountain road with the highway, and the
goddess presiding was offered coconut and camphor flame
by every vehicle going up the mountain road.

Vasu pulled up his jeep and asked the man at the tea-
shop, "What's the news?"

The man said, "Good news. There was a prowler last
night, so they say. We saw pug marks on the sand, and
sheep were bleating as if they had gone mad. Not where I
live. But I heard Ranga talk of it today."

"Did he see anything?" asked Vasu, and he added
eagerly, "What did he see?"

The tea-shop had a customer at this moment, and the
man mechanically handed him a bun, drew strong red tea
from the sizzling urn, and poured it into a glass tumbler.
I had been starving. I cast longing looks at the brown buns
arranged on a shelf, although normally I would not dare
to eat anything out of a shop like this. Flies swarmed over
sugar and everything else, with nothing washed or covered,
and road dust flew up at the motion of every vehicle and
settled on all the bread, buns, fruit, sugar, and milk. The
shop had a constant crowd of visitors; buses and trucks
climbing to the coffee estates, bullock carts in caravans,
pedestrians—everyone stopped here for refreshment.

When I put my finger into my pocket I did not find a
single coin, but only the stub of a pencil with which I'd
been correcting the proof of the invitation. I called pathetically, like a child at a fair tugging at the sleeve of
his elder, "Vasu!" He was busy discussing the pug marks,
and his circle was growing. A coconut seller, the village
idiot, the village wag, a tailor, and a man carrying a
bundle of tobacco on his head—each was adding his own

to the symposium on the visit of the tiger and enlarging on the story.

Vasu did not hear me call him. I had to cry out, "Vasu, lend me some cash; I want to try the tea here."

He paused. "Tea? Why?"

I felt silly with my shirt open at the chest and the dhoti around my waist. "I'm hungry. I had no time for breakfast this morning."

He looked at me for a minute and resumed his discussion about the pug marks. I felt slighted. Hunger had given an edge to my temper. I felt indignant that I should have been dragged out so unceremoniously and treated in this manner. I called out, "Have you or have you not any loose coin on you? I'll return it to you as soon as I am back home."

"So you think we are going back home, eh?" he said irresponsibly.

I was struck with a sudden fear that this man was perhaps abducting me and was going to demand a ransom for releasing me from some tiger cave. What would my wife and little son do if they were suddenly asked to produce fifty thousand rupees to get me released? She might have to sell the house and all her jewelry. I had not yet paid the final installment on that gold necklace of hers that she fancied only because someone she knew had a similar one. Good girl, this had been her most stubborn demand in all the years of our wedded life, and how could I have denied her? Luckily I had printed the Cooperative Bank *Annual Report* and paid off half the price of the necklace with those earnings. But—but that necklace cost in all only seven hundred rupees; how would she make up fifty thousand? We might have to sell off the treadle; it was rickety and might fetch just thirteen thousand—and then what should I do after my release, without my printing machinery? What was to happen to Sastri? He'd be unemployed—or would he go over to operate the Heidelberg? If my wife appealed to him would he have the sense to go to the police and lead them to the tiger cave guarded over by this frightful man with the dark halo over his head? Suppose the tiger returned to the cave and found him while he mounted guard over me, would the beast have the guts to devour him first and then, retching at the sight of any further food, leave me alone?

All this flashed through my mind in an instant, and it made me swallow my temper and smile ingratiatingly at Vasu, which had a better effect than any challenge. He relented enough to say, "You see, when I'm out on business I rarely think of food." (Because you'll not hesitate to make a meal of any fool who has the ill luck to go with you, I remarked mentally.) Then he suddenly left me, got into his jeep, said, "Come on," to someone in the group, and was off.

I felt slightly relieved at his exit, but cried like a lost child, "When . . . ? When . . . ?"

He waved to me, saying, "Stay here, I'll be back," and his jeep raced up the mountain road and disappeared around a bend.

I looked down at my chest, still unbuttoned. I felt ridiculous, standing where I was. This was no doubt a very beautiful place—the hills and the curving village road, and the highway vanishing into the hills, but I'd hardly have chosen to be dragged out and stranded here. The hills looked blue, no doubt, and the ranges beyond were shim-

mering, but that could hardly serve as an excuse for anyone to take liberties with my person in this manner. I sat
down on a wooden plank stretched over two empty tins,
which served for a bench at the tea-shop.

"Is there a bus for Malgudi from here?" I asked the
tea-shop man.

"Yes, at two o'clock, coming from Top Slip."

It would be a nice idea to catch it and get back to town,
but how was one to pay for the ticket? I didn't have even
a button to my shirt. I cursed myself for entertaining and
encouraging Vasu. But I also felt relief that he had gone
away without a word about the ransom. I explained my
situation to the tea-shop man. He was very happy when he
heard that I was a printer and eagerly said, "Ah, I'm so
happy, sir, to know you. Can you print some notices for
me, sir?"

"With pleasure," I said, and added, "I'm here to serve
the public. I can print anything you may want, and if you
prefer to have your work done on a German machine, I
can arrange that too. My neighbor has an original Heidelberg, and we are like brothers."

The man explained, "I have no time to leave this place
and attend to any other business in the town; and so I have
long been worrying how to get some printing work done."

"Oh, you don't have to worry as long as I'm here. Your
printing will be delivered to you at your door, that's how
I serve my customers. I print for a wide clientele and
deliver the goods by bus or train, whichever goes earlier."

"Ah, that's precisely how I would like to be served," he
said. And then he launched on his autobiography. He was
a self-made man. Having left his home in Tirunelveli when
he was twelve years of age, he had come to Mempi in

search of work. He knew no one, and he drifted on to the tea plantations on the hills and worked as an estate laborer, picking tea leaves, loading trucks, and in general acting as a handyman. In the August of 1947, when India became independent, the estate, which had been owned by an English company, changed hands, and he came downhill to look for a new job. He established a small shop, selling betel nuts, peppermints, tobacco, and so on, and expanded it into a tea-shop. Business prospered as new dam construction was started somewhere in a valley ten miles out and engineers, ministers, journalists, builders, and laborers moved up and down in jeeps, trucks, and station wagons; the place buzzed with activity night and day. His tea-shop grew to its present stature. He built a house, and another house, very near the shop in a back street. "I can go home in five minutes for a nap or to snatch some food," he boasted. And then he took an interest in the shrine at the confluence of the mountain and plains. "Hundreds of vehicles go up to those summits, and to this day we have never heard of an accident— although some of those roads are narrow and twisting and if you are careless you'll dive over the ridge. . . . But there has not been a single accident—you know why?" He pointed at the little turret of the shrine showing above the roadside trees. "Because the Goddess protects us. I rebuilt the temple with my own funds. I have regular *pujas* performed there. You know we have also a temple elephant; it came years ago of its own accord from the hills, strayed along with a herd of cattle returning from the hills after grazing. It was then about six months old and was no bigger than a young buffalo. We adopted it for the temple. His name is Kumar, and children and elders alike adore him and feed him with coconut and sugar cane and rice all day."

After all this rambling talk he came to the point. He was about to celebrate the consecration of the temple on a grand scale, carrying the Goddess in a procession with pipe, music, and everything, and led by the elephant. He wanted me to print a thousand notices so that a big crowd might turn up on that day.

I readily agreed to do it for him, and asked, "When do you want it?"

He was flabbergasted. "I don't know. . . . We shall have to discuss it at a meeting of the temple committee."

I was relieved to note that it was only a vague proposal still and said, "Write to me as soon as your plans are ready and I will do my best for you. I will print anything you want. By the way, why don't you let me taste your tea, and a couple of those buns? Who is your baker in the town? He has given them such a tint!" He concocted a special brew of tea for me and handed me a couple of brown buns on a piece of old newspaper. I felt refreshed and could view my circumstances with less despair now. At the back of my mind was a worry as to whether the adjournment lawyer might still be sitting waiting for my return. Return home? Ah, there was no such prospect. I should have been wiser if I had written my will before venturing out with Vasu. "I'll pay your bill next time when I come to you," I said, "maybe with the printed notices. You see I had to come away suddenly and didn't know I'd come so far." And then I made another request. "Do you know these bus people? What sort are they?"

"Every bus must stop here for tea," he said boastfully.

"I knew it'd be so," I said. "Can you do me a favor?

Could you ask one of these conductors to take me back to town and collect the fare at the other end? The bus has to pass in front of my press, and I could just dash in—"

"Why do you want to go away? Won't you wait for Vasu?"

I felt desperate. Was this man in league with Vasu? Probably they had plans to carry me to the cave at night —all ransom-demanding gangsters operated only at night. They were perhaps saving me up for their nocturnal activities. I said, "I must get back to the press today; the lawyer will be waiting for me, you know. Wedding invitation. You know how important it is."

"But Vasu, he may ask why I didn't keep you here. I know him, and he is sometimes strict, as you may know."

"Oh," I said casually. "He is a good fellow, though his speech is blunt sometimes. We are very close, you know, and he knows all about this marriage invitation. He'll understand and—he is a good friend of mine. The trouble is I came away without picking up my buttons or cash." I laughed, trying to import into the whole situation a touch of humor. "I wonder when Vasu will be back!"

"Oh, that nobody can say. When he hears about a tiger, he forgets everything else. Now he'll be right in the jungle following the pug marks."

"Fearless man," I cried in order to please the tea-seller. "What is your name?"

"Muthu," he said. "I have four children, and a daughter to marry—"

"Oh! so you will understand more than anyone else how anxious that lawyer will be."

"Which lawyer?" he asked.

"Our adjournment lawyer, whom I left sitting in my office—"

"I'm sure you will help me to find a good bridegroom for my daughter." He lowered his voice to say, "My wife is scheming to marry her off to her own brother's son. But I have other ideas. I want the girl to marry a boy who is educated."

"She must marry someone who is at least a B.A.," I said.

He was so pleased with this that he gave me another bun and another glass of tea. "This is my treat. You don't have to pay for this cup of tea," he said.

Presently his customers began to arrive—mostly coolies carrying pickaxes, crowbars, and spades on their way to that mysterious project beyond the hills. Caravans of bullock carts carrying firewood and timber stopped by. Loudspeaker music blared forth from the tent cinema, where they were testing their sound again and again—part of a horribly mutilated Elvis Presley tune, Indianized by the film producer. I sat there and no one noticed me: their arms reached right over my head for the glasses of tea; sometimes brown tea trickled over the side of a tumbler and fell on my clothes. I did not mind it; at other times I'd have gone into a rage at any man that dared to spill tea over my clothes. Today I had resigned myself to anything—as long as I could hope for a bus ride back to town on credit and good will. I glanced at the brown face of a very old timepiece kept on a wooden shelf inside the tea-shop. It was so brown that I could hardly make out the numerals on it. Still an hour more before the bus would arrive, and two hours since Vasu had gone. I only hoped that he would not return before the bus arrived. I prayed he would not. I reassured myself again by asking, over the babble of the tea-shop, if Muthu could tell when Vasu would be back, and he gave me the same reply as before. This was the only silver lining in the cloud that enshrouded my horizon that day. Even then my heart palpitated with apprehension lest Vasu should suddenly appear at the tea-shop and carry out his nefarious program for the evening. He could pick me up between his thumb and first finger and put me down where he pleased. Considering his enormous strength, it was surprising that he did not do more damage to his surroundings.

I sat in a trembling suspense as men came and went, buying tobacco, betel leaves, and cigarettes and tea and buns. I could hardly get a word with Muthu. I sat brooding over what I'd have to face from Sastri or my wife when I got back. . . . Got back! the very words sounded remote and improbable! The town, the fountain, and my home in Kabir Street seemed a faraway dream which I had deserted years ago. . . .

The crowd at the tea-shop was gone in a while. I sat on the bench and fell into a drowse. The hill and fields and the blindingly blue sky were lovely to watch, no doubt, but I could not go on watching their beauty forever. I was not a poet. If my monosyllabic friend were here, perhaps he would have enjoyed sitting there and watching forever; but I was a businessman, a busy printer and so forth. . . . I felt weak; I might eat all the buns in the world, but without a handful of rice and the sauce my wife made, I could never feel convinced that I had taken nourishment.

The air far off trembled with the vibration of a motor. Muthu declared, "The bus should be here in ten minutes."

Amazing man, with ears so well attuned! I said so. I wanted to do and say everything to please this man, whom at normal times I'd have passed as just another man selling tea in unwashed glass tumblers.

The bus arrived, on its face a large imposing signboard which called it "Mempi Bus Transport Corporation," although the bus itself was an old one picked off a war-surplus dump, rigged up with canvas and painted yellow and red. It was impossible to guess how many were seated in the bus until it stopped at the tea-shop and passengers wriggled and jumped out as if for an invasion. They swarmed around the tea-shop, outnumbering the flies there. The conductor, a very thin man in a peaked cap and khaki shirt over half-shorts, emerged with a cash bag across his shoulder, and the driver jumped out of his seat. Men, women, and children clamored for attention at the tea-shop. The driver and the conductor exchanged a few words, looked at the cash bag, took out some coins for themselves. And the conductor addressed the gathering in general: "I am not stopping more than five minutes. If anyone is left behind, he will be left behind, that's all. I warn you all, don't blame me later," and he looked around like a headmaster watching his pupils and passed into the tea-shop.

He was given a seat of honor beside the owner at the tea-shop. He called for a glass of tea and buns. He lit a cigarette. After he was well settled, I went up to show my-self to Muthu, who I feared might forget me in the midst of his booming business—a fear which was well founded, for as soon as he saw me, he said, "Ah, I'd forgotten about our printing master." He told the conductor, "Brother, give him a seat for the town; he will pay at the other end."

The brother took time to grasp the meaning of the proposition. He looked at me with sour suspicions. "Why should he not pay now?"

"Because he has left all his cash in the town."

"Then why did he come here? You know how many tell me that each day?" He moistened his upper lip with his tongue as smoke emerged from his nostrils. Another monster in league with Vasu, I thought, and felt desperate. He demonstrated with his hands the act of wringing a neck. "I'd like to do this to anyone who comes up with such a proposal. If our inspector checks midway, it'll end my career, and then I and my family will have to take a begging bowl and go from door to door." This man had a far-fetched imagination. Having always lived within the shelter of my press, I had probably grown up in complete ignorance of human nature, which seemed to be vicious, vile, vindictive, and needlessly unfriendly everywhere.

I went up to him with chest drawn up and said haughtily, "I'll guarantee that you will not have to carry a begging bowl. Today I am stuck here, but generally I'm not a passenger for any bus, as I have a car—if not mine, my friend's, which is as good as mine."

"What car do you use?"

"Well . . ." I said, reflecting, "a Morris, of course," mentioning the first make that came to my head.

"Model?" he asked, pursuing the subject.

"Fifty-one, I think."

"Four-door?"

"Yes."

"Oh, you are lucky, it's worth its weight in gold, this particular model. I know more than one man who is searching for this model desperately. Do you think you would care to quote a price for it?"

I shook my head. "Oh, dozens of persons ask me that every day, but I want to keep it till it falls to bits, you know. I don't want to sell."

Now he developed a wholesome respect for me as a member of the automobile fraternity. He was prepared to overlook my unbuttoned shirt and disheveled appearance and ticketless travel; I wished I had acquired some more jargon of the auto world in order to impress him further, but I had to manage as best I could with whatever rang in my memory as a result of printing for Ramu of Ramu's Service Station, who sometimes dropped in to talk of the state of the nation in the motoring world.

The bus conductor said, "Any time you want to dispose of your Morris, you must tell me." He turned to Muthu and confided, "Sooner or later I want to give up this endless ticket punching and drive a baby taxi. I know a man who earns a net income of fifty rupees a day with just one baby vehicle. I have saved enough to buy a car now."

Muthu nudged him in the midriff and muttered, "Don't I know!" darkly, at which both of them simpered. I knew at once they meant that the conductor made money by pocketing a lot of cash collected from the passengers. I said, to add to the mood of the hour, "One has to make money while one can. Otherwise, when one is old or down and out, who would give a paisa?"

When he started out, nearly half an hour later, I walked along royally with the conductor and took my seat in the bus. I had taken leave of Muthu briefly but in touching terms: he assured me that he would write to me for any

help he might need. I sat beside the driver. The conductor
leaned over my shoulder from behind to say, "You will
have to move and make space at the next stop; the Circle
is expected." The word "Circle" in these circumstances indicated the inspector of police for this circle, whose seat
at the front was always reserved. If another passenger
occupied it, it was a matter of social courtesy to vacate it
or at least move up closer to the driver and leave enough
space at the end of the seat for the Circle. The historic
variation of this pattern occurred long, long ago, when a
planter returning to his estate created a lot of unpleasant-
ness by refusing to make way for the Circle, with the result
that the Circle was obliged to travel in one of the ordinary
seats inside the bus, with the rabble, and at the next stop
he impounded the whole bus with the passengers for overcrowding.

The bus traveled for an hour. I felt happy that I'd
slipped away from Vasu after all. I cast a look behind
once or twice to see if his jeep was following us. Coming
back from his tracking of tiger, he might want to embark
on the bigger expedition of tracking a printer escaped
from the tea-shop.

The bus stopped under a tree on the roadway, the conductor warning, "We are not stopping for more than a
minute. If anyone is impatient to get out, let him get out
forever. Don't blame me afterwards." In spite of this
threat a few of the passengers wriggled out and disappeared behind the bushes on the roadside. A constable in
uniform was seen coming across the maize field, sweating
in the sun and bearing under his arm a vast load of
papers and files. He gesticulated from a distance to catch
the eye of the driver. He arrived and placed the files on

the seat next to me. I moved over to the inner side of the seat close to the driver and cleared a space for the Circle. I couldn't, after all, be choosy, being there on sufferance.

The constable said to the driver, "The Circle is coming; you'll have to wait."

"How long?" asked the conductor.

The constable clung to the rail, rested his feet on the step, pushed his turban back on his head, and disdained to answer the question. Instead he asked, "Give me a *beedi*," and held out his hand for it. The driver produced matches and a *beedi* from his pocket.

The constable smoked; the acrid smell of *beedi* leaf and tobacco overpowered the smell of petrol. The constable's face shone with perspiration. He said, "I feared I might lose the bus; the Circle would have chopped off my head." A couple of children started crying, a woman sang a soft but tuneless lullaby, someone was yawning noisily, someone was swearing, a couple of peasants were discussing a litigation, someone asked wearily, "Are we going to go on at all?" and someone else joked about this. I looked back furtively for Vasu's jeep coming in pursuit. I grew tired of the policeman's face, and the road ahead, and everything. I was beginning to feel hungry, all the buns having been assimilated into the system long ago. The whole of the passenger crowd subsided into an apathetic, dull waiting—and finally the Circle turned up, a swarthy man in khaki uniform; he suddenly appeared beside the bus on a bicycle. As soon as he jumped off, the constable held the handle of the machine, and the conductor heaved it up to the rooftop. The Circle climbed into his seat and just said, "Start." The driver squeezed the bulb of the rubber horn, and its short raucous bark resounded along the

highway, past the hill, and brought running a dozen
passengers who had strayed away from the suffocating
bus into the surrounding country. For a brief while there
was the disorder of people trying to clamber back to their
original seats. One heard grumblings, "I was sitting here,"
and rejection of such claims, until the conductor said,
"Keep quiet, everyone," in deference to the presence of
the Circle. The Circle, however, sat stiffly looking ahead;
it was evident that he did not want to embarrass the conductor by noticing the overcrowding.

I was overwhelmed by the proximity of this eminent
personage, who smelt of the sun, sweat, and leather belt.
I hoped he'd not take me for an ex-convict and order me
out. He had a nice downward-directed short mustache. He
wore dark glasses, and his nose was hooked and sharp;
his Adam's apple also jutted out. The driver drove with
great caution; this man who had been swerving away from
collisions for over an hour (a pattern of driving to which
Vasu had already accustomed me) never drove now at
over twenty miles, applied the brake when a piece of paper
drifted across, and gently chided any villager who walked
in the middle of the road. At this rate I felt that he'd reach
the town only at midnight. His speed depended on where
the Circle was getting out. I felt it imperative to know at
once his destination. "You are going to the town, I suppose?" I said to the Circle. Where was the harm in asking
him that? There was no law against it.

He turned his sunglasses at me and said, "I'll be getting
off at Talapur."

"Is that where you stay?" I asked.

"No. I'm going there for an investigation," he said,
and I shuddered at the thought of the poor man who was

going to be investigated by him. He talked to me about
the crime in his area. "We've a lot of cattle-lifting cases in
these parts, but the trouble is identification when the
property is traced; they mutilate the animals, and then
what happens is the case is dismissed and all the trouble
one takes to frame a charge-sheet is simply wasted. We
have a few murders too, and a certain amount of prohibition offenses around the dry-belt areas." I found that he
was a friendly sort of man, in spite of all his grim looks.
"This is a difficult circle," he said finally. "Offenders often
disappear into those jungles on Mempi, and one has to
camp for days on end sometimes in those forests."

At the Talapur bus stand, which was under a tree, with
a replica of Muthu's tea-stall, a constable was on hand to
receive the Circle and haul down his bicycle from the bus
roof. He got on his cycle and pedaled away. Talapur was
a slightly larger town than Mempi and was viewed as an
important junction on the road. It had more shops lining
the street. The bus conductor uttered the usual warning to
the passengers and vanished into the tea-shop. Most of
the passengers followed suit, and some dispersed into
various corners of the city. I sat in the bus, nursing my
hunger in silence, having no credit in this town.

When the bus started again, every breath of it demonstrated that the Circle was no longer there to impede its
freedom. It was driven recklessly and brought to a dead
stop every ten minutes to pick up a wayside passenger. The
conductor never said "no" to anyone, as he explained to
me, "These poor fellows will get stranded on the highway
if we are not considerate. After all, they are also human
creatures." He was a compassionate conductor who filled
his pockets with the wayside fare, never issuing a ticket.

At this rate he could buy a Rolls-Royce and not a Morris Minor, I thought. The bus left the highway and darted across devious side tracks through cornfields in search of passengers. It would draw up at a most unexpected spot, and the driver, sounding the horn, would cry, "Come on, come on, Malgudi, last bus for the town. . . ." The bus penetrated into the remotest hamlet to ferret out a possible visitor to the town, and all the passengers had to go where the bus went and sit there patiently watching the antics of the driver and the conductor, who seemed to have fixed a target of income for the day and were determined to reach it. That was how a three-hour jeep ride in the morning was stretched out to eight on the return journey, and it was eleven at night when the bus came to a halt at the public square beyond the market in Malgudi.

At eight o'clock next morning I sat correcting the proof of the adjournment lawyer's invitation. Sastri came in half an hour after I had opened the door of the press. He stood transfixed at the sight of me and said, "We all waited till nine last night."

"I've always told you that you should lock up the door at your usual time, whether I am in or out," I said grandly, and added, "I sometimes get so much else to do."

"But that lawyer would not move. He kept saying you promised to be back in five minutes, in five minutes . . . and then the fruit-juice labels. He was very bitter and said—"

"Oh, stop that, Sastri," I said impatiently. I did not like the aggrieved tone he was adopting. I had had enough of nagging from my wife all night, after she had to get up from sleep and feed me at midnight. If I disappeared abruptly it was my own business. Why should I be expected to give an explanation to so many?

"Stop that, Sastri. If the fruit-juice man wants to print his labels elsewhere, let him clear out, that's all. I can't be dancing attendance on all and sundry, that's all. If he can find any other printer to bring out his magenta shade in the whole of South India . . ."

Mr. Sastri did not wait for me to finish my sentence but passed in, as it seemed to me, haughtily. I sat correcting the proof; the corrections were where I had left them the previous day. "Mr. . . . requests the pleasure of your company . . ." Wrong fonts, and the bridegroom's name was misspelled. "Company" came out as "cumbahy." I never cease to marvel at the extraordinary devils that dance their way into the first proof. The sight of "cumbahy" provoked me to hysterical laughter. I was feeling light-headed. Would not have to beg at a tea-shop and starve or go about without a button to my shirt. I had a feeling of being in an extraordinarily fortunate, secure position, enough to be able to say "fie" to Sastri or anyone. Life on Market Road went on normally. It was good to watch again the *jutkas* and cycles going round the fountain and the idlers of our town sitting on its parapet and spitting into it. It produced a great feeling of security and stability in me. It could last only for a few minutes. The adjournment lawyer, looking unshaven as ever, draping his shoulders in a spotted khadi shawl, and clad in a dhoti above his knees, with an umbrella dangling from his arm, stepped in, his face set in a frown.

"Do you think—" he began.

One look at him and I knew what he was going to say. "Won't you come in and take a seat first?"

"Why should I?" he asked. "I'm not here to waste my time."

I still motioned him to a chair, but he seemed to be afraid that, once he sat there, I'd abandon him and disappear again for the day. He briefly said, "I'm printing my invitation elsewhere, so don't trouble yourself."

"Oh, no trouble whatever, this is a free country, you are a free man, our constitution gives us fundamental rights, how can I compel you or anyone to do what you may not want to do?" I knew he was lying; if he had wasted his time till nine last evening and was back so soon, when did he find the time to seek a printer? Anyway it was not my business; this was a free country, fundamental rights, every citizen was free to print his daughter's marriage card where he pleased, but if he had his wits about him he'd watch out where he got the best results.

"Sastri!" I called aggressively. "Bring this gentleman's original draft. Lawyer so-and-so's daughter's wedding."

Sastri from his invisible world responded with his voice but made no effort to come up with the original. It gave everyone time to cool—signalized by the lawyer's edging a step nearer the chair. "Won't you take your seat, please? Mr. Sastri should be with us in a minute." He sat down. He remained in a state of hostile silence.

I asked, "I suppose all your other arrangements are ready?"

He shook his head and said, "Truly have our elders said . . ." He quoted a proverb which said that building a house and conducting a marriage were the two Herculean tasks that faced a man. I added a further sentiment, that a man who marries off his daughter need perform no other meritorious acts in life as he is gifting away the most precious treasure, a daughter—which moved the lawyer so deeply that the tears came to his eyes. He said, blowing his nose, "Susila is the gentlest of my children. I hope she will have no trouble from her mother-in-law!" He sighed deeply at this thought.

I said consolingly, "Mother-in-law! Down with them, says the modern girl, college-educated and modern-minded."

"I've given her the best possible education," he said morosely. "What more could I do? I pay her music master fifteen rupees a month, her school fees amount to fifteen rupees, and I pay ten rupees for her school bus."

And you have to manage all this, I thought, by securing endless adjournments—but I said aloud, "Yes, life today is most expensive." After all this agreeable tête-à-tête, I cried suddenly, "*Sastri*, here is the gentleman waiting to take away his invitation copy; after all, we must give him time to print elsewhere"—at which the lawyer behaved like one stung. "Oh no, oh no," he cried, "even if it means stopping the marriage, I will not go for my printing anywhere else."

I said, "I'm here to help humanity in my own humble way. I will never say no to anyone. Don't hesitate to command me for whatever you may want me to do."

He took my offer promptly and said, "A thousand cards — or do you think we could do with less?"

Late that evening Vasu's jeep drew up before my press. It was past eight and the traffic in the street was thin. Vasu looked at me from his driving seat. His hair was dust-covered and stood up more like a halo than ever. He beckoned to me from his seat. I was overworking today in order to finish the lawyer's invitations, and I had even undertaken to address and distribute them if he ordered me to. He had worked up so much confidence about me that he did not feel the need to sit up with me, and had gone home. I shouted back to Vasu, "Why don't you come in?" I was now on my own ground, and I had no fear of anyone.

He said, "Hey, come on! I want you to see what I have here." I went out, making up my mind not to step onto the jeep, whatever might happen. I'd stand at a distance to see whatever it was that he was going to show me. There was dust and grime on his face, but also a triumphant smile exposing his teeth; his eyes had widened, showing the whites. I edged cautiously to the jeep. I only hoped that he would not thrust his arm out, grab me, and drive off. He took a flashlight and threw the beam on the back seat, where lay the enormous head of a tiger.

"Where did you manage it?" I asked, there being no other way of talking to a man who had brought in the head of a tiger.

A couple of curious passers-by slowed their pace. Vasu shouted to them, "Get away and mind your business." He started his car to take it through the side gate and park it in the yard. I went back to my seat and continued my work. I could hear his steps go up the wooden stairs. When the breeze blew in from his direction, there was already a stench of flesh—it might have been my imagination.

The curtain parted; he came in and took a seat. He lit a cigarette and asked, "Do you know what he measures? Ten and a half tip to tip, head is almost eighteen inches wide! I got him finally in the block, you see; they will have a surprise when they next check the tiger population in

their block." He then narrated how he got information
from various persons, and followed the foot marks of the
tiger from place to place. He had to wander nearly six
miles within the jungle, and finally got it at a water-hole,
at about two in the night. He showed me the bleeding
scratches on his feet from having to push his way through
thicket; at any moment it might have sprung on him from
some unsuspected quarter. "I was prepared to knock him
down with my hands and ram the butt of my rifle between
his jaws if it came to that," he said. It was evident that he
was not going to wait for others to pay him compliments.
He showered handfuls of them on himself.

"What about permit? You didn't have it?"

"Anyway the tiger didn't mind the informality!" And
he laughed aloud at his own humor. "That swine double-
crossed me! Probably because you didn't print Golden
Thoughts for him." He never let slip an occasion to blame
me or accuse me.

I gave no reply. I became curious to see his animal. He
took me to his room. Since he had occupied it, this was my
first visit there. He had his bed draped over with a mosquito net, a table in a corner, heaped over with clothes
and letters, and a trunk with its lid open with all his
clothes thrown about. He had tied a string across the
room and had more clothes on it. On the little terrace he
had put out some skins to dry; there was a tub at a corner
in which the skin of the tiger was soaking. Skins of smaller
animals lay scattered here and there—jungle squirrels—
and feathered birds lay heaped up in corners. A lot of
wooden planks and molds and all kinds of oddments were
about. Ever since I had given him the attic I had left him
fairly alone, not wanting to seem an intrusive host. And

all the while he had been surrounding himself with carcasses. The room smelled of decaying flesh and raw hide. This man had evidently been very active with his gun, which now rested on his bed. "I'm a man of business, and I cannot afford to waste my time. Each day that I spend without doing my work is a day completely wasted."

There was a resinous odor in the air which made me retch. I couldn't imagine any human being living in this atmosphere. Sastri had come now and then in the past weeks to complain of a rotting smell somewhere. We had searched our garbage cans and odd corners of the press to see if the paste we were using had gone bad. Once I had to speak severely to our binder; I called him names for possibly using some nasty slaughterhouse material in binding. He was apologetic, although he had used no such material. Even after his promise to improve his material, the smell persisted. It was pervasive and insistent, and Sastri found it impossible to stand at the type board and compose. Then we thought a rat might be dead somewhere and turned up every nook and corner of the press, and then we blamed the health department. "Next time that fellow comes around for votes, I'll make him stand at the type board and perform inhaling exercises," I said bitterly. Sometimes my neighbor of the Heidelberg came to ask if I noticed any smell around. I said emphatically that I did and asked him his views on the municipal administration, little thinking that it emanated from my own building, the reservoir, the fountainhead of all the stink being the attic over my own machine.

There was an iron chair on which I sat down because the whole problem loomed before me enormously. If this man continued to stay here (I had really no idea how long he proposed to honor me with his presence) what was to happen to me and to my neighborhood?

Vasu was stirring the broth in the tub with a long pole, at which the stench increased. I held my nostrils with my fingers, and he ordered, "Take off your fingers. Be a man." When I hesitated, he came up and wrenched my fingers apart. "You are imagining things," he said. "What do you think that tub contains? Tiger blood? Ha! Ha! Pure alum solution." And he led me into the higher realms of carcass treatment. He said, "Actually the whole process of our work is much more hygienic and cleaner than paring the skin of vegetables in your kitchen." I shuddered at the comparison. "After all, one takes a lot of care to bleed the animal, and after all, only the skin is brought in. In order to make sure that there is no defect, I attend to everything myself. The paws and the head are particularly important." He lifted the paw of the dead tiger and held it up. "If there is the slightest flaw in incision you will never be able to bring the ends together. This is what Suleiman taught me; he was an artist, as good as a sculptor or a surgeon, so delicate and precise! I killed the tiger last night. What do you think I was doing till tonight?"

Hiding yourself and the carcass from the eyes of forest guards, I thought.

"Bleeding, skinning, and cleaning it so that sentimentalists may not complain. To make sure further, we pack —rather, pickle—the skin in tons of salt immediately after flaying. So you will understand it is all done under the most hygienic conditions." He swept his hand around. "I do everything myself—not because I care for anyone's comments, but—"

"Bits of flesh still there," I said, pointing at the new tiger skin.

"What if! Don't you have flesh under your own skin? Do you think you have velvet under your skin?" This was his idea of humor, and I had no way of matching it.

I looked around. On his work bench in a corner stood a stuffed crow, a golden eagle, and a cat. I could recognize the cat as the one that used to prowl in my press hunting for mice. "Why did you shoot that cat? That was mine!" I cried, shuddering. I fancied I could still hear its soft "mew" as it brushed its back against my legs at the treadle.

"I didn't know," he said. "I only wanted it for a study —after all, the same family as the tiger. I am trying to make a full mold of the tiger. There are some problems of anatomy peculiar to the *Felis* family in this area, and I needed a miniature for study and research. Without continuous application one cannot prosper in my line," he said.

"What did that crow do to you?" I asked.

"It's to serve as a warning to other crows to let Vasu's skins alone and not to peck at them when they are put out to dry."

"And that golden eagle?"

"It was wheeling right over that tile four days ago; it's only five days old, do you notice any smell?" he asked victoriously. He had such a look of satisfaction and victory that I felt like pricking it a little.

"Yes, of course, there is a smell."

"Oh, come on, don't be a fussy prude, don't imagine that you are endowed with more sensitive nostrils than others. Don't make yourself so superior to the rest of us.

These are days of democracy, remember," and I was appalled at his notion of democracy—that there should be a common sharing and acceptance of bad odor.

"What did that poor eagle do to you?" I asked. I could not bear to see the still, glazed look of that poor bird. "See its stare!" I cried.

"Aha!" he cried. He picked it up, brought it closer to me. "So you think it's looking at you with its eyes!" Its dilated black pupils set in a white circle seemed to accuse us. He was convulsed with laughter and said, his voice splitting with mirth, "So you are taken in! You poor fool! Those eyes are given by me, not by God. Now you will understand why I call my work an art." He opened a wooden chest and brought out a cardboard carton. "See these." He scooped out of it a handful of eyes—big round ones, small ones, red ones in a black circle, the ferocious, striking, killing glare of a tiger; the surprise and superciliousness of an owl; the large black-filled softness of a deer—every category of look was there. He said, "All these are from Germany. We used to get them before the war. Now, you cannot get them for love or money. Just lens! Sometimes I paint an extra shade on its back for effect. The first thing one does after killing an animal is to take out its eyes, for that's the first thing to rot; and then one gives it new eyes like an optician. I hope you now appreciate at least what an amount of labor goes into the making of these things. We have constantly to be rivaling nature at her own game. Posture, look, and the total personality—everything has to be created." This man had set himself as a rival to nature and was carrying on a relentless fight all his hours.

"You have no doubt excelled in giving it the looks, but, poor thing, it's death, especially this one. Don't you see that it is a *garuda*."

"What if?"

"Don't you know that's sacred? That it's the carrier of God Vishnu?"

"I want to try and make Vishnu use his feet now and then."

"You may be indifferent, but haven't you seen men and women stopping in the road to look up and salute this bird when it circles in the sky?" I wanted to sound deliberately archaic and poetic.

He ruminated for a second and added, "I think here is a good business proposition. I can supply them stuffed eagles at about fifty rupees each. Everyone can keep a sacred *garuda* in the *puja* and I'll guarantee that it won't fly off, thus they may save their eyes from glare. I want to be of service to our religious folk in my own way."

I shivered slightly at the thought of this man and his mental working. Nothing seemed to touch him. No creature was safe if it had the misfortune to catch his eye. I had made a mistake in entertaining him. I should send him out at the earliest possible moment. His presence defiled my precincts. My mind seethed with ideas as to how to throw him out. But he noticed nothing. He settled himself down on the easy chair, stretched his legs, and prepared for a nice long chat. "This is all a minor job. I really don't care for it. My real work you will see only when you see that tiger made up. You see it now only as a beast with a head and a lot of loose skin soaking in alum. But I'll show you what I can do with it."

Chapter Five

He was a man of his word. He had said that he never wasted his time. I could see that he never wasted either his time or his bullets. Whenever I heard his jeep arrive, I could see some bloody object, small or big, brought in, if I cared to peep out. But nowadays, as far as possible, I tried to shut my eyes to it. I was having a surfeit of it. Not in my wildest dream had I ever thought that my press would one day be converted into a charnel house—but here it was happening. And I was watching it helplessly. Sometimes it made me very angry. Why couldn't I ask him to get out? This was my own building, laboriously acquired through years of saving and scraping, and the place would not have come to me but for a good Moslem friend who migrated to Pakistan and gave me the first offer. If I opened the back door, I stepped into Kabir Street, and right across it to my own home. But all this for harboring the murderer of innocent creatures!

I was brought up in a house where we were taught never to kill. When we swatted flies, we had to do it without the knowledge of our elders. I remember particularly one of my grand-uncles who had the little room on the *pyol*, who used to give me a coin every morning to buy sugar for the ants, and he kept an eye on me to see that I delivered the sugar to the ants in various corners of our house. He used to declare, with approval from all the others, "You must never scare away the crows and sparrows that come to share our food; they have as much right as we have to the corn that grows in the fields." And he watched with rapture squirrels and mice and birds busily depleting the granary in our house. Our domestic granary was built not with concrete in the style of these days, but with a bamboo matting stiffened with mud and rolled into a cylinder, into whose wide mouth they poured the harvest as it arrived in laden bullock carts. That was in the days before my uncles quarreled and decided to separate. . . .

Where am I? Yes. I was appalled at the thought that I should be harboring this destroyer. Frankly speaking, I had no courage to go up to him and say, "Take yourself and your museum out!" He might do anything—bawl me out, or laugh scornfully, or rattle my bones. I felt dwarfed and tongue-tied before him. Moreover, it was becoming difficult to meet him; he was always going out and returning home late at night, sometimes being away for three days at a stretch. He returned home late at night because he did not want his booty to be observed by anyone around. When he was home he was busy upstairs with the broth and molds; one heard the hammering, sawing, and other sounds pertaining to his activity, and sometimes during the day he hauled down packing cases and drove off to the railway station. I noted it from my seat in the press and said to myself: From this humble town of Malgudi radiate stuffed carcasses to the four corners of the earth.

He worked single-handed on all branches of his work. I admired him for it, until I suddenly realized that I too labored single-handed at my job, with the slight difference that Sastri was with me; but he had, I suppose, all those ruffians of Mempi lending him a hand in his nefarious trade. I do not know why I should ever have compared myself with him, but there it was. I was getting into an abnormal frame of mind. There was no person in whom I could confide and from whom I could seek guidance—having always played that role myself. My visitors were, as usual, the journalist and the poet, both of them worthless as consultants. All the same I made an attempt to ascertain their views.

The journalist was frankly dumfounded when he realized that in this particular problem there was no point which he could blame directly on the government. He merely snapped, "Why do you tolerate these things? As a nation, we are what we are today because of our lack of positive grip over our affairs. We don't know where we are going or why. It is a part of the policy of drift, which is our curse."

I left him alone. After all, one should learn to bear one's burdens. Still, two days later the oppression on my mind was so great that I buttonholed the poet when he was struggling to start on the seventh canto of his opus. I asked what he would do in my place—and immediately almost feared that the poet might suggest reading poetry aloud as a possible step to drive out the killer. He took time to comprehend my problem; even for myself, the more I attempted to speak it out, the more incomprehensible it seemed to me. It left me wondering if I was making too much of a very simple matter. When he did comprehend, the poet asked, "Why don't you to try to raise the rent?"

I beat my brow. "Oh, *Kavi!* Do I have to tell you that I am not a *rentier?* I let him in as a friend and not as a tenant. Do you want to heap on my head the reputation of being a man who takes rent for his attic space?"

The poet looked bewildered and said, "Then you could surely tell him to go. Why not?" It was impossible to explain.

My wife also said the same thing. Though I rarely discussed my problems with her, I had become abnormal and turned to her in my desperation. I was brooding too much on Vasu. His footstep on the wooden stairs sent my heart racing. I knew that it was involuntary anger which stirred my heart; the trouble was that it was both involuntary and suppressed! My wife said simply, sweetly, as she served my supper, "Ask him to go, that's all. Babu is frightened of him and refuses to go up when I send him to you."

All this worked in my mind. I waited for a chance to have a word with the man. It was like waiting for my father in my childhood. I often had to spend days and days hoping to catch my father in a happy mood to ask him a favor, such as cash for purchasing a bat or ball or permission to go out on a scouting trip. He was most times preoccupied and busy, and I lost the taste for food until I was able to have a word with him. I would confide in my grand-uncle and he would help me by introducing the subject with my father at the appropriate moment, when my father was chewing betel leaves after a contented dinner. When my father turned to question me, I would squirm and find myself tongue tied, unable to go on with my proposition. I was in a similar predicament now, with the added handicap of not having my grand-uncle around.

I recollected that on the day I saw his dead body stretched
out on the bier my first thought was, "Oh, Lord, who is
going to speak for me hereafter?"

I stuck a note on Vasu's attic door when he was away—
"May I have a word with you when you have the time?"—
and waited for results. One morning three days later he
parted the curtain and peeped in while I was at the treadle
printing the monosyllable forms. I had now barricaded
the passage beyond from the attic stairs to my treadle
with steel mesh, so that Vasu always had to come by the
front door whenever he wanted to see me. Now the first
thing he said was "You take pleasure in making me go
round, is it?"

My heart sank at the sight of him. There was a frown on
his terrible brow. Perhaps he missed a mark or his gun
backfired! I commented to myself when I saw him. More
dangerous than asking for a concession from my father.
He flourished the note and asked, "Is this for me?" He
seemed to possess a sixth sense. He looked grim and unfriendly. I wondered if someone had been talking to him.
Where were the expansive villainies of this man? I missed
them badly. I looked up from my proof and just said,
"Nothing urgent. Perhaps we could meet later, if you are
busy just now."

"If *you* are busy it is a different matter, but don't concern yourself with whether I am busy or otherwise. I am
always busy."

Yes, I added mentally, as long as the forests are full.

He added, "I cannot afford to lounge, if you know what
I mean. If I had the same luck as your other friends that
congregate in your press, reading verse or criticizing the
government, I might . . ."

That settled it. He was in a mood of challenge. I suppressed the qualms I had had all along and said, "Will you kindly take a seat; I will join you in a moment." When I went to him two minutes later, taking just enough time to put away the paper in hand, he was sitting in his chair, but he said, "You have made a fetish of asking people to sit in this room." This was a surprise attack.

"I like to observe the ordinary courtesies," I said.

"Do you mean to say that others don't?" he asked with his face puckering into the usual lines, and I knew that he was getting back into his old mood of devilish banter. I felt relieved. I would have gone to the extent of inquiring even about his dead or dying animals, but I checked myself, feeling an aversion to the subject.

I said, "Vasu, I don't want you to mistake me; have you been able to secure a house?"

"Why?" he asked, suddenly freezing.

"I just thought I might ask you, that is all."

"Not the sort of question a supposedly hospitable person should ask of his guest. It is an insult."

I fought down my racing heart and my tongue ready to dart out like a snake's. I said very casually, "I asked because I require the place for . . ."

"For?" he asked aggressively, cocked his ear, and waited for my answer.

"Someone is coming to stay with us, and he wants . . ."

"How many rooms in your own house are occupied?"

"Should one go into all that now?"

"Yes, the question is of interest to me," he said, and added, "Otherwise I would not mind if you got all your relatives in the world to come and live with you."

I suppressed the obvious retorts. Aggressive words only

generate more aggressive words. Mahatma Gandhi had enjoined on us absolute non-violence in thought and speech, if for no better reason than at least to short-circuit violent speech. I toned down my reply to a cold, businesslike statement. "My guest is a man who likes to stay by himself."

"Then why should he want to stay in this noisy press?"

I had no answer for him, and he said after some reflection, "For years you did nothing more than house old decaying paper there. Now that I have made it slightly habitable you are getting ideas. Do you know how much it has cost me to make it livable? The mosquitoes and other vermin eat you up if you are slightly careless, and the roof tile hits your head; there are cobwebs, smoke, and in summer it is a baking oven. No one but a fool like me would have agreed to live there."

All that I could say in reply was something obvious like, "Is this the return I get for giving you shelter?" or "After all, if you remember, you volunteered to stay," et cetera, et cetera, or "After all, you are living on my hospitality; get out if you do not like it." I swallowed back all these remarks. Instead I said sentimentally, "I never expected you would be so upset."

"Who says I am upset? You are fancying things. It takes a lot more to upset me. Well, anything else?" he asked, rising.

Not until his jeep moved did I realize that he had given me no answer to my question. He had treated it lightly, viciously, indifferently, but all to no purpose. He was gone, and my problem remained unsolved, if anything made worse by my having irritated the man. Stag heads, tiger skins, and petrified feathers were going to surround me forever and ever. My house was becoming a Noah's Ark, about which I had read in our scripture classes at Albert Mission. There was going to be no help from anywhere. Nobody seemed to understand my predicament. Everyone ended up with the monotonous conclusion, "After all, you invited him to stay with you!" I felt completely helpless.

Sastri alone grasped the situation and now and then threw in a word of cheer such as, "These things cannot go on forever like this, can they?" Or sometimes he was brazen enough to say, "What can he do, after all, if you really want him to clear out?" as he piled alphabet on alphabet in the composing stick in his hand. He felt it necessary to cheer me up nowadays, as I was involving him in a lot of worrying transactions with our customers. The cooperative society report and ledgers were overdue because I could not muster enough sharpness of mind to check the figures. The cash bill of Anand Bhavan Hotel remained half done for the same reason, and it was he who had to battle with the customers and send them back with a convincing reply. Anyway he was a slight comfort in a world where there seemed to be no other comfort whatever.

I was lulled into a state of resignation. Vasu saw me less and less. I could hear his steps treading the staircase more emphatically than ever. I detected in that stamping of feet a challenge and a sense of ownership. I raged within myself every time I heard those footsteps, and I knew I had lost him as a friend. Hereafter our relationship was going to be the coldest, and I would be grateful if he left me alone and did not think of bringing that terrific fist of his against my chin.

That he had not been idle came to light very soon. Five

days passed uneventfully. And then came a brown envelope brought by a court process-server. I mechanically
received it, signing the delivery note. Opening it, I read,
"You are hereby asked to show cause why proceedings
should not be instituted against you . . ." et cetera. It
was from the House Rent Controller, the most dreaded
personality in the town. The charges against me were: one,
that I had given part of my press for rent without sanc-
tion to one Mr. Vasu; and, two, that I was trying to evict
a tenant by unlawful means. It took me time to understand
what it meant. Vasu had filed a complaint against me as a
landlord. There was also a complaint that I was not
maintaining the house in a habitable condition, which involved the said tenant in great loss and damage and
expense.

This took me into a set of new activities. So far I had
not known what it was to receive a court summons. I really
did not know where to start and what to do next. Litigation was not in my nature. It was a thing I avoided. I had
a shuddering fear of courts and lawyers, perhaps since the
days when my uncles let them loose on my father and
there was no other topic of discussion at home for months
on end. I put the summons away; they had given me three
days' time to attend to it—a sort of reprieve. It gave me
a feeling of being on parole. I did not confide even in Mr.
Sastri. I spoke to no one about it. I realized that it would
be futile to speak about it to anyone; no one was going to
understand. Everyone would treat me as if I had done
some unlawful act on the sly and was now caught, or trot
out the old advice, "After all, it was *you* who agreed to
take that man in. You have only yourself to blame."

The situation seemed so dark that I surrendered myself

to it in a mood of complete resignation. I even began to look relaxed. I attended to my work normally, listened to jokes and responded to them normally at my press. I counted the days—seventy-two hours more, sixty, twenty-four . . . Tomorrow I should probably be led off straight from the court to the jail, and everyone was going to have a surprise, and Vasu would probably chase out Mr. Sastri and my customers and utilize my front room and all the rest of the space for arranging his "art" pieces. People would get used to it in due course and cease to refer to the place as a press, but rather call it a museum. My wife and child would fend for themselves and visit me in the prison on permissible days. A strange sense of relief came over me when, as it seemed to me, my mind had been made up on all these issues and I knew where I was going to end. People would no doubt sympathize with me but always conclude with "Who asked him to encourage that man, anyway? He brought it all on his own head. Let him not blame others."

On the last day of my freedom, at dawn, I had gone as usual to the river for a bath and was returning to my house at five-thirty. This was where I always used to meet the adjournment lawyer. An idea struck me; it had never occurred to me till now that he could be of use. I'd viewed him only as a printing customer. Since I had printed his cards, he had been avoiding me, because of the unpaid bill. The marriage was over, and the bill had become stale; after all I only charged him ninety rupees for the entire lot of one thousand cards. Nowadays I never saw him even in my morning walk back from the river. Perhaps he detoured and took a parallel road. But today, as my luck would have it, the man came up, face to face.

A great feeling of relief came over me. "Ah, my friend," I cried at the sight of him. "Just the person I was hoping to meet."

He looked panic-stricken. Luckily I cornered him at the bend of Kabir Street where the house of the barber abuts the street, and with the storm drain on the other side a man cannot easily slip out if his path is blocked. He said awkwardly, "Just today I was planning to see you at the press. You know, with one thing and another, after my daughter's marriage . . ."

I felt overjoyed to see him, and asked him breezily, "How is your daughter? Has she joined her husband? How is your son-in-law? How do you fare in the role of a father-in-law?"

He said, "Most people think with the wedding all one's troubles are over. It's only half the battle! Ha, ha!" I laughed in order to please him. I didn't want him to think that I had accosted him so early in the day for my unpaid bill. He said, "It's only after a marriage that one discovers how vicious one's new relatives can be. How many things they demand and keep demanding! Oh, God."

"That's true," I said, "taking your daughter up and down to visit her mother-in-law."

"That I wouldn't mind," he said. "After all, she is our child; it's my duty to help her travel in comfort."

"Yes, yes," I said, wondering what it was that he really minded.

His answer was not long in coming. "All sorts of things, all sorts of things . . ."

The first rays of the sun touched up the walls of the barber's house with the glory of morning. Sparrows and crows were flying already in search of grain and worms.

As I looked at them, a part of my mind reflected how lucky they were to be away from Vasu's attic windows.

The lawyer was talking, habituated to rambling on with a sentence until the court rose for lunch. "The presents demanded are enough to sink one," he was saying. "The new son-in-law must be propitiated all the year round, I suppose," he said with a grim humor. "He must be given a present because it's the sixth month after the wedding, because it's the month of Adi, because it is Deepavali, because it is this and that; every time you think of the great man, you should part with a hundred rupees in cash or clothes! It's all old, silly custom; our women are responsible for keeping up these things. I would not blame the young man; what can he do? It's his mother who demands them, and the bride's mother at once responds by nagging her husband. These women know that if a man is sufficiently nagged he will somehow find the cash."

So, I thought, May I know if the good lady can be made to take an interest in the payment of my bill?

The man said, as if reading my thought, "Now you know why I could not really come over to see you. In spite of one's best efforts, small payments get left out. In all I had to find about ten thousand rupees for the marriage—savings, borrowings, loans, all kinds of things; anyway, it is all over. I will not have to face a similar bother for at least a decade more. My second daughter is just six years old."

"That gives you a lot of time," I said, and I hoped he would now let me say a word about my own problem. But he added, "I am sorry I kept your bill so long; it escaped my notice."

"Oh, that's all right," I said reassuringly. "I knew you

must have been busy. Some of my customers are like a safe-deposit for me, I know. I can ask for my money whenever I want. Don't worry, sir, I would not mistake you. Don't trouble to come to my press. I can send Sastri to collect the amount from you." This I added out of a sudden apprehension that he might think I was writing off the account. The sun had grown brighter now, and still I had not told him of my problem. I did not know how to make a beginning in a litigation. He was bestirring himself to move off, having had his say and left nothing unsaid. I said quickly, "I want to see you on a legal matter."

He drew himself up proudly now. He was on his own ground. He asked brusquely, "Any more problems coming out of your property matters? I thought they had all been settled once for all."

"No, no, it's not that—" I began.

"Or are you thinking of a partnership deed? Lot of businessmen are doing it now, you know."

"Oh, no, I am not such a big businessman."

"Or estate duty; have you any trouble on that account?"

I laughed. "Fortunately I own nothing to bring the estate duty on my head."

"Or Shop Assistant's Act, or sales tax? You know half the trouble with sales-tax problems is due to lack of definition in the phrasing of the act. Today I could tweak the nose of any sales-tax official who dared to tamper with my client, with all their half-digested manuals!"

"I have a summons from the Rent Controller."

"What for?" he asked. "Do you know how many persons—" he began, but I wrested the initiative from him and cut in. "It is some fancy summons, as you'll see. Can I meet you at home?"

"No," he said. "Come to my office." His office was above
a cotton warehouse, or rather a bed-maker's shop, and
cotton fluff was always flying about, and clients who went
to him once never went there again, as they sneezed
interminably and caught the death of cold; it was particularly upsetting to asthmatics, who were ill for weeks
after a legal consultation with him. His clients preferred
to see him as he lounged about the premises of the district
court in search of business, and he tackled their problems
standing in the veranda of the court or under the shade
of a tamarind tree in the compound. But he liked his in-
experienced clients first to meet him at his office and catch
a cold. I tried to dodge his proposal, but he was adamant;
I should meet him in the narrow room above the cotton
shop.

I went sneezing up the wooden stairs. The staircase was
narrower than the one leading to my attic devoted to dead
wild life, and creaked in a manner which dimmed the
sneezings of a visitor. Although I was born and bred in
that district, this was the first time I had been in Abu Lane,
which was only four roads from my press, conveniently
tucked away from the views and turmoils of Market Road.
There you saw the lawyer's signboard, bleached by time
and weather, Mr. ———, Pleader, nailed to a pillar on
which a more aggressive board announced Nandi Cotton
Corporation, where you saw no one at first but only bales
and bales of cotton, and then a heap in a corner with some
women beating them into fluff for bed-making. It was this
process that spread tuberculosis and asthma to would-be
litigants. Our lawyer's chamber was right on the landing;

it must have been a modified landing space converted into a room, where he had one table, one chair, and one bureau full of law books. His clients had to stand before him and talk. His table was covered with dusty paper bundles, old copies of law reports, a dry ink-well, and an abandoned pen; his black alpaca coat, going moss-green with age, hung by a nail on the wall. Down below, the cotton-fluffers kept up a rhythmic beating. He had a very tiny window with wooden bars behind him, and through it one saw the coconut tree by a neighboring house, a kitchen chimney smoking, and a number of sloping roof tiles, smoky and dusty and with pieces of tinsel gleaming in the bright sun.

"Allergy?" he cried on seeing me. My sneezings had announced my arrival. I stepped in, blowing my nose and rubbing my eyes. There was a beatific smile on his face, and his single tooth was exposed. He sat at the table and commented, "Some people suffer from allergy to dust and cotton. But I never notice such things." He seemed gratified at the superior physique granted to him by God, almost seemed to feel that it was through a special arrangement between himself and God that it was made possible; he enjoyed the sight of allergy in others, as it seemed to give him an assurance that God was especially good to him. "Allergy, they say, is just mental, that's all," he said. "It is something you should overcome by your own resolution," he said grandly.

I stood at the edge of his table like a supplicant and placed before him the brown cover. He put on his spectacles, opened out the paper, spread it out with the palm of his hand, put a weight on it (the inkless bottle), reared back his head in order to adjust his vision, and read. His unshaven jowl and chin sparkled as if dusted over with silver powder.

He sighed deeply. "Of course you have given him no sort of receipt?"

"Receipt? What for?" I asked.

"For the rent, I mean, and I believe you have been sensible enough not to take a check from him?"

I was appalled. This man was falling into the pattern of all the others, including my wife. I simply declared, "I have not rented him the house."

"Have you taken a lump sum?" he asked.

"Look here, he is not my tenant."

"Whose tenant is he, then?" he asked, cross-examining me.

"I don't know. I can't say." I was losing my equanimity. Why were people so pig-headed as not to know or want to understand my position? My legs felt heavy with the climbing of this ladder, and this man would not give me a seat. He seemed to delight in punishing people who came to see him. I could hardly recognize my own voice, it sounded so thick with the cotton dust.

The man was pursuing his inquiry. "If he is not your tenant, what is he?"

"He is not a tenant but a—a friend," I said, almost unable to substitute any other word.

He was quick to catch it. "Friend! Oh! Oh! What sort of friend that has gone and filed a complaint against you! This is a fairly serious offense, according to the present housing act. Why could you not have straightaway gone through the usual formalities, that's—"

"Stop! Stop!" I cried. "I swear that I gave the attic free, absolutely free to that man, because he asked for it."

"If I were a judge, I would not believe you. Why should you let him live with you? Is he a relative?"

"No, thank God; it's the only thing that is good about the present situation."

"Are you indebted to him in any way?"

"No. On the contrary, he should feel himself in debt to me, and yet he doesn't hesitate to hang me!" I cried. I explained at length how Vasu had come in search of me and how it had all come about. Finding that perhaps this lawyer was feeling too sympathetic to my enemy, I tried to win him over by saying, "You remember that day when you came to print the wedding invitation, and how he pulled me out and left you—that's how he does everything. You now understand what he is capable of?"

That prejudiced his mind. He reflected with some bitterness. "And I had to sit there and waste a whole day to no purpose!" He spoke to me on many legal technicalities and took charge of my paper. He pulled out of his drawer a sheet of paper and took my signature. Then he put away the whole thing with relief. "I'll deal with it; don't worry yourself any more about it. How much money have you now?"

"Not an anna," I said, and showed him my pocket to prove it. He looked gloomy at my bankruptcy.

"I would not charge more than a minimum, you know. Some routine charges have to be paid—stamp charges, affidavit charges, and coffee charges for the bench clerk. He is the man to help us, you know."

"Oh, how?"

"Don't ask questions. Now I'm wondering how to pay these charges—absolutely nominal, you know. If you can spare about five rupees—"

"I thought since—since you have—you might adjust your account with me."

He threw up his arms in horror. "Oh, no, never mix up accounts. Two different things, absolutely different situations. Don't mix up accounts. Whatever else you may do. It always leads to trouble. Can't you send someone to your press to fetch your purse, if you have left it there?"

I felt like banging my fist on his table and demanding immediate settlement of my press account, but I felt humbled by circumstances; the lawyer had to save me from prison now. So I said, "If you will manage it somehow today, I shall send the amount to your house as soon as I'm back at the press."

"I am not going home. There is no time today for me to go to the court if I go home, and so, I don't want to seem to trouble you too much, but I thought one wouldn't start out on a business like this without cash of any kind."

"I came out only to consult you," I said.

"I hope you have found it satisfactory," he said ceremoniously.

"Yes, of course," I said. I felt like a pauper petitioning for help. How long would he keep me standing like this? I could not afford to be critical. So I asked breezily, "Now what is to be done?"

"First things first." He studied the sheet of paper intently. "The summons is for eleven a.m. tomorrow, Tuesday the twenty-fourth; today is Monday the twenty-third. It is ten-thirty now. I must file your application for nonappearance almost at once. The rule gives twenty-four hours if a summons is to be non-responded. It would have been a different matter if you had dodged the summons. Did you sign that little paper the fellow had?"

"Yes, of course."

"Ah, inexperience, inexperience," he cried. "You should have consulted me before touching it or looking at it."

"I had no idea it was coming," I said, putting into it all the shock I had felt at Vasu's treachery.

"That's true, that's true," he said. "You must have thought it was some printing business from the district court, ha?"

"Now, is that all?" I asked.

"Hm, yes," he said. "I can always depend upon the bench clerk to help me. I'll do what I can. You must feel happy if you are not on the list tomorrow. I'll have to plead that you are away and need more time or notice."

"But everybody can see me at my press," I said.

"Oh, yes, that's a point. But how can the court take cognizance if you are there? In any event, it'll be better if you don't make yourself too conspicuous during the hours of the court sitting."

"Except when I am called out, I'm most times behind the blue curtain," I said.

"That's good, it is always helpful," he said.

"And what's the next step?"

"You will be free at least for four weeks. Rent court is rather overworked nowadays. They won't be able to reissue the summons for at least four weeks," he said. I felt grateful to the man for saving my neck for four weeks; and now he added a doubt. "Perhaps the complainant will file an objection."

"He may also say that I've not gone anywhere, as he lives right over my head."

"But the court is not bound to take cognizance of what he says. It's not that way that your *mala fides* can be established."

I didn't understand what he meant.

"I have some work now," I said apologetically. I did not want to hurt his feelings with the least hint that I didn't like to be kept standing there while he talked; though as a matter of fact my legs were paining.

"You may go," he said grandly. "I'll be back home at three o'clock. I will manage it all somehow. If you are sending anyone at all to my house, send an envelope with ten rupees in it. Anyway, I'll give you a complete accounting when it is all over."

The proof of the lawyer's handiwork: I was sitting unscathed at my press, printing three-color labels, on the day following my D Day. I gladly sent him ten rupees through Sastri. He would account for it all at the end. I was not to mix up accounts. Great words of wisdom, it seemed to me in my fevered state.

Chapter Six

Fifteen days passed uneventfully. We left each other alone. I heard Vasu come and go. His jeep would arrive at the yard; I could hear that mighty fist pulling the brake, and feet stumping upstairs. Amid all his impossible qualities, he had just one virtue: he didn't try to come to my part of the building; he arrived and departed as he liked. Only the stench of drying leather was on the increase. It disturbed the neighborhood. I had a visitor from the health department one fine day—a man in khaki uniform. He was a sanitary inspector whose main business was to try to keep the city clean, a hard job for a man in a place like Malgudi, where the individual jealously guarded his right to independent action.

The sanitary inspector occasionally came to my press and sat quietly in a chair when his limbs ached from too much supervision of the Market Road. He would take off his pith helmet (I think he was the only one in the whole town who had such headgear, having picked it up at an army disposal store), place it on the chair next to him, wipe his brow with a checked colored handkerchief, sigh, and pant and call for a glass of water. I could not say he was a friend, but a friendly man. Today he leaned his bicycle on the front step of my press and came in, saying, "There is a complaint against you." He produced from his pocket an envelope, took out a sheet of paper, and held it to me.

I was beginning to dread the sight of brown envelopes nowadays. A joint petition from my neighbors, signed by half a dozen names, had been presented to the municipal authority. They complained that on my terrace they noticed strange activities—animal hides being tanned; the petitioners pointed out that tanning and curing of skins was prohibited in a residential area as it gave rise to bad odor and insanitary surroundings. They also complained of carrion birds hovering around my terrace. One part of my mind admired my neighbors for caring so much for sanitation, while the rest of it was seized with cold despair.

I requested the inspector to take a seat and asked what he expected me to do. He said, "Can I have a glass of water?" I called Sastri to fetch the water. After gulping it down in one mouthful, the sanitary inspector (the most parched and dehydrated man I had ever seen in my life) said, "By-Law X definitely prohibits the tanning of leather indiscriminately in dwelling areas; By-Law Y specifies exactly where you can conduct such a business. I did not know you were engaged in this activity. Why? Is your press not paying enough?"

I slapped my brow with my palm in sheer despair. "I have not turned a tanner!" I cried. "I am still a printer. What makes you think so?"

"Where is the harm?" asked the inspector. "There is dignity in every profession. You don't have to be ashamed of it, only you must carry it on at the proper spot without violating the by-laws."

"All right, I'll do so," I said meekly.

"Oh, it's good you will cooperate with us! That is the difference between educated people and uneducated ones. You can grasp our problems immediately. Of course people will do wrong things out of ignorance. How can we expect everyone to be versed in municipal by-laws? I never blame a man for not knowing the regulations, but I'm really upset if people don't mend their ways even after a notice has been issued. May I have another glass of water, please?"

"Oh, surely, as many as you want. Mr. Sastri, another glass of water." I could hear Sastri put away the urgent job he was doing and prepare to fetch the glass.

The inspector emptied the second supply of water at one gulp and rose to go. He said while parting, "I'll send off an endorsement to the parties, something to silence them."

"What will you say?" I asked, a sudden curiosity getting the upper hand.

"We have a printed form which will go to them to say that the matter is receiving attention. That is enough to satisfy most parties. Otherwise they'll bombard us with reminders."

I saw him off at the step of my press. He clutched the handle of his bicycle, stood for a moment thinking, and said, "Take your time to shift, but don't be too long. If you get a notice, please send a reply to say that you are shifting your tanning business and pray for time."

"Yes, sir," I said, "I'll certainly do all that you say." I was beginning to realize that it was futile to speak about any matter to anyone. People went about with fixed notions and seldom listened to anything I said. It was less strenuous to let them cherish their own silly ideas.

The septuagenarian came tapping his stick; he stood on the road, looked up through his glasses, shading his eyes with one hand, and asked in a querulous voice, "Is Nataraj in?"

The usual crowd was in. "Now is the testing time for Nehru," our journalist was saying. "If the Chinese on our border are not rolled back . . ." The poet had brought the next canto of his verse and was waiting to give me a summary of it.

The septuagenarian asked again, "Is Nataraj here?" unable to see inside, owing to the glare.

"Yes, yes, I'm here," I cried, and went down to help him up the steps.

He seated himself and looked at the other two. "Your friends? I may speak freely, I suppose?" I introduced them to him, whereupon he expatiated on the qualities of a poet, and his duties and social relationships, and then turned to me with the business at hand. "Nataraj, you know my grandson had a pet, a dog that he had been keeping for two years. He was very devoted to it, and used to play with it the moment he came back from school." I almost foresaw what was coming. "Someone killed it last night. It lay under the street lamp, shot through the heart; someone seems to have shot it with a gun, you know. Who has a gun here in these parts? I thought no one but the police had guns."

"Why did you let it out?"

"Why? I don't know. It generally jumps over the wall

and goes around the neighborhood. It was a harmless dog, only barking all night, you know, sitting under that street light. I don't know what makes these dogs bark all night. They say that ghosts are visible to the eyes of a dog. Is it true? Do you believe in ghosts?"

"I haven't been able to see any—" I began.

"Oh, that's all right. Most people don't see them. Why should they? What was I saying?" he asked pathetically, having lost track of his own sentence. I was loath to remind him. I hesitated and wavered, hoping that he'd forget the theme of the dead dog and concentrate on the ghosts.

But the journalist said, "You were speaking about the dog, sir."

"Ah, yes, yes. I could not bear to see its corpse, and so I asked the scavenger to take it away. I don't know what you call that breed. We called it Tom, and it was black and hairy, very handsome; someone brought it from Bombay and gave it to my son, who gave it to this little fellow—quite a smart dog, very watchful, would make such a row if anyone tried to enter our gate. . . . Would wait for me to get up from my morning prayer, because he knew he would get a piece of the bread I eat in the morning. The last three years doctors have asked me to eat only bread, one slice of it. Before that I used to take *idli* every day, but they think it's not good for me. My father lived to be a hundred and never missed *idli* even for a single day." He remained silently thinking of those days.

I was glad he was not asking to be reminded of his main theme. I hoped he would get up and go away. Everyone maintained a respectful, gloomy silence. If it had continued another minute, he would have risen and I'd have helped him down the steps. But just at the crucial moment Sastri came in with a proof for my approval. As soon as he entered by the curtain, instead of handing me the proof and disappearing, he stood arrested for a minute, staring at the old man. "What was all that commotion at your gate this morning? I was coming to the press and had no time to stop and ask. But I saw your grandchild crying."

"Oh, is that you, Sastri?" asked the old man, shrinking his eyes to slits in order to catch his features. "How are you, Sastri? It's many months since I saw you. What are you doing? Yes, of course I know you are working with Nataraj. How do you find his work, Nataraj? Good? Must be good. His uncle was my classmate, and he had married the third daughter of . . . He used to come and play with my nephew. Where do you live, Sastri? Not near us?" Sastri mentioned his present address. "Oh, that is far off, Vinayak Street; ah, how many centuries it seems to me since I went that way. Come and see me sometime, I'll be pleased."

Sastri seemed the more pleased of the two to be thus invited. He said, "I must, I must come sometime."

"How many children have you?" Sastri mentioned the number, at which the old man looked gratified and said, "Bring them along also when you come. I'd like to see them."

Instead of saying "Yes" and shutting up, Sastri said, "Even this morning I could have come for a moment, but there was too much crowd at your gate."

"Oh, idiot Sastri! What on earth are you becoming so loquacious for?" I muttered to myself. "Leave him alone to forget this morning's crowd."

But he had stirred up mischief. "Didn't you know why there was a crowd?"

"No, I only saw your grandchild crying."

The reminder of his grandchild nearly brought the septuagenarian to the verge of a breakdown. The old man almost sobbed. "That boy is refusing to cheer up. I can't bear to see that youngster in such misery."

"Why? Why? What happened?" asked Sastri.

"Someone had shot his pet dog," said the journalist.

"Shot! Shot!" cried Sastri as if he had been poked with the butt of a rifle. "When? Was it shot dead? Oh, poor dog! I have often seen it at your gate, a black one!" Why was he bent upon adding fuel to the fire?

"Do you know who could have shot it?" asked Sastri menacingly.

"For what purpose?" said the old man. "It's not going to help us. Will it bring Tom back to life?"

But Sastri insisted on enlightening him. He gave the old man the killer's name, whereabouts, and situation, and added, "He is just the man who could have done it."

The old man tapped his staff on the floor and shouted at me, "And yet you said nothing? Why? Why?"

"It didn't occur to me, that is all," I said hollowly.

The old man tapped the floor with his staff and cried, "Show me where he is, I'll deal with him. I'll hand him over to the police for shooting at things. What's your connection with him? Is he related to you? Is he your friend?"

I tried to pacify the old man. But he ignored my words.

"In all my seventy years, this is the first time I've heard of a shooting in our street. Who is this man? Why should you harbor him? Tomorrow he'll aim his gun at the children playing in the street!"

Knowing Vasu's style of speech with children, I could agree with the old man's views. The old man's hands and legs trembled, his face was flushed. I feared he might get a stroke and collapse in my press—anything seemed possible in my press these days. I said, "Be calm, sir, it will not do to get excited. It's not good for you."

"If it's not good for me, let me die. Why should anything be good for me? Death will be more welcome to me than the sight of my unhappy grandson."

"I'll get him another dog, sir, please tell him that, a beautiful black one. I promise."

"Can you?" asked the old man, suddenly calming down. "Are you sure? You know where one is to be found?"

"Oh, yes," I said. "Easiest thing. I know many planters who have dogs, and I can always get a puppy for our little friend."

"Will you accompany me now and say that to him?"

"Oh, surely," I said, rising.

Sastri chose just this moment to thrust the proof before me and ask, "Shall I put it on the machine?"

I didn't want anything to stop the old man from getting up and going, so I said, "Wait a moment, I'll be back." But Sastri would not allow me to go. "If you pass this proof, we can print it off, everything is ready. They are shutting off power at eleven o'clock today. If we don't deliver—"

"Oh, Sastri, leave everything alone. I don't care what happens. I must see the child first and comfort him." I was desperately anxious that the old man should be bundled off before someone or other should offer to point out Vasu.

As he became more aloof, he became more indifferent, and everything that he did looked like a challenge to me. I was, I suppose, getting into a state of abnormal watchfulness and challenge myself; even the sound of his footstep seemed to me aggressively tenant-like, strengthened by the laws of the rent-control court. He pretended that I never existed. He seemed to arrive and depart with a swagger as if to say, You may have got an adjournment now, but the noose is being readied for you. He brought in more and more dead creatures; there was no space for him in his room or on the terrace. Every inch of space must have been cluttered with packing boards and nails and skins and molds. The narrow staircase, at which I could sometimes peep from my machine, was getting filled up with his merchandise, which had now reached the last step; he had left just enough margin for himself to move up and down. He had become very busy these days, always arriving, departing, hauling up something or hauling down packing cases, doing everything single-handed. I had no idea where his market was. In other days I could have asked him, but now we were bitter enemies. I admired his capacity for work, for all the dreadful things he was able to accomplish single-handed. If we had been on speaking terms, I'd have congratulated him unreservedly on his success as a taxidermist; his master Suleiman must really have been as great as he described him. He had given his star pupil expert training in all branches of his work. Short of creating the animals, he did everything.

Vasu was a perfect enemy. When I caught a glimpse of him sometimes while I stood at the treadle, he averted his

head and passed, perhaps stamping his feet and muttering
a curse. He seemed to be flourishing. I wondered why he
should not pay me the charges for printing his forms and
letterheads. How to ask him? I did not want to do anything that might madden him further.

I was beginning to miss his rough company. I often
speculated if there could be some way of telling him that
all was well, and that he should not give another thought
to what had happened between us; that he could stay in
my house as long as he pleased (only don't bring too many
carcasses or keep them too long; this is a fussy neighborhood, you know). I could never be a successful enemy to
anyone. Any enmity worried me night and day. As a
schoolboy, I persistently shadowed the person with whom
I was supposed to be on terms of hate aand hostility. I
felt acutely uneasy as long as our enmity lasted. As we
started home from school, I was never more than a few
paces away from the boy who declared himself my enemy.
I sat in a bench immediately behind him and tried to
attract his attention by coughing and clearing my throat
or by brushing against his back while picking up a pencil
deliberately dropped on the floor. I made myself abject in
order to win a favorable look or word from my enemy and
waited for a chance to tell him that I wanted to be friends
with him. It bothered me like a toothache. I was becoming
aware of the same mood developing in me now. I was longing for a word with Vasu. I stood like a child at the
treadle, hoping he would look at me and nod and all would
be well again. He was a terrible specimen of human being,
no doubt, but I wanted to be on talking terms with him.
This was a complex mood. I couldn't say that I liked him
or approved of anything he said or did, but I didn't want

to be repelled by him. My mind seethed with plans as to how to re-establish cordiality. I was torn between the desire to make a grand gesture, such as writing off his print bill, and my inability to carry it out—as I didn't like the idea of writing off anything. I liked to delude myself that I collected my monies strictly and never let anyone get away with it. So I decided not to rake up the question of the bill with Vasu until a smiling relationship could once again be established between us and I could refer to the question in a sort of humorous manner.

While I was in this state of mental confusion, Sastri came up with a new problem. There was a hyena at the foot of the stairs, the sight of which upset him while he was composing the admission cards of Albert Mission High School. I was at my usual place, and he parted the curtain and cried, "How can I do any work with a wolf and a whatnot staring at me? And a python is hanging down the handrail of the stairs."

I was all alone in the parlor. "Sastri, I saw it; it is not a wolf but a hyena. Don't you think it surprising that we should be having all this life around us in Malgudi? So near—they are all from Mempi hills!"

The educational value of it was lost on Sastri. He simply said, "Maybe, but why should they be here? Can't you do something about it? It's repulsive, and there is always a bad smell around. All my life I have tried to keep this press so clean!"

I could see that Sastri was greatly exercised. There was no use joking with him or trying to make him take a lighter view of it. I feared that he might take steps himself, if I showed indifference. He might call Vasu through the grille that separated us and order him to be gone with the wolf. I didn't want Sastri to risk his life doing it. So I said placatingly, "Sastri, you know the old proverb, that when your cloth is caught in the thorns of a bush, you have to extricate yourself gently and little by little, otherwise you will never take the cloth whole."

Sastri, being an orthodox-minded Sanskrit semi-scholar, appreciated this sentiment and the phrases in which it was couched; and capped it with a profounder one in Sanskrit which said that to deal with a *rakshasa* one must possess the marksmanship of a hunter, the wit of a pundit and the guile of a harlot. He quoted a verse to prove it.

"But the trouble is that the marksmanship is with him, not with us. Anyway he'll soon deplete the forest of all its creatures, and then no doubt he will have to turn to a tame life, and our staircase will be clear again."

"He fits all the definitions of a *rakshasa*," persisted Sastri, and he went on to define the make up of a *rakshasa*, or a demoniac creature who possessed enormous strength, strange powers, and genius, but recognized no sort of re-straints of man or God. He said, "Every *rakshasa* gets swollen with his ego. He thinks he is invincible, beyond every law. But sooner or later something or other will destroy him." He stood expatiating on the lives of various demons in puranas to prove his point. He displayed great versatility and knowledge. I found his talk enlightening, but still felt he might go on with the printing of the school admission cards, which were due to be delivered seventy-two hours hence; but I had not the heart to remind him of sordid things.

He went on talking; his information was encyclopedic. He removed his silver-rimmed spectacles and put them away in his shirt pocket as being an impediment to his discourse. "There was Ravana, the protagonist in *Ra-mayana*, who had ten heads and twenty arms, and enormous yogic and physical powers, and a boon from the Gods that he could never be vanquished. The earth shook under his tyranny. Still he came to a sad end. Or take Mahisha, the *asura* who meditated and acquired a boon of immortality and invincibility, and who had obtained the special favor that every drop of blood shed from his body should give rise to another demon in his own image and strength, and who nevertheless was destroyed. The Goddess with six arms, each bearing a different weapon, came to fight him riding on a lion which sucked every drop of blood drawn from the demon. Then there was Bhasmasura, who acquired a special boon that everything he touched should be scorched, while nothing could ever destroy him. He made humanity suffer. God Vishnu incarnated as a dancer of great beauty, named Mohini; the *asura* became infatuated with her and she promised to yield to him only if he imitated all the gestures and movements of her own dancing. So a dance began: the demon was an accomplished one; at one point of the dance Mohini placed her palms on her own head, and the demon followed this gesture in complete forgetfulness and was reduced to ashes that very second, his blighting touch becoming active on his own head. Every man can think that he is great and will live forever, but no one can guess from which quarter his doom will come."

Vasu seemed to have induced in Sastri much philosophical thought. Before he left, his parting anecdote was, "Or think of Daksha, for whom an end was prophesied through the bite of a snake, and he had built himself an island fortress to evade this fate, and yet in the end . . ."

and so on and so forth, which was very encouraging for
me too, as I felt that everything would pass and that my
attic would be free from this man. I hoped we would part
on speaking terms, but Sastri did not think it necessary.
I was glad he found a solution to his problem through his
own research and talk, and left me without asking me to
throw out the hyena. He vanished behind the curtain as
he suddenly remembered that he had left the machine idle
and that the ink on the plate was drying.

My only aim now was to save the situation from becoming worse and gradually to come back to a hello-
saying stage with Vasu. But it was not destined to be so.
One fine morning the forester came to my press to ask if
Vasu was still with me. I thought he had come to get his
book of morals printed, and said, "I have not forgotten
my promise, and just as soon as I am able . . ."

He didn't seem interested, but said, "All right, I am in
no hurry about anything, but I am here on official work.
Is Vasu still here? If he is I'd like to speak to him."

A sudden doubt assailed me whether it would be safe
to be involved in this. The forester might have come as
a friend, or he might not. So I said dodgingly, "I'm not
seeing much of Vasu nowadays, although he lives upstairs.
He seems to be very busy nowadays. . . ."

"With what?"

I became cautious. "I don't know. I see him coming
and going. He has his own business."

"Has he? That's what I want to find out. Would you
answer some questions?"

"No," I said point-blank. "I wish to have nothing to
do with anything that concerns him."

"Rather strange!" he said. He had seemed such a timid morals-compiling man some months ago when he first visited me. It surprised me to find him adopting a tough tone. He continued, "He is your tenant, as everybody knows, and he claims your friendship. What do you mean by disclaiming all knowledge of him? Is it believable?"

"Yes. You should believe what I say. Won't you sit down and talk?"

"No, I'm spending the government's hours now, I'm here on official duty, and they are certainly not paying me to lounge in your chairs. I must get busy with what I'm here for."

This thin, cadaverous man, whose neck shot straight out of his khaki collar like a thin cylindrical water-pipe, was tough. He said, "Any man who violates the game laws is my enemy. I wouldn't hesitate to shoot him if I had a chance. A lot of game has been vanishing from our reserves, and even tigers disappear from the blocks. Where do they go?"

"Perhaps to other forests for a change," I said.

He laughed; it was a good joke, in his view. I hoped that this piece of humor would establish a bond between us. "That shows your ignorance of wildlife."

I felt relieved that he recognized it. That would certainly induce him to view me with greater toleration and absolve me from all responsibility for what Vasu was doing. He recovered his composure, as if he realized that he should not spoil me by smiling too much, and suddenly compressed his lips into a tight, narrow line and became grim. He said, "Joking apart, I shall lose my job if I don't track down this mischief going on in the forests of Mempi. Somebody is busy with his gun."

"Can't you watch out?" I asked.

"Yes, but in a forest of hundreds of miles you can't watch every inch of ground, especially if the thief operates at night. Some of our guards are none too honest. We depend in some places on the jungle dwellers, and they are not wholly dependable. I must first have a talk with your tenant."

"He is not my tenant. I take no rent from him."

"Then he must be your friend," said the man, and I recognized the pincer-movement in which this man was trying to trap me as all the others had done.

I said, "He is not even my friend. I never knew him before." This sounded even worse than the others—much better remain his friend or landlord than his business associate. I could see the cadaverous face before me hardening with suspicion.

He thought over his situation for a moment and asked, "Why don't you help me?"

"In what way?"

"I want to get at this man who is destroying game. Can't you give me some clues?"

We came around to the same starting point again, and I said, "I wish to have nothing whatever to do with this business of yours. Leave me out of it. What makes you think I should have anything to do with it?"

"Since you are not his friend, why don't you help me?"

"I am not your friend either," I said.

It seemed silly to carry on a talk like this early in the day, while the Market Road traffic was flowing by and the treadle was rolling on nicely with the admission cards—carry on a vague talk on friendship with an obstinate cadaver! I said with an air of finality, "If you want to rest, come in and take a chair."

"Do I go through here to reach his room?"

"No, it's blocked this way. He has his own door. . . ."

He stepped down without a word and went away. I could read his mind. He was now convinced that I was a joint owner of the poaching and stuffing factory. He went out with the expression that when the time came, he'd round up the gang.

I heard him go up the staircase and knock on the door. Vasu was unused to having visitors. He shouted from inside, "Who is it?"

I heard the other reply, "I wish to see you for a minute. Open the door, please."

"I asked who are you? What is your name?"

"I am Ramaswami. I want to see you."

"Ramaswami, whoever you may be, go down and wait near my jeep. I will be coming down in a short time."

"Why don't you let me in now?"

Vasu shouted from inside, "Don't you stand there and argue. Get out and wait."

I heard the forester go down the staircase, pausing for a moment to study the hyena. Half an hour later, steps once again tumbling down the stairs; and voices from the yard where the jeep was parked. "So you are Ramaswami, are you? To what do I owe the honor of this visit?"

The cadaver was a match for Vasu. He said something that wasn't clear to me. I had to follow all their conversation through the wall at my back, and it filtered out their exchanges in the lower octaves. I stood on a chair and opened slightly a high-up ventilator in the back wall in order to follow their conversation better. The cadaver was repeating his statement about the disappearance of game from Mempi Forest. And all that Vasu asked was "Why not?" The other merely said, "Game in the sanctuaries is expected to be preserved."

"Of course it will be preserved if you take the help of a taxidermist who knows his job," said Vasu jocularly.

"Well, we may not take the taxidermist's help, but the taxidermist himself."

By this time Vasu had climbed into his seat in the jeep; the forester was standing beside it. What a contrast to the first day when he brought the forest official into my office and seated him and flattered him as a noble writer!

"We will watch, and when we get at the man who is depleting the reserve, well, the law is pretty clear on that—"

"If your department needs my cooperation in any matter, don't hesitate to tell me," said Vasu with that crude cynicism he was capable of. The forester ignored it, but said, "How do you account for the hyena that you have on the staircase?"

"That hyena came in search of me. I shot it right where you are standing now," he said.

"What about . . . ?"

"What about? Nothing, that's all. I am not bound to say anything."

"From which forest did you get them?"

"Not from your jungle. Go and look again to see if there is any trademark on them proving that they are from Mempi. India is a big country with many jungles, and you get everything everywhere. For your information, I've also some tiger skins. Are they yours? Claim them if you

can. I am hungry; I'm going out for breakfast. No time
to waste. Don't bother me unless you come with some more
practical proposition."

He drove off unceremoniously. The forester stood where
he was for a second and moved away.

Nothing happened for two days. I was in my usual chair
one afternoon when Vasu's jeep pulled up at my door.
My heart gave a thump. He sat in the jeep and said,
"Nataraj, come here."

I had an impulse to drop whatever I was doing and rush
up to him to seize the chance to make friends with the
monster again. But my pride was stronger. I suddenly
resented all the trouble he had caused me. "Come in and
speak if you have anything to say." I was amazed at my
own temerity.

He grinned. "Ah, you are showing some spirit after all.
That's good."

I didn't like the paternal tone he adopted. I asked again,
"What is your business with me? I'm rather busy."

"Yes, yes," he said mockingly. "I see it, and it's good
to see a man do an honest job at his office instead of chat-
ting away the time with friends who treat the place as a
club lounge." He went on shouting from his jeep, "I appreciate your guts, Nataraj. I had thought that you were
rather spineless. I now know that you have a spine. I'd
never have dreamed that you would set that ghost in khaki
on me! You were smart to think it up. So that's your move;
you want to know what I'll do next?"

"No, I'm not interested. I'm busy."

"You showed him the way to my room. What of it? He
sees all the things there. But hereafter ask your friend to

put a rubber stamp on the backs of all the beasts in Mempi, so that he may identify them later and not make a fool of himself, and not make a fool of you either." And he drove off.

Sen said, "I don't envy your luck in getting a man like that to live with."

I wondered what Vasu's menacing words might mean. Legally he had trapped me at the Rent Controller's court, and the adjournment lawyer was tapping me every now and then for a five or ten; but I now learned that he was satisfied if I gave him just a couple of rupees and made no mention of the money he owed me for printing his daughter's wedding card. I thought Vasu had done his worst, but now what did he mean? I hoped he was not planning to abduct my son and hold him for ransom. He might be up to anything. That evening I told my wife, "If you have any urgent business to call me about, wait till I come home. Don't send the little fellow across."

She grew slightly nervous and asked, "Why? Why?"

I just said, "I don't want him to come there and make a fuss, that's all."

"You see so little of him," she complained. And added, "You leave before he wakes and come home after he is asleep, and if he wants to see his father, he shouldn't even come to the press, I suppose?" And then I had to explain and she grew really frightened.

She was in a panic. She kept the front door shut. She grew completely demoralized if the boy did not come home at six. She behaved as if the monster would be unleashed and come rushing in to swallow up the family if the back door of my press was opened. My son seemed to enjoy the thrill of the situation as long as there was daylight. He spoke to his friends about the dangers that surrounded his life, and I saw batches of schoolboys standing around in knots in front of my press, looking up at the attic window, during the afternoon recess at school. I became curious and beckoned to a couple of children to come in.

"What are you all doing here?"

"Nothing," said one of them. "We are going home from school."

"What are you looking for?" I asked.

"Babu said there was, was—some giant here . . ."

"You want to look at him?" They nodded. "Better not. Go home, boys. There is no such creature here." I was anxious that they should not see Vasu, as they might shout and circle round him and infuriate him. Knowing his attitude to children, I did not want to risk a meeting.

One of them asked slyly, "Is it true that he eats dogs?"

"Oh, no," I said immediately. "He eats rice and other stuff just as we do. That's all false."

"Then why did he shoot Ramu's dog?"

"Oh, that! It was shot by mistake. He was expecting a black bear and had his gun ready, but just at that time this dog came. . . ."

"It was called Lily," said one boy.

Another contradicted, "No, it was Tom."

"No, it's Lily," persisted the boy. "Yes, what'll you give me if it is Lily? Shall we go and ask Ramu?"

"Yes, come on." And they ran off as if they were a couple of birds that had alighted at the window and were flying off again. Two other children who were watching the scene also ran off happily, shouting, "Let us ask Ramu."

My son came up with Ramu one afternoon two days later. Ramu said, "My grandfather asked me to see you."

My son added, "He has come to ask for his dog." Several
weeks had gone by since I had promised the septuagenarian
that I'd replace his grandson's dog. Although at that time
it had seemed a perfectly feasible thing to find another dog,
as days passed it began to look more and more difficult.
I had promised in a moment of emotional stress, and now
in the cold light of day it appeared to me an unreal, impossible task. I did not know how to acquire a puppy or
where one was to be had. I had no doubt mentioned some
planter with a dog. I had had in mind Achappa, a coffee
planter on Mempi for whose estates I used to do printing
work at one time. I remembered his saying that he had a
great Dane pair with nine puppies. Did I need one? That
was years ago. Achappa was not to be seen nowadays; occasionally his manager was noticed at my neighbor's press.

I walked across to the Star and said, "If you see anyone
from Consolidated Estates, please call me." He replied
that it was months since he had seen anyone from Consolidated Estates and suspected that Achappa was getting
his printing done at Madras. So there it was. The dog-
sources were drying up. I needed some expert help in
the matter. I sincerely wanted to help the boy get another
dog. But my resources were poor. I had no time, either.

Every day the boy came to my press and he always
said, "My grandfather asked me to see you." And every
day I gave him some reply and sent him off. It was becoming a mechanical action. And the boy went away satisfied with any answer I gave. My intentions were absolutely honest; but the press work was heavy nowadays and
I did not have a moment to spare. In addition to other
work, Sen was giving me manifestoes to print and the poet
was fetching his cantos with greater speed. With one thing

and another my time flew swiftly each day. I had to work hard and make enough money at least to pay the lawyer whenever he held out his hand for cash! I had not given up hopes of recovering my dues from him, but I obeyed his advice not to mix up accounts.

I had no time actually to go out in search of a dog for the boy, but I had several plans in my head. I'd make a list of all my friends with dogs, tabulate each breed, note down their breeding time, fasten one or another of them to a promise that one of the litter would be given to me, make a round of visits on every Sunday afternoon, and finally pick up one for the young fellow. My son asked me at nights as he nestled close to me (as night advanced the fear of the monster grew in him and he refused to sleep in a separate bed), as if he were a sharer of my dream, "Get me a puppy too, Father, when you get one for Ramu."

"Yes, yes," I said. "Why not?"

At the hyena corner one day, Sastri heard the jingling of bangles and turned to see a woman go down the steps and out of the building. He had been at the machine. I was in the front office, and presently the curtain parted and he peeped in. A look at his face and I knew something was wrong—some matter referring to Vasu. His face was slightly flushed, and his spectacles wobbled as he raised and lowered his brow.

There was no need for preambles, and so I asked straightaway, "What is the latest?"

He swallowed once or twice before saying, "All sorts of low-class women are wandering around this press nowadays. . . ."

"Where? Who are they?"

He flourished his arms upward, and I knew that he was indicating not the heavens, but Vasu. I did not like to pursue the subject because I had a couple of visitors waiting to discuss a printing job. "Sastri, I will be with you in a moment."

He took the hint and vanished into the wings. After persuading my would-be customers to patronize the original Heidelberg, I went in to conduct the research with Sastri. He was printing the leaves of a bank ledger with a sullen face. I had never seen him so worried before. Even the first shock at finding a hyena beyond the grille was nothing to what he seemed to face now. I stood beside him without a word except to sound bossy. "There is too much ink. Watch the inking."

He ignored my fussy advice and said, "If this sort of thing goes on, our reputation in the town will be ruined. I saw Rangi going downstairs. Is it the sort of person we should encourage here? Is this a printing press or what?"

"Who is Rangi?"

He looked desperate, shy, and angry. I was enjoying his discomfiture immensely. "Oh, you are asking as if you didn't know!"

"How should you expect me to know anything of Rangi, Sastri? I have so much to do!"

"As if I had nothing else to do."

"I don't know anything about these people."

"Best thing, under the circumstances. . . . We should not have this kind of person seen in a place like this, that's all."

"I don't know what you are saying, Sastri. What is it all about?"

"That man has started bringing all these disreputable people here; and then where are we?"

Little by little I got it out of him. Rangi was a notorious character of the town. She lived in the shadows of Abu Lane. She was the daughter of Padma, an old dancer attached to the temple of God Krishna, four streets off, our ancient temple. Padma herself had been an exemplary traditional, dedicated woman of a temple, who could sing and dance, and who also took one or two wealthy lovers; she was now old and retired. Her daughter was Rangi. Sastri darkly hinted that he knew who fathered her into this world, and I hoped it was not himself. His deep and comprehensive knowledge of the dancer's family was disconcerting. I had to ask him to explain how he managed to acquire so much information.

He felt a little shy at first and then explained. "You know where my house is, and across from our road is Abu Lane, and so we know what goes on there. To be frank, I live in a portion of the house; the other half is occupied by Damodar, who has a wholesale grain shop in the market. For many years he was keeping that woman, and after this daughter was born, he suspected Padma's fidelity and gave her up, but she threatened to go to a court to prove that he was the father, and finally he had to accept the situation and pay her a lot of money to get out of her clutches. He used to be a chum in our schooldays and he would never conceal his exploits from me."

He went on to say that Padma was now retired, being old, fat, and frightening, like the harem guards of Ravana. Her daughter Rangi had succeeded her at the temple. Before that she studied in a school for a while, joined a drama troupe which toured the villages, and came back to the town after seducing all the menfolk she set eyes on. According to Sastri, she was the worst woman that could ever have come back to Malgudi. Whatever it was, she seemed to be a subject of constant reference in Abu Lane and responsible for a great deal of the politics there.

Next morning I was at the machine, after sending away Sastri to the binder's to look to something. I heard the sound of a bangle, and there she was—Rangi, stepping between the hyena and the mongoose and making for the door. She was dark, squat, seductive, with big round arms and fat legs, wearing a pink sari and overloaded with jewelry, and she was going out with the flowers in her hair crushed, and her clothes rumpled. She evidently didn't care how she looked now; this was her off-hour. I couldn't imagine any woman who would be prepared to walk along the streets in this deshabille. I felt curious to know what she would look like in the evenings. Perhaps she would powder her face, talcum floating uneasily over her ebonite skin; anyway, whatever might be the hour, every inch of her proclaimed her to be what she was—a perfect female animal. But when did she come in? How did she get home? She just walked off, was it? Going about her business with such assurance! Walking in and out of a place like a postman! My mind seethed with speculations. Did Vasu bring her in his jeep at the darkest hour? Not likely. What a man, who could turn his mistress out in cold blood when morning came!

My further speculations on the theme of lust were cut short by the arrival of Sastri, who said, "The binder says that one of his office boys is down with mumps, and that he cannot do the ruling until Friday." He said this in a tone of utter fatalism.

"The sky is not going to fall because he puts it off till Friday," I said.

"Unless the ruling is done, the ledger for the bank won't be ready and they'll come down on us."

Why was this Sastri always in a state of panic lest we should fail one or another of our customers? He had no trust in my ability to manage things and no sort of confidence in me. I felt indignant. "No need for panic! I have run this press for how many years? I've managed to survive and flourish, and so far not made a fool of myself. So why do you worry?" I could not conclude. There was no conclusion as there was no basis at all for beginning the sentence. My mind was busy following the fleshy image of Rangi, and perhaps I resented the intrusion!

I was mistaken in thinking that Rangi was all. I had only to stand there between seven and eight in the morning—and it became a sort of game to speculate who would be descending the stairs next. Sometimes a slim girl went by, sometimes a fair one, sometimes an in-between type, sometimes a fuzzy-haired woman, sometimes another, some mornings a fashionable one who had taken the trouble to tidy herself up before coming out; most times, Rangi also, along with one or another of them, or by herself. Brisk traffic passed on the staircase. I guessed that after the challenge from the cadaver, Mempi Forest was watched more carefully, and Vasu's activities were neutralized, and so he had turned his tracking instinct in another direction. I had no notion that our town possessed such a varied supply of women.

Chapter Seven

It took me time to make him out. His face was familiar. I had seen those slightly finlike ears and round eyes somewhere. He stood on my threshold and brought his palms together and cried, *"Namaskaram."*

Oh, that voice, with its ring—I knew it. It was the afternoon hour. The Market Road was sleepy, a donkey was desultorily chewing an old newspaper at the fountain parapet, the black cow and its friend the free bull had curled up for a siesta right in the middle of the road, obstructing the traffic as was their wont. A couple of late schoolchildren were dawdling along the edge of the road, gazing with fascination into the gutter; a bright, scalding sun was beating down; the woman sitting under the acacia, selling a ripped-up jack fruit, was desultorily waving a stick over its golden entrails, trying to keep off a swarm of flies; a *jutka* was rattling along on the granite metaled road; a sultry, sleepy hour. I had returned to my seat after lunch; Sastri had not yet arrived. My brain was at its lowest efficiency and I had to battle within myself to wrench myself away from a siesta. I had arrears of work to clear. I sat on the Queen Anne chair and stretched my legs on the ancient table as a compensation for forgoing my siesta.

"Come in, come in," I said as a general courtesy to whoever it might be that said "*Namaskaram.*" He came in, with an umbrella tucked under his arm, hesitantly and lowered himself gingerly into the first chair.

"I came by the morning bus—not the one that brought you but the earlier one."

Oh, yes, now it came like a flash. "Oh, Muthu!" I cried, almost jumping at him and hugging him. "Whom have you left to mind the tea-shop?"

"Oh, those boys are there, they can manage it. I am returning by tonight's bus."

"How is your business?"

"Doing very well, sir."

"How are your children? Have you found a bridegroom for your daughter?"

His face fell at the mention of it. I would normally not really have troubled him with any reminder of his daughter's marriage, but in order to cover my initial lapse I now tried to show off my knowledge of his problems. I could not be blamed for my initial lapse. At his tea-shop he had been bareheaded; now he had donned a white khaddar cap, and wore a long mull jibba and a dhoti, and had a lace upper cloth over his shoulder—he had dressed himself to come to town, I suppose. I was very happy to see him. He had rescued me from Vasu that day. I had always anticipated another meeting with him, at least, in order to pay off the tea bill. I opened the drawer of my table and took out a rupee and held it to him. I was suddenly inspired by the lesson taught by my adjournment lawyer not to mix accounts.

He looked at the rupee with some surprise and asked, "What is this for?"

"I have long wanted to pay you that bill for the tea and buns." Even as I was speaking, I realized how silly it sounded. The lawyer had taught me a rather coarse lesson.

Muthu looked rather hurt as he said, "I have paid a bus fare of fourteen annas for coming and will pay fourteen annas for going back; do you think I am spending all that in order to collect—how much was it?"

I was abashed, but said, "My duty, you know. Can I get you coffee or tiffin or anything?"

He shook his head. "I never eat anywhere outside when I travel, and it keeps me fit. I like and enjoy a good meal when I go home."

And now that all the awkwardness was gone, I asked, "What's your command? Tell me what I can do for you." A sudden fear assailed me lest he should ask me to go up to tell Vasu that his old friend was come. I said testingly, "I saw Vasu go out in his jeep."

"We too see him at Mempi going up the hill now and then, but he doesn't stop to speak to us nowadays."

I was pleased and relieved. "What is the reason?"

"Why go into all that?" he said, gently tapping his umbrella on the floor. "He is a man with a gun. Why speak of him? He doesn't care for us now."

"He may have no more use for you," I said, adding fuel to the fire.

"He has other people, who are more suitable to his temperament," he said, hinting at a vast army of undesirable men, trailing behind this man, looking for mischief.

I didn't want to pursue the subject further. I merely said, "He may drop them off when he finds someone more useful," once again a sentiment on which we both immediately concurred. And then a final statement: "After all, it may be for the best; it'd be best to be forgotten by him and have nothing whatever to do with that man." I elaborated the statement with an account of all the happenings since he had stepped on my threshold. "He stood just where you stood; I welcomed him, he sat where you are sitting now. I make no distinction between men——"

Muthu sprang up as if he had occupied a wrong place and said, "I am not that kind."

"I know, I know," I said. "Don't I know? You are a helpful man. You cannot see a man stranded. I know you."

He was pleased and said, "We helped that man so much. Now he thinks that we have informed against him, and he came and created a scene at my shop and threatened us with his gun." He laughed at the memory of it. "As if we wouldn't know what to do, as if we would sit back and let him shoot us! We don't want to bother about him and so leave him alone. He still passes up and down, but never stops for tea and doesn't seem to carry home much from the forests either——and he thinks we are responsible for it! Why, there are hundreds of people going up and down to the project or somewhere on that road, and anyone was bound to notice his activities."

"It's all for the best if a *rakshasa* ceases to notice you," I said, and that put an end to our discussion of Vasu. I was very happy to note that he was no longer liked by Muthu. My enemy should be other people's enemy too, according to my age-old practice.

After all this preamble, he mentioned his business. "You remember our temple elephant I spoke to you about, though you couldn't see it that day? It had gone into the jungle. It's sick, and we want your help to find a doctor!"

Our doctor, Dr. Rao of Town Medical Stores, how would he react to the presence of an elephant in his clinic? I said doubtfully, "I don't know if our doctor knows enough about elephant-sickness."

"Oh, no," he said. "We have heard of a government hospital for animals recently opened here. We want your help to get our Kumar treated there."

A new set of circumstances seemed to approach me in an enveloping movement. This was the first time I had heard of an animal hospital. I could have just said, "I don't know anything about it," and ended the matter there. But my nature would not permit it. I had to get into complications. So I said, "All right, let us see what we can do for poor Kumar. What is the matter with him?"

"He is not taking his food at all nowadays. He shuns it."

What a mighty problem was coming onto me! The enormity of it oppressed me. This was not something I could evade by suggesting that they look over Heidelberg. At the same time I felt flattered. That someone should think of me for tackling such a profound problem was itself an honor. I felt too proud to say that I knew nothing about elephant doctors; after all, the man who had come all this way expected me to do something about it. Suppressing my astonishment at being involved in it, I asked, "Is there any hurry about it? I mean, can't the elephant wait?"

He looked doubtful. "I came to you because, more than others, I knew you would be able to do something for me. You were kind enough to say I could ask you for any help. That poor Kumar, he used to be so lively, playing with all the children, and now for the last ten days he is suffering, he accepts no food. I don't know, something is wrong with him. There is a fellow there in Top Slip, an elephant trainer, who looks after some of the elephants working in the timber yards, but he says that he can't really judge what is the matter."

"All right. I'll do my best. Now what are his symptoms? At least tell me that."

He thought it over for a moment and said, "He seems to get cramps—he lies down on his belly and howls. Have you ever seen an elephant lie down? I have never seen it before; he has to be coaxed and cajoled to accept a ball of cooked rice."

I felt genuinely concerned about poor Kumar now. I said, "I'll go and meet this doctor you mentioned, and we will see what we can do. How shall I communicate with you?"

"Please drop a card, or send a note with any of the Mempi bus drivers, and I'll be here next minute."

I noted down various details officiously. Before leaving he said, "Nothing is more important to me than this, sir."

I had to overlook the responsibilities on hand. Kumar's welfare became an all-important issue. The visiting card that I was printing could wait, but not Kumar.

Later in the day I asked Sastri, "Where is the animal hospital that was recently opened?"

"No idea," he said. "Lost interest in animals five years ago; after the death of my cow, I vowed never to have another. I'm the first person in our whole family to buy milk from street venders! My relations laugh at me for it."

I inquired here and there. Two days were gone. I had the feeling of being a defaulter. As each hour and day passed I grew nervous and finally on the flash of an idea sought my friend Sen, who lived all alone in a converted garage in the compound of a house in Lawley Extension. I had to take a cycle on hire for this expedition. Sen was pleased to see me in his shed. He had surrounded himself with books and stacks of newspaper, which were all over the floor. He sat on a rush mat and worked by a small kerosene light.

I burst in on him at about seven in the evening. He had a sloping board on which was fixed a sheet of paper for writing. It had been a warm day, and he sat barebodied. He was delighted to see me. I sat on his mat.

"I can't give you coffee or anything, but if you like, let us go to a restaurant, there is one not too far off." He was visibly overwhelmed by my visit. All along he was used to visiting, and this was one of the rare occasions when he was receiving.

I said, "I don't need coffee, please. I have come for some information. As a newspaperman, you'll be able to help me." He liked to be called a newspaperman, and I hoped sincerely that some day he would see his views in print. He was always saying that he was about to secure the finances, was on the verge of it, and something always happened; and he sat back, wrote his editorials, and waited for the next financier. But he was equipping himself for the task all the time. Part of his equipment was to know what was going on in the town all the time—in the past and in the present. I asked him about the animal hospital.

"Oh, yes, I remember something about it. . . ." He frowned for a moment at all the accumulation of the past, got up, pulled down some stacks of old paper, turned them over, blowing the dust in my face. He thrust an old newspaper under my nose and tapped his finger on a news item. It gave a description of a Deputy Minister laying the foundation for a veterinary college and animal-welfare hospital on the other bank of Sarayu, for which ten acres of land had been gifted by the municipality and some foundation had given dollars and equipment for a start, and the government had promised to take it under its wing during the third Five-Year Plan, and so on and so forth. A lengthy speech was reported in which the Deputy Minister dwelt on the importance of *ahimsa* and the importance of animals in human economy, and then he was garlanded and made to tread the red carpet. I wondered how I had missed it.

"Do you know how you missed it? Like the rest," Sen said. "They mismanaged the whole thing. The printed invitations went out late, and reached most people a day too late."

"I wonder where they got them printed," I said to ward off any suspicion that I might be responsible for the mess.

"The result was that no one turned up at the function except the organizers and the Deputy Minister—and he was furious at the mess. They had platform, decorations, and an elaborate tea, but only a handful of audience; the Deputy Minister made his speech all the same. Anyway, it looks dignified and impressive in print," he said fondly, looking at the printed column. "However, the doctor is already on the scene, although little else is ready."

Next afternoon I went in search of this animal doctor. I crossed Nallappa's Grove on my cycle. It was about one o'clock, and the sands were hot. A few bullock carts were crunching their wheels along the sand. The mango trees cast a soft shade, and the air was thick with the scent of mango blooms. The river flowed on with a soft swish. It was so restful that I could have set my bicycle against the trunk of a tree and gone to sleep on the mud under the shade of the tree. But duty impelled me onward. I cycled up the other bank across a foot track and suddenly came upon a bare field enclosed within barbed wire. The gate was barricaded with a couple of bamboo poles. A tablet on a short masonry work commemorated the laying of the foundation. The south side of the barbed-wire enclosure was bounded by a wall of the cremation ground, where a couple of funeral parties were busy around smoky pyres. A howling wind blew across the fields; there was a single palmyra tree standing up in the middle of this desert, although across the road tops of green corn rippled in the air.

I left my bicycle at the gate and walked around to read the signboard over the entrance: DEPARTMENT OF ANIMAL WELFARE, WORLD Q.R.L. (World Quadruped Relief League, California). I saw the roof of a hut shining in the sun and sent off a shout in that direction, "Hi! Who is there?" I was enjoying this hunt. I shouted without any hope, expecting the Mempi hills shimmering on the horizon to echo back my call without an interruption.

But I got the answer. "Who is there?" a voice called back.

"I have come for the doctor," I said.

It seemed absurd to be calling for a doctor out of empty space. But it worked. A man appeared at the door of the hut and gesticulated. He cried, "Come along!"

"The gate is barred," I cried.

"Come through the fence," he called. I slipped through the fence, the barbed wire slightly gashing my forearm and tearing my dhoti. I swore at it, but it gave me a feeling of shedding my blood for a worthy cause.

The man stretched his hand. "I'm Dr. Joshi."

"My name is Nataraj," I said as the wind howled about my ears.

He was a short man wearing a shirt over white pants, with a small face and a brow knit in thought. "Come in," he said, and took me into the hut. A tin roof arched overhead; there were a bamboo table, a couple of folding chairs, and a charpoy with a pillow. He had a few books in a small wooden rack, a kerosene lamp and a stove and pots and pans in a corner. Here was a man with a mission, definitely. He seated me in a chair and drew the other close to me and said, "Yes, Mr. Nataraj? What can I do for you, Mr. Nataraj?"

I looked around; there was very little of the hospital or dispensary or college about it. I told him about the elephant. He listened to me with the characteristic patience of a doctor and said, "Hm, I'd like to have it under observation and then I'll see what we can do."

I had not visualized this prospect. I had thought that he would go and examine the elephant. I suggested it. He said, "It's impossible. The equipment for tests is here."

"He is sick and keeps throwing himself down. How to bring him so far?"

The problem looked frightening, but he had an absolutely simplified view. He brushed aside all my doubts and said, "He has his mahout, hasn't he? Tell him that he must come here and he will prod him and prick him and make him walk. . . . Animals, once they realize the pleasure of sitting, will always sit down," he said. "It doesn't mean anything. It's our business to prod them and keep them on their feet. Unless I have him here, I shall have no means of handling him or testing him. You see there . . ."

He walked over to a chest and threw it open; it was crammed with all kinds of shining instruments, tubes, bottles, and a microscope. "This is the standard equipment that our League ships to every center; it contains everything that a veterinarian will need, but you see, we are doing so little with it now."

"Why so?" I asked.

"Our League provides equipment and a basic grant for a doctor like me, but the local organizations will also have to do their bit. For instance, the college and the hospital must go up before we can do anything."

"When do you expect it all to be ready?"

"How can we say? It is full of politics; people do not want it here, but somewhere else. Our Deputy Minister has no interest in this project, and so it goes on at its own pace. The Public Works should give us the building and the sheds for the animals, but they are still in the stage of estimates and sanctions. I really cannot imagine when we will get going and what we can do. I'm the only one ready, because I'm being maintained by the League and there's a lot of equipment to guard. As matters stand, I'm only a watchman. I'm sticking on because I feel that if I leave even this will be gone. I have a hope that things will be okay sometime. I'm not allowing things to rust, you know. I'm all the time bombarding the headquarters with letters and so forth. . . . I'm happy that you have heard about us and want our service."

"It was in the papers," I said knowledgeably.

"Bring your elephant over, I'll do what I can for the poor creature. I have always wanted to try my hand at an elephant."

"What could be wrong with him?"

"Well, anything. Colic, or an intestinal twist, or he might have swallowed a sugar cane without chewing it and that sometimes causes trouble."

"Do you know all about all animals?"

"Oh, yes, about most of them. Our League headquarters in California has one of the biggest collections of animals in the world, and I went through a four-year course. Our main job will be to treat the cattle of our country, but we like to do our best for any creature. Most animals and man arc alike; only the dosage of a medicine differs," he said. He was a completely serious man, completely living in a world of animals and their ailments and diseases.

At Mempi it caused a sensation. The village elders gathered together in front of the tea-shop and a great debate started over the question of the elephant. Muthu was all for bringing the elephant over. They all trooped, after carrying on their discussion in front of the tea-shop, to the little temple. Trucks and cars passed by. I marched with them to the little shrine at the crossroads; the four-armed Goddess watched our proceedings serenely from her inner sanctum. Within the yard of the temple the elephant was tied by his hind leg to a peg under a very large tree. It had flopped itself down like a dog, with its legs stretched out. Its trunk lay limp on the ground; its small eyes looked at us without interest; its tail lay in the dust; its tusks seemed without luster. Muthu patted its head and said, "He has been like this for days now." He looked unhappy. A few boys stood outside the ring of elders and watched the elephant and commented in whispers.

Everyone looked at me sourly as a man who had come to abduct their elephant and make things worse for them. I said, "If you do not send the elephant along, what is the alternative?"

"Bring the doctor here," said the tailor, who had his machine next to the tea-shop and who was one of the trustees of the temple. There was a schoolmaster in their gathering who was not sure what he wanted to say but kept interrupting everyone with his reminiscences. "There was once," he began, "an elephant . . ." And he narrated a story which was considered rather inauspicious as at the end of it the elephant had become incurably ill. "Oh! Master!" appealed Muthu. "Should I teach a wise one like you what to speak and when and what not to speak?" He looked sadly at the teacher.

I began the whole proposition over again. "Our main business will now be to see that the elephant Kumar gets well." It received common agreement, the only part of my statement which met with universal accord. "And so," I began, "what is most important is that we should see that he gets onto his feet and moves freely." This was the same sentiment in another form. They hesitated for a moment, examining it critically, but accepted it eventually as one without any trap in it. And now I mentioned something really dangerous: "And so he should be made to get up on his feet and move in the direction of the doctor."

"No," said the obstinate tailor. "The doctor must come to here. Have you no pity? How can a sick animal tramp fifty miles? It'd be cruel." For a moment everyone made noises of sympathy for the tailor. This brought the question back to its starting point. The tailor had won his point; he looked triumphantly obstinate, and moved away.

I felt desperate. Between an immobile elephant, an equally immobile doctor, and a mentally immobile com-

mittee there seemed little to do except pray for the elephant. I realized that in a committee there was likely to
be no progress, and so I didn't press the point. I knew that
the tailor would not go on standing there forever; sooner
or later someone was likely to come to his shop and demand his clothes back. So we spent the time morosely
watching the recumbent elephant and suppressing the
obvious suggestions. The ring of children was growing
smaller, as they had grown bored with watching the gloomy,
theory-speaking elders and had exhausted themselves in
suppressed giggles (for fear of the serious elders, who were
constantly turning to them and ordering them to shut up).
There were really five on the committee of the temple but
except for Muthu and the tailor the rest were men of no
consequence. All that they did was to simper and evade any
commitment. I had not too much time to waste today. I had
come by the first bus in the morning, and the last bus was
leaving at six; at four o'clock there was still no sign of
any agreement on the elephant question. I was still hoping
that the tailor would be called off; and as if some customer
of his had been hit by a thought wave from me, an errand
boy from the tailory came panting with the statement:
"The trouble-maker is back, and won't go until he can
talk to you."

The tailor lost his head at the mention of the trouble-
maker, whoever that beneficent soul might be. "Has he no
business except to come for those miserable jackets of his
wife's? Fifth time he is visiting me!"

"Perhaps his wife has barred the house to him until he
brings home the jackets," I commented under my breath.

"Throw his pieces out. Fling his pieces in his face," cried
the irate tailor.

"But you have locked them up," said his errand boy seriously.

"That settles it. . . . I'll be back soon," he said and rushed out in a rage. I felt relieved, lighter in my chest. This was my chance. Now I had the committee in my pocket. I told Muthu hurriedly, "Before my bus leaves, I must see this elephant on his feet. We will discuss the other things later."

"How to get him up? Kumar!" he appealed, "please, please stand up."

One of the stragglers, a young urchin who had been watching us with a thumb in his mouth, took out his thumb and said, "I know how to make an elephant get up."

"How? How? Come on, do it," I said eagerly, pulling his hand out of his mouth and propelling him forward. He grinned, showing a toothless gum, and said, "If you get me a frog, I can make him get up."

"What! How will you do it?"

"When a frog is put under an elephant, it'll jump, and the elephant will jump with it," he said.

I was even prepared to dig a crowbar under Kumar and lever him up if necessary, but a mahout arrived at the crucial moment. He was attached to the timber yard five miles up in a mountain jungle. They had desperately summoned him four days ago through a truckdriver passing that way, and the man found the time to turn up only today. He arrived just when we were hesitating between applying a jumping frog or a crowbar to make Kumar get up, wanting to do something before the tailor should return. The mahout wore a knitted vest and over it a red sweater and a white dhoti coming down to his knees, a combination calculated to strike terror into the heart of any recalcitrant elephant. He pushed his way through the ring of watching loungers and looked us all up and down questioningly. "Why is he lying down?" he asked.

"That is what we should like to know," said Muthu. "He has been like this for four days."

The mahout looked at Kumar questioningly, put his face close to the elephant's, and asked, "What is your secret?" in a soft murmur. He told us, "Keep away. He doesn't like a big audience for his speech, you understand? Move off, and he will tell me." We moved away. He put his face close to the large trunk of the elephant, murmuring something, and after a while we turned to look as we heard a swish, proceeding from a very thin green switch in his hand, which lashed the underside of the elephant within his reach; he repeated it at intervals of a second, and the elephant was on its feet.

He flourished the green switch, which looked no different from any trailer of a plant, and said, "This is . . ." And he gave us the name of some obscure plant grown in mountain thickets. "This is more serviceable than one's own brothers emanating from the same womb," he explained. "I have yet to see an animal that does not respect this stick." As he flourished it the elephant blinked and gave a loud trumpet. I only hoped that it would not bring the tailor scrambling in. The trumpeting was loud and prolonged.

The mahout leaned on the elephant's side, as if posing for a photograph, and smiled at the gathering. He seemed to fall into a mystic trance as he drew the switch across his nose. "Now get me a broken coconut and a little jaggery and a piece of sugar cane."

We sent a youngster running to fetch these. While waiting for the youngster's return, the mahout leaned on the elephant and he regaled us with his memoirs; he recounted the tales of all the elephants that he had coaxed and taken to the various zoos in the country and he spoke of a chance that he had had of taking an elephant to Tokyo or New York, which was frustrated by his brothers, who did not like the girl he had married and wanted to punish him for not marrying according to their own arrangements. From Kerala, far-off Kerala, this mahout had brought a girl to marry, but his brothers advised him to pay off the woman and raised among themselves two hundred rupees. The mahout went up to her with the money and asked her to go back to Kerala. She quietly said, "Keep your money, only tell me if there is any deep well or tank nearby where I can drown myself. I want you to know that I have come to you not for your money. . . . If I can't be worthy of being your wife, I shall be quite happy to be dead at your feet, rather than to go back to my village with two hundred rupees." He explained, "Two hundred rupees, not just two rupees, and she did not want it. I immediately told my brothers that I did not care for them, told them to do their worst, and married the girl. You think that I married her on the money from them? Not me. I returned it to them, I actually threw it out of the door and told them to pick it up, and borrowed a hundred rupees on which I am still paying interest of five rupees a month, and married her. Such a wonderful woman. She won't eat her food unless I am back home, even if it is midnight. What can I do? Sometimes I have to be out for days and days, and what does she do? She starves, that is all," he said. "A dutiful wife."

He never finished his narrative to tell us how it prevented his going to Tokyo or New York, for at this moment the elephant coiled its trunk around his back, and he patted it and said, "Now we are friends, he wants me to sit on his back." He tapped the elephant's knee and took hold of its ear, and pulled himself up even as he was talking. By this time the youngster had brought coconut and jaggery. The mahout stooped down to take it and held it for the elephant, saying something. The elephant just picked up the bamboo tray, raised it, and sent it flying across the field.

Muthu was crestfallen. "See, that's what he does to food."

"Never mind," said the mahout, "he is not hungry, that is all. I would fling the dinner plate at my wife's face myself if I did not feel hungry and she persisted. Now I am ready ; where is he to go?"

"Ride him to the town," I said promptly. "I will meet you at the toll-gate outside the city." And before we knew what was happening, he had flourished his green switch and was off, with all of us trooping along. The children let out a shout of joy and ran behind the elephant. I was not very happy about the amount of public notice the whole business was receiving. It might stir up the tailor once again. Muthu walked with a look of triumph beside the elephant. I felt triumphant too in a measure. To put our ideas in proper perspective, the mahout leaned down to say, "Because he is trotting, don't imagine he is not ill. He is very sick. I have my own medicine for his sickness, but you want to see an English doctor ; try him and come back to me. I never want to stand in anybody's way of doing something, although I know what English doctors can do. They will sooner or later call people like me. . . ."

This made Muthu once again thoughtful. He suddenly remembered that he had come out without thanking the Goddess. He ran back to the temple, lit a piece of camphor before the Goddess, and rejoined the procession. At the

Market Road, when the procession passed in front of the tea-shop, he invited the mahout to stop for a moment and ran into his shop.

The mahout said, "If you can, reach me a glass of tea here. I can't get down. If I get down, Kumar will also sit down immediately; that is his nature." Kumar seemed to understand this comment; I could detect a twinkle in his small red eyes, and he swayed his head in appreciation of this statement. Muthu brought out a tray covered with buns and a tumbler of tea, and held it up to the mahout. The flies that swarmed in his shop sought a diversion by coming on in a mass and settling on the back of the elephant for a ride. The mahout sat comfortably in his seat, set the tray before him, and started to drink his tea. And now the tailor came flouncing out of his shop, demanding, "Everyone get out of the way and tell me what is happening."

The mahout thought the remark beneath his notice and looked down from his eminence with indifference. This irritated the tailor. He said, "This is our elephant, where are you taking him?" The tailor's sense of ownership over the elephant was comical, and everyone laughed. Muthu, who had gone back to his seat at the counter, now said, "He knows how to handle the elephant, don't worry. He is taking it out for its own good."

"What—to the city? I will never have it, never, never." The tailor stamped his feet like a petulant child.

The mahout was confused. He looked puzzled and asked, tying a towel around his head as a turban, "What does it mean? Am I stealing an elephant?"

Muthu came out of his shop, put his arm around the tailor, and said, "Come and have tea," and managed to say at the same time to the mahout, "Yes, yes, you go, it is getting late, remember where you will be met. . . . We will look to other things. . . ."

The mahout flourished his green switch ever so gently, and the elephant was on the move again, with the trail of children behind it. Soon the green turban vanished from the landscape, around a bend. The tailor was disconsolate until Muthu poured oblatory tea into him, unwashed glass after unwashed glass. At this rate, I said to myself, Muthu will be a bankrupt treating all his elephant associates to tea. He will close down his business, and then who will pay the elephant doctor at the other end?

I sat on the plank bridging two empty kerosene tins in front of Muthu's shop, watching the scene with detachment. Now that the elephant was gone, a big worry was off my mind. I didn't care what the tailor thought or said. Refreshed by tea and buns, he came out of the shop and passed me without a word. But the brief look he cast in my direction was enough to indicate what he thought of me—an abductor of elephants. He stepped out, wiping his mouth with the sleeve of his shirt, and was soon out of view in his own shop four doors off. I could hear him say to someone, "Take away those pieces if you cannot wait. I promised you the jackets only at the end of this week."

I could not hear the rest of his sentence as the dreaded jeep drew up on the road in front of me. Vasu had come downhill. He looked at me from his seat and said, "Coming along? I am going back to the town."

I hesitated for a moment. The bus had been due any time for the last ninety minutes. Still there was no sign of it. But how could I go with this man? I didn't like to tell him about myself or my mission here. I would be at his

mercy if I climbed into his jeep. I said, "I am not coming
back yet."

"Why not?" he asked persistently. "What do you want
to be doing here? You want to spend the night here?"

He was blocking the road; a truck was trying to pass;
the truckdriver sounded his horn impatiently. Vasu merely
waved his arm. "You have enough clearance there."

"There is a ditch."

"All right, get into the ditch. Don't disturb me now.
Don't you see that I am talking to a gentleman?"

The truckdriver edged close to the drain and passed.
Vasu said to me, "I will take you back home."

"You may go," I said.

He indicated the back seat. "I have nothing there today.
I knew that you would swoon at the sight of a dead creature.
That is why I came without any today."

How did he know my movements? Perhaps he had been
watching me all the time. In any case I did not like to talk
to him about it. I merely said, "I have other conveyance.
You may go, thank you."

"What other conveyance?" he persisted. "Your bus has
broken down at the tenth mile up, axle gone. Men, women
and children sitting on the roadside. They will have to be
there until—I don't know. If anyone has a gun there he
may shoot a tiger or a rogue elephant that may prowl
around them tonight. If you are keen on catching the bus,
I will take you there and leave you with that crowd."

I wondered for a moment if there might be truth in his
report. As I hesitated he commanded, "What are you waiting for? Or if you want to spend the night with that tea-
shop crowd, go ahead—please yourself. I have things to
do, if you don't mind," he said sarcastically.

It irritated me at first, but I suddenly realized that this was a good chance to establish contact with this man again. He spurned me when it suited him and picked me up again as it suited his fancy. This was a galling thought, no doubt, but it was better than being continuously ignored by him. So I climbed into the jeep without a word. He drove off. We remained without speech for some time; he drove at his usual scaring, reckless speed, swearing at bullock carts, threatening to smash them up and calling all passers-by names. He was disappointed when they accepted his bullying unprotestingly, but when one or another of the cartmen turned round with a frown or a swear word he was delighted, and he nudged me and confided, "That is how I like to see my countrymen. They must show better spirit; they are spineless, and no wonder our country has been a prey to every invader who passed this way."

I could not accept his view of our countrymen, and so I asked, "Do you want everyone to be a blustering bully in this country?"

"Yes," he said simply. He was in an extraordinarily good humor. I wished he would continue thus. It was becoming dark, and the lights were up on the homesteads in farms on the way. He said, "How busy are you nowadays?"

"Well, the usual quantity of work."

"And the usual quantity of gossipmongering?"

"What do you mean?" I asked rather sharply.

"No offense, no offense," he said with mock humility. "Just for fun, that is all. I meant the chair fixtures of your press."

"Why can't you leave them alone?" I asked. "They hardly ever think of you; why should you bother about them?"

"No offense meant, no offense meant," he said with great display of humility. "I just wanted to know, that is all. I am their well-wisher, and I just wanted to know how well they are faring, that is all."

"Look here, Vasu," I said, on a sudden access of fool-hardiness, "you should leave others alone; it will make for happiness all round."

"I can't agree with you," he said. "We are not lone dwellers in the Sahara to live self-centered lives. We are members of a society, and there is no point in living like a recluse, shutting oneself away from all the people around."

There was no use arguing with this man. I once again became aware of a mounting irritation and wanted to guard against it. I said, moderating my tone, "After all, that poet has done a remarkable performance with his life of Krishna. He is completing *Radha Kalyan,* that is the marriage of Krishna with Radha, and his book will be out soon."

"Hm," Vasu said with a half-interest in the program. "And what about the other?" He was referring to his favorite target, the journalist. . .

"Well," I said, with considerable pride, "his plans are almost ready for starting a small news sheet in this town; he is already issuing printed manifestoes now and then."

Now he seemed impressed with all this achievement. He remained thoughtful for a moment and said, "I like people to do something, whatever it may be."

So the journalist and poet had secured this man's approval, I reflected. I wanted to tell him, but could not, that it was impertinence on his part to think that the world waited for his approval. However, he was pleased to think that humanity could move only after securing a clearance certificate from him. There was no use arguing with him, as he was one of those strong men who had no doubt at all about their own conclusions. He asked suddenly, "I want to know if you are willing to print a book I am writing. I have been busy with it for some weeks now."

"Aha!" I cried, unable to restrain myself. It was unthinkable that this man should be busy with a literary composition. He brightened up on hearing my interest and said, "It is a monograph on wildlife. Every day our papers are full of speeches and meetings on the problem of preservation of wildlife, and most of the folk do not know what they are talking about. I have some very important points on the subject, and I am making them in my book. What has happened in this country is that amateurs have invaded every field. People just talk their heads off. I have many important points in my book, and I want it to be ready for the conference on wildlife coming off at the end of this year."

"But that conference will be for the preservation of wildlife?" I asked.

"What if? My book is also on the better methods of preserving wildlife. It is not to be achieved by refusing game licenses for honest folk, or by running behind the animals with cries of sympathy."

I restrained my interest in his talk. I did not want to get involved in his affairs again. I dreaded the prospect of having him again in my parlor, sharpening his wits against the poet and my other visitors. I maintained my reserve and silence for the rest of the journey as the jeep sped along the dark highway.

Chapter Eight

The poet was in an exalted mood. He had completed
the portion where Krishna meets his future wife Radha
and their marriage is to be celebrated. He had several
hundred lines of crystal-clear monosyllables; he had
evolved his own prosody and had succeeded. His manuscript
was ready, several little exercise books stitched by himself and wrapped in brown paper, closely filled with writing
in green ink. He had written till late on the previous night.
His eyes were red with sleeplessness. But his face glowed
with triumph. With the marriage, the book would make
about ninety-six pages. Sastri had printed the book at the
rate of four pages a month over a space of countless months,
and it had now assumed the shape of a volume. Sastri himself was excited at the completion of the volume with the
marriage episode. He brought in proofs of some pages and
hesitated for a moment. When Sastri stood hesitatingly
this way, I always knew he would have something to say
and hoped that if I did not turn round and meet his eyes
he would be gone. As I bent over my paper, I was aware of
his shadow behind me.

"What is it, Sastri?" I asked sharply.

He looked at the poet and both of them smiled. So I

knew it was a piece of good news and felt relieved. "When a poet has arrived at the stage of the marriage of a God, it'll be auspicious to celebrate the occasion." And then he went on to explain how it was to be conducted. I was fond of the poet, and anything that was going to give him a place in our society was welcome.

Enormous preparations started. Once again my normal work of composing and printing was pushed to the background. The fruit-juice man prospered more than ever and wanted four thousand more of the three-color labels, but I was not prepared to give him his labels yet. I had only time to print the first basic gray; I put it away to dry and said so every time the messenger came from fruit-juice. Let him try and print it elsewhere and I should not object to it. But where would he get the magenta, that thirst-creating shade of color which drew people in a rush to wherever his bottles were displayed? The sixth time I turned back the boy, K.J. himself came thundering in and shouted at Sastri from beyond the curtain. He did not know that I was also there; I was behind the curtain, helping Sastri to compose an appeal for our function ahead. We needed funds for the celebration. We were also in a conference with an astrologer in the composing room. We did not want to be disturbed; there now hung a thickly woven bamboo mat screening us off from whatever might be on the other side of the grille. Vasu might have all the dead animals in creation there, but it was not going to affect us. He might have all the prostitutes in the town marching up and down the steps, but that was not going to distract either me or Sastri. We could hear footsteps moving, but that didn't distract our attention. We went on with our jobs, although if I felt too curious I could always peer through a pinhole in the bamboo curtain and get a lovely circular vision of a hyena's snout or the legs of some woman or the hefty feet of Vasu himself stumping up. But it was a luxury that I permitted myself only under some very special or extraordinary condition; never when Sastri was around, as I did not want him to get into the habit. I don't think he ever knew of the existence of the peephole.

The astrologer was sitting on the floor beside the treadle. He had a page of an almanac open before him, held at arm's length, for want of focus, and was explaining, "On the full moon, the moon is in the sixth house, which is the best place we can have for the moon, and the presiding star that day is . . . , which means—" He shrank his eyes to catch the figure in the column and muttered, "I've left my glasses at home," whereupon Sastri took his own glasses off his nose and handed them to him. He put them on and said, "You see this here. . . . What's the number?" It was now Sastri's turn to snatch the almanac from the other man's hand and hold it at arm's length. Still not being able to see, he held out his hand for the glasses, which the other man removed from his nose and handed to him. Now Sastri saw the number and said something, and the other man, wanting to verify it, held his hand for the glasses—and thus Sastri's silver-rimmed glasses were bandied back and forth. The conference proceeded on these lines—I'd not much to do, a veritable ignoramus among the stars. The idea was to fix a day suitable to the poet, also coinciding with the spring festival at the Krishna temple.

A loud voice called through the curtain, "Sastri!" I was offended by the commanding tone. I signaled to Sastri to find out who it was on the other side of the curtain, but before Sastri could take a step forward the voice continued, "Are you delivering the labels or not? If you can't, say so, instead of making our boy run to you a dozen times."

Now I knew who it was. He went on in a big way, cataloguing his grievances and our lapses, and threatening us with dire consequences. Sastri and the astrologer looked intimidated. I could notice in Sastri's face a slight satisfaction too on the realization that he had said so and that I had not heeded his warning. So it was time for me to show myself. I said, "Who is it? Is it K.J.?"

There was a pause, and the man said from the other side of the curtain, "Mr. Nataraj, you are letting me down. How can you expect us to deliver our bottles when . . ."

I could say it for him. I knew all his points. So I cut him short with: "Why don't you take your seat, my friend? I'll be with you in a minute." I had hesitated for a moment whether I should tell him to come through the curtain as a special gesture, but abandoned it for fear it might create a bad precedent. People respected the curtain, and it had better be so. Vasu alone had pierced the privacy and it had turned out to be a nuisance in every way. I did not want it to happen again, and so I said to the angry fruit-juice seller, "Sit down comfortably in that big chair, and I'll join you in a moment."

A silence ensued, and I heard the movement of a chair and guessed he must have acted on my advice in a mood of sullen compliance. I allowed him to wait, giving him time to cool off. We resumed our conference with the astrologer, who sat carrying on his investigation among the planets unruffled by the happenings round him. After half an hour's silent calculations, with Sastri's spectacles

perched over his nose, the man lifted his head slightly
but would not speak. He behaved like one not yet out of a
trance. I knew that the man in the other room was impatient. He was kicking the floor and clearing his throat
in order to attract my attention. I felt satisfied that I had
cowed the irate customer. The astrologer sat beside the
treadle and still said nothing. Sastri stood respectfully
looking down at him. I asked, "What are we waiting for?"
The astrologer merely looked up. The visitor in the other
room again cleared his throat. Sastri said, "He may take
another fifteen minutes." I thought it would be best to dispose of the visitor. I passed through the curtain.

The drink-seller sat cross-legged in the Queen Anne
chair; he had left his sandals on the floor under the chair.
He was an old-type orthodox man, who wore a red caste
mark on his forehead. It was clear that he was there to
see this thing through and to have it out with me. Initiative
was half the victory in a battle, and so before he could
open his mouth I remarked, wearing a look of the utmost
grievance, "What's the use of my friends losing their
temper in this place? I never delay anyone's business without a reason."

"What is it this time?" K.J. asked cynically. "Blocks
not ready? Ink not available? That's why I made sure to
send along with my order that can of ink which I got from
Madras."

"And your can of ink is perfectly safe here," I said,
producing it out of my drawer. I turned the can in my
hand, scrutinized the label, and gave it to him. "This is
unsuitable. If I had used it, people would have run away
from your bottles. Do you know what it looks like when

it dries? It assumes the pink of an old paper kite picked out of a gutter."

"I got it from Madras, the same brand you suggested."

"But I use only the imported variety. This is canned in Delhi. Did you know that?"

This was a good development, as it made K.J. look so ignorant, wrong, and presumptuous that he remained dumb. I said, "I wouldn't use stuff like this on your work even if you forced me at the point of a gun. I have my responsibility."

He asked like a child, "So what shall we do about it now?"

"Well, I won't let you down, an old, valued customer. If you have trust in me, I'll never let you down," I said as if I were a god speaking to a sinner. "Sastri!" I shouted. "Please bring that magenta ink." Turning to K.J., I said, "You can see the difference for yourself. . . ."

There were some vague movements of response inside the curtain. I knew Sastri would not pay any attention to my call unless I called him again. K.J. grew interested and asked, "Is Sastri in?"

"Why?" I asked.

"He never answered, although I called him," he said.

"He is a very busy man," I said. "He carries a hundred things in his head."

"Except my work, I suppose," K.J. said with a sort of grim humor.

"Don't blame him; he has a hundred different things to do."

"May I know the nature of his hundred activities?"

I could easily have snubbed him, but I said quietly, "A

poet is going to be launched in this world soon, and he is busy with the arrangements connected with it." I realized that in the last resort truth was more convincing and effective than any fabricated excuse.

K.J. looked stunned on hearing it, and asked, "Does it mean that nothing has been done about our labels?"

"Yes," I said, "the main reason being that we could not use your ink and we had to wait for our usual brand. The other reason was that this poet's business came up suddenly. We are in search of a good day for the function; as soon as the date is settled, we'll approach you. It's a good cause for which everyone should do his best."

"How? How? What do you expect me to do? Give money?"

"Yes, that'd be best, but we leave it to you. The only thing is that a good man like you must share the honor with us in doing this noble task; in what way, we leave it to you to decide."

He was afraid to ask further questions for fear of involvement, but still he was curious to know. "How am I concerned? What do you want me to do?" he asked.

I could see that he was scared. He was not one who gave a donation cheerfully, or mustered the courage to say no straightaway. He was an in-between type. So I said, "Some people give a hundred rupees, some have promised to give more. How can anyone set a limit on these things?"

He mumbled faintly, "A hundred rupees! I'm not so big, sir."

"What is a hundred rupees to you!" I asked. "You make it every hour. Don't I know how you sell?"

He looked forlorn. He felt sorry that he had walked into this trap today, and wished that he hadn't ventured out of his orbit. He looked as if he were facing the Income Tax Commissioner.

"No compulsion, no compulsion," I said. "Whatever is given must be given out of free will; otherwise the money will be worth nothing. Another thing, even in accepting donations we are selective. We don't care to take money from all and sundry. Money is not our main consideration. I mentioned the matter to you because your name is first in our list, and you came just when we were discussing you."

He began to fidget in his seat; he was eager to get up and get out of view. I was unwilling to let him go. I practically held him down and enjoyed it immensely. I said, "What do you propose to do for us? It's always easy to adjust these things, and I'd hate to trouble you unnecessarily. What exactly would you like to do for us?"

"I'm very busy now; I am going round organizing our sales in the surrounding country, where we are facing a certain amount of competition. A host of imitators have come into the field—"

"It's perfectly all right. We are not suggesting that you should disturb yourself. All that we want is encouragement from people like you. After all, you are an important citizen of this town, and we feel honored when people like you are associated with us." I laid it on thicker and thicker till he became panic-stricken. He got up suddenly and dashed out, muttering that he would see me again.

After he was gone the astrologer and Sastri emerged from their seclusion. The astrologer clutched a sheet of paper and the open page of his almanac in his right hand, and in his left dangled Sastri's silver spectacles. "I have a date for you—no, actually I have three dates: good, not so good, and half-good," he said. "You may make your choice according to your convenience. Each man should choose what is convenient."

The good date was five months hence; the poet would not survive such a delay. I knew him. He was impatient to launch his work within the next twenty-four hours. We rejected the half-good date, and so there remained only the not-so-good day, which came four weeks hence, when the full moon came up a second time over the muncipal tower, and coincided with the festival at the temple. The astrologer now said, "This is as good a date as the best one, but do you know why it's classed not so good? You see there is a slight aspecting of Jupiter, and the poet's ruling star is ——, and it might not prove so beneficial after all. Jupiter's aspects remain for four and a half hours; that will be until five twenty-five and it may mean a slight setback in one's efforts, that's all."

"What sort of setback?" I asked, rather worried.

"Well, it's hard to describe it. It may be nothing more serious than a stumped toe. Or the milk kept for coffee may turn sour. Are you going to give coffee for all the guests that day?"

"Certainly not," I said.

Now he wondered how he should describe the impending setback. "Or the water in the tap might suddenly stop flowing."

"Or flow into K.J.'s bottles a little too much," I said. "K.J. was here and he will probably offer to serve drinks to all the visitors and fill up his bottles with just water and nothing more."

"Oh, that's possible," echoed the astrologer. "Or anything else in a general way."

Sastri now interpreted, "You see in astrology anything is a setback. If a fly settles on your nose at a crucial moment and annoys you, you may treat it as one astrological setback worked off"—and laughed, and the astrologer laughed, and both of them said more or less simultaneously, "When it comes, it comes, when it goes, it goes, but it is useful to know ahead approximately." "Or the ink in the pen may not flow," added the astrologer. "Or it may be . . ." They were now at the game of drawing up a list of minor annoyances. Jupiter's aspecting seemed to bring about another set of worries. The astrologer probably felt that he was belittling the planet too much and suddenly drew himself up to explain, "He could be very vicious, left to himself—bring enough harm to a man's life itself or to his limbs; but when the presiding planet is Saturn, he yields place to him. You understand me? Saturn has more powers, although Saturn will not actually interfere with Jupiter's activities."

I really had to send people to be served by Heidelberg, as neither myself nor Sastri had any leisure to attend to our profession. I sent my printing customers in a steady stream next door. Sastri and I had a hundred things to do, morning till night. I kept walking in and out of my office— saw very little of my wife and child. I went home for dinner late every night. We printed appeals for donations in the form of a letter, setting forth our cultural heritage and so forth. We had to gear up our press to compose the final forms in readiness for the great day. I went out to meet the town folk and get their subscriptions for our function, by no means an easy job, as every one of our citizens had the same temperament as K.J.—afraid to reject an appeal, but unwilling to open the purse. We needed a lot of money.

We were planning an elaborate ritual, procession, and feast for a thousand. A few of the persons we approached asked point-blank why we wanted to do anything at all if we had no money in hand—a perfect question, but we did not contemplate a retreat. We had to keep going on, and the city was flooded with copies of my notice. Sen was good enough to compose it for me, and he had written a few hundred words, beginning with the origin of the world: writers' duty to society; greatness of the tale of Krishna and our cultural traditions; the merits of the monosyllable. He concluded with spicy remarks on the Nehru government's attitude to creative writing, which was totally censored by Sastri himself before he set up type. "Let Sen write a separate book on Nehru if he chooses. Why should he try to display his wisdom at our cost?"

Our appeal was scattered far and wide, and its effect was to draw Vasu into our fold again. He caught me late one evening as I was opening the door of my press in order to pass through to the back door. His jeep stopped at my door, and he followed me in. I hadn't even switched on the lights. I was for passing straight in. He followed, asking, "Are you in a hurry?"

"Yes. I'm—"

"Then slow up. Such frenzy will do your heart no good. Slow down, or slow up. Why stand in the dark and talk? Switch on the light. Where is the switch?" He fumbled along the wall and found the switch. He sat in his usual chair and ordered me to be seated too.

I said, "I'm hungry, I have to go in and have my dinner."

"I too am hungry," he said. "You are not the only man who eats, are you?"

I sat down reluctantly on the edge of my table. "Well, what is it?" I asked.

"Look, Nataraj, I'm trying to be good to you. Don't be naughty. I don't like anyone to talk to me in that tone."

"Can't we meet sometime tomorrow? I am very tired, that's all," I said.

"What has tired you? Being a busybody? Do you think I don't know what's going on?"

"What do you know?"

He produced one of our notices from his pocket and flourished it. "I'm as good a citizen as any, and even if you don't send me one, I can always get one. You print it right under my floor"—I winced at his expression of "my floor" —"and yet no one has the courtesy to send me a copy! Strange world!"

I had no answer for him. While we had posted out several hundred envelopes, I had deliberately avoided sending him one. I'd some kind of uneasiness at the thought of him, and though our cold relationship was slightly improved, I could not bring myself to send him an invitation. There was an uneasy thought at the back of my mind that it would not go right, that something might go wrong if this gunman was called in. But he was not the kind that would wait to be called. I merely said, "I knew you would get it, and so I did not think it was particularly . . ."

"Important?" he said while I was fumbling for expression. "Why did you think I'd not be good enough to give you money, or that I have no money?"

This was really crushing me. Why was he trying to have

a fight with me? "Do you want to find a reason for a fight with me?" I asked.

He said, "I'm not going to fight with anyone. If I had to fight, there'd be no half-measures. It will not be at all good for the man who asks for it. You want to fight?" he asked solicitously, as if he were asking "Would you like to wash?" or "Do you want a cup of coffee?"

I adopted diplomacy and said, "I thought of coming to you late, because I knew you would be here."

"That's better," he said. "Now you sound better. Hm, I had no notion that the poet had gone so far. Hard-working fellow!" he said with a sort of appreciation. He took out his purse and held out to me a ten-rupee note, holding it carelessly at the tips of his fingers. "Well, this is my contribution, although you wouldn't ask for it."

I stared at the note uncomprehendingly for a while and then said, "Is this all? I was going to ask you for a hundred . . ."

"A hundred! Hm, that's interesting. If my business were as good as it used to be . . . Those bastards are trying to lock away the animals, very unhelpful," he said, thinking of a big army of forest guards. "Still, they can't put me down, you know. It only makes my business a little complicated, that's all. Who are they to tell me how to shoot or when!"

"You are right in a way," I said in order to sound agreeable, without bothering to think what it meant—without thinking of the river of animal blood that would flow if he had his way.

He looked at me for a moment. "Nataraj! You really think so? I don't really need anybody's support or encouragement. I can get on very well by myself." The ten-rupee note still fluttered at his fingertips. "Well, do you want this or not?" he asked with a sudden aggressiveness coming into his voice.

My matching mood was coming on. "I said I want a hundred from you, not less."

"Okay," he said and put the money back into his pocket. "Now you will have to tell me how much you have collected in hundred rupees."

It was a challenge, and I said, "So far I have got fifty donors of the hundred-rupee class." That made him thoughtful.

"So, five thousand rupees! How much of it is in your hands?"

That was a point. I said, "I don't want to take it yet. I'll wait till nearer the time of the function. Why should we burden ourselves with the custody of so much cash?"

He made a sound of depreciation with his tongue and said, "What big cash! After all, five thousand rupees, not five lakhs!"

"It is big enough from our point of view," I said. "Someone else's money is always a burden to carry."

"That's an unphilosophical way of looking at things. Money is only a medium of exchange and it has no value by itself, and there can be no such thing as your money and my money. It's like the air, common to mankind."

"Then why not let me take your purse?"

"Why not indeed!" he said, took it out of his pocket, and dropped it on my lap. He rose and strode away to his jeep and drove off.

I sat transfixed. It was a large, well-stuffed purse of the size of a lady's handbag. I sat for a while wondering what to do with it. This was a most extraordinary situation for me. I had never expected that I'd be charged with the custody of this man's purse. Its flap was buttoned with an old-type metal head which could be pressed in. If you applied your thumb in the gap under the flap and lifted your finger, the flap snapped open. It had several compartments. It was stuffed with letters and currency. There was a photograph, plastic-covered, of a brawny young man with wavy hair standing up like a halo ear to ear, and bushy eyebrows. If you scrutinized it for a few minutes you would easily recognize the face—Vasu at eighteen or twenty; you would recognize him by his bull neck. There was a larger side-flap into which were stuffed currency, some letters, bills to be paid, and one letter in a blue envelope. The color of blue in notepaper or envelope always arouses my curiosity; and whoever might be the originally intended reader, I like to read it myself. I pulled it out, toyed with the idea of going through it, but put it back. I lacked the courage to read it. What if he came back suddenly and caught me reading! He might perhaps break my spine or hold me upside down and rattle my teeth out of my skull.

I also wanted to know urgently how much money he had in his purse and what were the unpaid bills standing in his name. But I lacked the courage to undertake this research now. I briskly folded back the purse and pressed down the metal buttons, put it carefully in my drawer, and locked it. I shut the front door and went in for the night.

Three days later Vasu came to claim his purse and peeped into my roll-top desk when I was looking through a list of persons who had promised us funds. He snatched the list from my hand, glanced through it, and asked, "How much money do you expect to collect?"

I opened a green folder in which all the papers relating to accounts, receipts, and cash already collected were kept. I examined the account and mentioned a figure.

"Give it here," he said, snatching away the green folder too. "I will double it for you. You mind the other things."

I stammered, "But—but—" and stretched my hand for the folder. He pushed away my hand. "Leave this to me, and attend to other matters." I tried to argue with him, but he didn't stop to hear me. He briskly walked to his jeep and drove away.

A week later he came into my office with a triumphant look. He flourished the green folder and asked, "Can you guess how much I have managed to get out of all the tight-fists in your town?"

I mentioned a figure.

He said, "You are wrong. Try again"—and went away.

After that, during my round of visits I met people who remarked, "What a money-gatherer you have engaged! One should sell the vessels in the kitchen, I suppose, and find the money, only to be rid of him! What a specimen!" There could be no doubt that he was extremely active. A variety of persons referred to him in a variety of ways.

I had to know exactly what he was up to. I waited patiently. When he came in one afternoon I asked him straightaway, "Where is the green folder?"

"It is locked up in an iron safe," he replied.

I ceremoniously showed him the Queen Anne seat and began, "We are all grateful to you for your help. You know a poet is—"

"Oh, no!" he cried. "I can't stand all this thanks-giving rigmarole."

"You are doing so much," I said, ignoring the insult. "Part of the collections will be utilized for expenses connected with the festival, and then whatever is left over——"

"Why do you tell me all this?" he snapped.

I said, "We need funds now for making a few advance payments."

He thundered, "So what?" He cooled suddenly and asked, "How much do you want, anyway?"

"At least five hundred rupees," I said.

"All right, you shall have it," he said without making any movement to fulfill it.

I asked, "When? When shall we . . . ?" He was trying to swat flies with a piece of cardboard.

"What when?" he asked, and added, "Why do you let these flies swarm here? Have you stored sweets in your desk for your favorite poet?"

"It is important that we should know how much you have been able to collect and from whom," I said firmly.

"All in proper time," he said. "Meanwhile, observe proper manners, keep your expenses down. Don't imagine you are millionaires!" He rose abruptly, glared at me for a moment, and was off.

Chapter Nine

We were a grim and silent trio that night. I had never worked harder as a printer. Details connected with the public function had kept us busy, so that I had had to neglect the most important item—the book to be dedicated on the day of the spring festival at the temple. I had to have at least one copy of the first volume ready in a special binding of hand-woven cloth. We still had a thousand lines of the verse to be printed to bring it up to the end of the marriage of God Krishna with Radha. The poet had given us the last installment of the manuscript weeks ago but it had lain in storage. I found no time even to open the cover. The poet was patient. He could not hustle me, as this was practically a free service I was doing. He had always said that if the whole of it could not be got ready, they could always make use of the manuscript for the ceremony. But it was a matter of prestige for me as a printer to get through it and have at least one bound copy ready.

So we were working on this desperately tonight—myself, Sastri, and the poet; Sastri to compose each page, the poet to pass the proof, and I to print off the page as it came through. We had a large flask of coffee among us. We were weary and tired. All speech had ceased. During the earlier

part of the night we discussed the various aspects of the
function ahead and cracked a few jokes, but it was now
an hour before midnight and we were irritated by one another's presence. My legs ached, my eyes smarted, and I
longed for a touch of the bed. There were moments when I
pondered why I should have involved myself in all this,
while I could have spent the time profitably printing K.J.'s
fruit-juice labels. The poet sat in the Queen Anne chair
and nodded; the sight provoked wild thoughts in me. I felt
like flinging a tumbler of cold water on his head. I felt
furious at seeing him nod as I sat in the chair opposite him.
We are doing all this for your sake. How dare you sleep?
was my thought. And I took pleasure in shouting in his
ears, "Here, should it be —— or ——?" a doubt, a query,
any excuse to pull him out of sleep. Looking at his mild
face one could not dream that he would be a fanatic in anything, but he was an implacable foe of all disyllables, which
drove him to attack and pulverize polysyllables in order
that they might fit into his scheme. A new syntax had grown
out of it, which caused Sastri endless doubts and headaches.
Every few minutes he called to me from the composing room
to clear doubts, and I in my turn prodded the poet to give
me an answer.

Strange problems faced us. The poet had used too many
Ks and Rs in his composition, and the available poundage
of K and R in our type board was consumed within the first
twenty lines; thereafter I had to request him to see if he
could not use some other letters of the alphabet in order to
facilitate our work. Sometimes he was obliging and sometimes he refused point-blank to countenance our suggestion. At such moments we managed to put in a star in place
of K or R and continue. Whenever he saw the star, the poet

went mad and every time asked, "What does it mean?" I answered pugnaciously, "Don't worry, we will take care of it while printing. Or we may add a footnote to readers to say that whenever they see a star . . ." all of which upset the poet very much, and kept him awake.

When I threw on the poet's lap a particularly complicated, star-filled galley, I watched him from my chair with calm satisfaction for a while. I told him each time, monotonously repeating myself, "Proof-correcting is like child-bearing. It is to be performed by you and you alone; no one else can step in and help you"—and slid down and rested my neck on the high back of Queen Anne and watched him. He was a man of few words, probably because most expressions are polysyllabic, and he just glanced at me and got absorbed in proof-correcting. He held between his fingers a very small white-handled pencil, and often nibbled its tip and brushed it against his cheek, the sight of which was somehow annoying and made me say, "Is your cheek a pencil sharpener?"

"I do that whenever I think."

"Shut up your thinking apparatus when you correct a proof. Let only your eye watch the right and wrong of word, letter, and mark. If you start thinking, we shall have to go on with corrections and proofs till eternity." I suddenly felt that perhaps I sounded like Vasu and said softly, "If we had more time I would not mind anything, you know."

"That's why I said—" he began, and I cut him short with, "Let us not waste the midnight hour. Go on, go on with the proof. Only after you have passed it can I print it." Watching him working under the twenty-five-watt bulb, my eyes swam. I ceased to notice anything. A radiant light gathered around him and isolated him as if he were within an illuminated capsule or cocoon. His frayed jibba and dhoti, and the silly jute bag on his lap in which he carried his papers, were no longer there; they became smudgy and vague. I could see only his face—unshaven (he was saving up a blade for the great day); the light fell on his nose-tip, and the rest receded in a shadow.

The policeman's whistle sounded far off somewhere; everything was conducive to a drugged state of mind. I felt light and floating and sank into sleep, forgetting everything for the moment—Sastri, temple, poet, the celebrations, the funds locked up with Vasu, pipe and drum, and the feeding arrangements and garlands. Like a dagger-jab, I heard the words, "Shall I stop with this line on this page?" Some silly doubts to be cleared, as Sastri stood over me and bellowed his question; and all the fine fabric of my oblivion completely gashed, torn, and messed up. Evidently Sastri got jealous when he saw me asleep and invented a doubt in order to pull me out of it.

Then it was Sastri's turn to seek a corner chair. He arranged it perfectly: dragged a chair, turned it away to face the wall, and curled up in it. Such deliberate preparations to sleep upset me, but I could do nothing about it, as he had an unchallenged right to doze off. It was my turn to work, for until I printed off the forms he had no type to compose with; the poet's work was omnivorous and swallowed up all the contents of the type cases. Until I released the type there was nothing for Sastri to do but sleep; and of course the poet was entitled to sleep, because until Sastri gave him a galley . . . I wished I could make them do something instead of letting them sleep; but my devilish brain was too dead at this hour, too tired to devise anything,

and so I stuck the type on the treadle, adjusted, and operated the pedal. . . . I could hear them snore in the other
room beyond the curtain. Perhaps I should splash a bucket
of water over them . . . but I felt unable even to contemplate the lifting of a loaded bucket. The sounds of the
treadle parts came in a series, *chug, gluck, pat, tap.* . . . I
was trying to classify their sounds. I poured out a little
coffee in the lid of the flask and paused ever so slightly to sip
it. Now over the *chug, gluck, pat,* and *tap* I heard a new
sound: a repeated tap on the grille that separated me from
Vasu's staircase. The stuffed hyena had not come to life,
I hoped. I tried to ignore it and go on with my printing.
Tap, tap, on the steel mesh. I applied my eye to the private
pinhole and tried to peer. I saw a vague outline stirring.
"Oh, the ghost of the hyena has come back!" I cried. I felt
a thrill of fear lifting the hair on my scalp and forearm.
I wondered if I should wake up the other two—perfect ex-
cuse for it—and make them share my fright.

"Sir, sir," whispered the animated hyena, "this is urgent."
I lifted the edge of the bamboo curtain. The light from
the treadle fell on the other side and illuminated the face
of Rangi. My hair stood on end. Rangi! The woman to
avoid. My first reaction was one of thanks that Sastri was
on the other side of the curtain, facing the wall. It was impossible—that woman whom I saw going down the steps
every morning with the flowers crushed in her hair, awful
fleshy creature whom Sastri considered it a sin to look at!
Was it possible that I was a prey to hallucinations? Perhaps overwork and the strain of the last few weeks had
done their trick. . . . After all! dream of Rangi, of all
things—and turned to my treadle, smiling indulgently
at the pranks my mind was playing.

But the phantom sounded husky as it called again, "Listen to me." Was this woman trying to seduce me at this hour? I looked around; if my wife happened to come in that would be the end of my domestic career. Although Rangi was black as cinder and coarse-looking, there was an irresistible physical attraction about her, and I was afraid that I might succumb to her charms. But there was the safety of the grille between us. I asked, with needless sternness in my voice, "Why do you disturb me at this hour of the night? Have you no—"

"Sh! Sh!" she said, gesturing with her fingers to cover her mouth. "You will wake him up if you talk so loudly. Listen to me, sir," she said. "I have very urgent news for you."

"What is it? Couldn't you have spoken to me earlier in the day?"

Nearer, after all, she wasn't so coarse. The light touched her high cheekbones. I found myself saying to myself: Not bad, not bad. Her breasts were billowy, like those one saw in temple sculptures. Her hips were also classical—I resented the attraction that exuded from a personality so rough. She wore a thin reddish sari. She interrupted my midnight dreaming with, "I must get back before he awakes. Listen: he is talking of shooting your Kumar tomorrow. Be careful."

I took time to grasp the sense of her information. The word Kumar stirred up in me all the necessary reaction— from the first day we had made him get up on his legs, through all our effort to restore him to health, to this day, when he was peacefully swaying and crunching all the sugar cane that the children of the neighborhood brought him.

For Dr. Joshi had done his work. The mahout had led
Kumar safely to town; I had taken them across the river
to the World Q.R.L., and the medications had begun at
once. During his convalescence, Kumar had become our own
temple elephant and was living in the compound. He was
to be a main feature of our festival, and afterward he would
be returned to Muthu.

"I am also a woman of that temple and I love that elephant," Rangi continued. "It must not be shot. Sir, you
must somehow see that he doesn't do it. Please save the
elephant."

"How? How can I shield the elephant? What sort of an
armor can we provide for him?" I asked. And then on a
sudden doubt I asked, "Are you in your senses? Or have
you been taking opium or something of that kind?"

She glared at me angrily. "Sir, I am only a public
woman, following what is my *dharma*. I might be a sinner
to you. But I do nothing worse than what some of the so-
called family women are doing. But I observe our rules.
Whatever I may do, I don't take opium."

I felt apologetic for uttering so outrageous a remark.
"What you say is so unbelievable."

She looked nervously up the stairs, as there was a slight
stirring noticeable above. "If he wakes up . . ." she whispered. "Wait here, don't go away," and she ran up the steps.
My blood tingled with an unholy thrill. I let my mind slide
into the wildest fantasy of seduction and passion. I was no
longer a married man with a child and home. I was like an
adolescent lost in dreams over a nude photograph. I knew
that I was completely sealed against any seductive invitation she might hold out for me, but—but I hoped I would
not weaken. . . . Still my mind speculated on how to

neutralize the grille between us if it came to that; the grille had a lock, and the key was in the drawer of my table in the other room. I stepped up to the curtain, parted the edge of it, and was relieved to see Sastri continuing his sleep, his position unchanged; the poet slept equally soundly, but he had drawn up his legs and curled himself in Queen Anne. If I approached the desk for the key, it was bound to disturb the sleepers. Anyway, I left the problem alone, resolved to tackle it somehow at the right moment.

When I tiptoed back to my place beside the grille, there she was, ready, as it seemed, to swallow me up wholesale, dissolving within the embrace of her mighty arms all the monogamous chastity that I had practiced a whole lifetime.

I found her irresistible. She stood on the last step, as it seemed to me a goddess carven out of cinder. The shadows cast by the low-powered lamp were rather tricky and created a halo around her. I pressed my hands close on the grille and took my face close, adopted the appropriate tone of a man about to succumb to seduction, and said, "Oh, you are back!" I tried to put into it all the pleasure I was anticipating.

She looked at me indifferently and said, "Only went up to see if he was sleeping; he was only rolling over, he won't get up till five, I know him." She sat down on the last step, took out of the folds of her waist a pouch and took out a betel-nut and leaf and two inches of a tobacco plug, put them into her mouth, and started chewing. She looked completely relaxed. In my fevered state I wanted to ask her if she was aware that the grille was locked and the key was where Sastri was sleeping.

She asked, "Are you going to save that elephant or not?"

"Should you ask? Tell me all about it."

"He will kill me if he knows I have been talking. But I don't care. He has been telling me his plans. Tomorrow night, what time does your procession pass this way?"

"Well, you should know; aren't you in it?" She was to perform her original function of a dedicated woman and dance in front of the God during the procession, although her dance would consist only of a few formal flourishes of her arms. She was perhaps the most indifferent dancer in India, but no one expected anything else of her. People were used to seeing her before the God and no one cared how she performed. Her place would be right between the decorated chariot and the group of pipers and drummers.

"He doesn't want me to go in the procession tomorrow," she said, "because he says it'll not be safe for me." She giggled slightly and threw the end of her sari over her face, feeling shy at the thought of Vasu's considerateness for her.

I asked in a panic, "Aren't you joining the procession?"

"Yes, I'll be there. It will be my duty."

"But—but what about Vasu?"

"Oh, let him say what he pleases; no man so far has stopped my doing what I like," she said proudly.

"Why doesn't he want you there?"

"He doesn't want me there when it happens."

"What happens?"

"When he shoots the elephant from his window."

"I never thought Vasu cared for anyone so much."

"He cares for me very much, although sometimes he is completely mad and picks up all kinds of women and expects me to quarrel with them—but not me. Let any man do what he fancies. I don't care what anyone does, as long as he doesn't dictate to me what I should do." She chewed her tobacco contentedly. "He wants to take me with him to Bombay—that's why he doesn't want me to get lost in the crowd."

"What will you do in Bombay?" I asked, my curiosity aroused.

"Cook for him. He likes the *pulav* I make, so he wants to take me along with him. I want to see new places too when the time comes. In a year or two, who will care to call me?"

Oh, you will have your charms, I wanted to say in my impassioned state. But I restrained myself. She treated me with much respect, always addressing me "sir," and she would have a shock if I spoke to her like a lover. Even at that mad hour, I am glad to think, I kept my head and tongue. "Good man, he cares for you so much!" I said.

"He is tired of his restaurant food, he says, and he doesn't want me to risk my life in the crowd when he shoots the elephant from his window."

"Why shoot that poor thing?" I persisted. "Who is going to let him do it?" I asked heroically. "I will tell the police."

"Oh, sir," she begged, "don't do that. How will it help? The police themselves may ask him to shoot. They may want someone able to shoot." And then she explained, "Somewhere along here, when the elephant is passing the road, it may go mad and charge into the crowd."

"Oh, God. Why?"

"Well, elephants are easily excited; and then he will take aim from his window and shoot it. He is certain that he can finish it. His aim is always accurate, you know," she said.

I said angrily, "If he is such a good shot, the place for him to demonstrate it is elsewhere, not here."

"Master," she implored, "don't be angry. Think calmly what you should do, and act before it's too late."

"Anyway, why does he want to shoot that elephant?" I asked.

"He says it's more useful dead. He may kill me for speaking, but I don't care. I want to save that poor Kumar."

"Neither you nor Kumar need have any fear," I said very heroically. "The time has come for me to hand him over to the police, the devil!" I said it with a lot of passion and heroism, but little idea of what I could do about it.

I finished the printing of the forms, woke up Sastri to do more, woke up the poet to proofread, printed four more pages, and by nine o'clock in the morning I saw the last page off the machine and two sets of sheets were assembled ready for the binder. The sacred copy was to be bound in Benares silk and kept in the temple. I said to the poet, "It's all right, go home and wash and be here in time. We have to be at the temple before three."

He yawned, scratched the back of his head, and went down the road, muttering, "I'll be back soon. Tell me if there is anything more I could do."

I sent Sastri with the two copies to the binder. Sastri hesitated for a second. "Can't I go home for half an hour, for a wash?"

I was irritated. "Why not me? I could also go home and sleep and wash and relax. . . ." As I was talking my little son came running down the road. "Father, Mother says—" Even before he finished his sentence, I said, "Tell your mother not to call me for the rest of the day. Tell your mother that even Sastri is not going home today. We are all very busy." I handed him a bunch of colored notices. I knew I could always bribe him out of his duties; he liked to collect them. "Give one to your mother and the rest to your friends or anyone you like. Let them all turn up at Krishna's temple. We'll all meet there. Tell Mother I'll come home, but I don't know when."

Even as I spoke I remembered Rangi, and for a moment I wondered why I should not ask my son and wife to keep out of the crowd. Damn it! I said to myself. Nothing shall happen. I shall have that Rangi and that paramour of hers in a police lock-up. This thought gave me strength, although I had no notion how I was going to achieve it practically. The police would just not listen to my orders if I said, "Lock up that man." Why should they?

Every hour of that day was like a tenth of a second to me, it was so compressed and so fleeting. After sending everyone away I sat down to take stock of all that I'd have to do between now and the grand function. I found my head in a whirl. I didn't know where to make a start in drawing a schedule. Every item appeared to be important and clamored for immediate attention. I could now understand why government officials liked to stack up on their desks IMMEDIATE, URGENT, and TOP PRIORITY trays. It was inevitable. Any man would feel choked in the midst of so much urgency. Today everything was on the top-priority level. Although we had been working madly for weeks, everything was getting crowded at the last minute.

First I must remind the flower-supplier to get us the first supplies for the decoration of the chariot by eleven.

We had engaged two specialists, brothers from Talapur, who were in demand all over South India. Given the foliage and the quantity of chrysanthemums they demanded, their decoration of a chariot was a masterpiece, but they needed a clear eight hours for arranging the flowers. The chariot should be ready for the procession at eight in the evening, and they would have to begin their work at eleven. I had paid a visit to them at Talapur ten days before. They accepted the engagement only because the police inspector whom I could influence interceded; otherwise they had a much bigger job to do at Madras. I gave them an advance of fifty rupees and noted down their requisition: seven thousand yellow chrysanthemums, four thousand of a certain green plant, two thousand red oleanders, two hundred thin bamboo splintered according to their specification, which they'd loop around the pedestal of God to work the flowers into, and seventeen bundles of banana fibers thinly torn off for binding the flowers. In addition to these basic requirements they had asked for a thousand roses, twenty measures of jasmine buds, and bouquets and garlands ready-made to be strung according to their specifications. These latter items could come after six, but the first supply of chrysanthemums must be there before eleven. The brothers were arriving by the bus at ten o'clock behind the market depot, and they were stars who expected to be received on arrival. I was the only one who had seen them, and it meant that I would have to wait for them at the Market Stand.

Also I had to visit the florist who had his shop at the farthest corner of Market Road, a man amenable only to my influence. He waited in his turn on the suppliers from the surrounding gardens. We were taking all the flower supply coming into the town that day, and the price of flowers for common folk shot up.

I had to make sure that our piper and the drummer, who lived not too far away, would arrive in time. Our chief piper blew through a silver-covered pipe, and the drummer had gold beads around his neck and beat his drum with ivory-tipped fingers; they were stars in their own line, and so expected personal attention from the organizers as represented by me. They were in demand all over South India for marriage and temple festivals, but they condescended to accept a local engagement because it was the first of its kind in our town. They lived right on the edge of the town, the last house in Ellaman's Street, but because they were cousins of the barber whose house abutted Kabir Street, we were able to exert pressure on them through him and set him to bring them to the temple at three in the afternoon.

We had an enormous program of feeding the public too. We had plans to offer the God rice cooked with jaggery and spiced with cardamom and coconut and distribute it to the crowd that might follow the procession. One of the rice merchants had donated us all the rice that would be needed, together with coconut, jaggery, and other stuff. All that he wanted in return was that, if there was going to be a public speech, there should be a mention of his shop. We had a kitchen in the temple, and an enormous caldron was fetched and mounted over a fireplace with half a ton of chopped wood burning under it. Four professional cooks were at it; several thousand little receptacles made of banana bark would be filled up with sweetened rice and distributed. And then Kitson lights and petrol lamps for the illumination of the temple and the procession, in addition to torches soaked in oil. And, above all, fireworks. . . .

The whole town was at it. The Chairman of our Municipal Council had agreed to preside over our function, the
advantage being that the municipal services were easily
secured for us! When it was known that the Municipal
Chairman would be around, the roads were swept and
watered, and the license for a procession was given immediately. Along the corridor of our Krishna temple we
had erected a *pandal* and a dais, on which the Mayor (he
liked to be called Mayor) would stand and harangue the
gathering before the dedication. All these tasks of public
relations and general arrangements at the temple were
undertaken by Sen, who never left the temple precincts for
seven days, working at them night and day. He had managed to get a band of young volunteers from Albert Mission
College and High School to assist him and run small errands for him. He had erected a *pandal* with coconut thatch
and bamboo; he saw to the decorations and kept a hold on
the Municipal Chairman by writing his speech for him.

Sen had also arranged to keep in readiness handouts and
photographs for newspapers. K.J., our aerated-water spe-
cialist, had opened a booth at the temple gate and offered to
open a thousand bottles free of cost and thereafter charge
only half-rate to the public gathered at the temple. There
were three donors who had offered five hundred rupees
each, and they expected me to go to them in a car and fetch
them for the function, although one had to be fetched from
New Extension, the other from Gandhi Park, and a third
from Lawley Road. I had fortunately the assistance of
Gaffur, who had his 1927 Chevrolet and ran it as a taxi—
always available around the fountain. "Any time, any-

where, this car is yours," he had declared. I had only to fill the petrol tank and give him ten rupees at the end of the day.

"First things first, and I have to be at the temple at three." Dr. Joshi, the elephant doctor beyond Nallappa's Grove, wanted a car to be sent for him. I must remember to take with me six bottles of rose water and the sandalwood paste, I said to myself. Items kept coming again and again, like the waves beating on a shore. Oh, and when Muthu and his party arrive, must leave a guide at the bus stand to take them to the temple. Everything was important and clamored for first attention.

I dropped everything, dashed through the press, opened the back door, and stepped across to my house. I'd have no time to visit the river today. I went straight into the bathing room, saw cold water in a brass caldron, undressed and poured the cold water over my head, and shouted through the door to my wife, "Bring me my towel and a change of clothes." Presently she thrust my towel through the half-open door, and now I cried, "I forgot to shave, bring me my safety razor and mirror. I'll shave here." And she ran back to fetch these items.

Presently my son entered, bearing these in his hands. I shouted, "You should not handle razor blades."

"Mother asked me to carry them." That excused the lapse.

I called his mother urgently and told her, "Hereafter take care not to let the young fellow handle razor blades."

"He insisted upon fetching them himself."

"That's no excuse," I said. "You must watch him."

"What else do you think I am doing?" she asked. "But now I have your breakfast on the fire, and I know how you will dance for it and make us dance who serve you, the moment you come out of the bathroom."

"No time for arguments today." Within fifteen minutes, out of the house again, completely refreshed by a bath and food. I took leave of my wife. "Try and manage to come to the temple at five with Babu. I'll give you a good place for watching the show. And you could come back home and come again before the procession. The decoration will be the finest. . . . Come with some of our neighbors." I was off. Across the street, back at my press. Even as I was uttering my invitation to my wife I was troubled with a secret uneasiness, that perhaps I should ask her to stay at home in view of Rangi's warnings. First I must . . . If I started out to do all my things one by one, devoting four minutes to each task, I could get through everything and reach the temple in time for the Chairman's arrival. But— but I had to get this information straightened out, and no one but Vasu could be useful for it. I stayed for a second to look through the sample binding Kandan had brought in, and prepared to face Vasu. I did not want to give myself any time for it. If I thought it over I'd find an excuse to go away, while the lives of thousands of men and women would hang by a thread depending upon my interview with Vasu—above all, the survival of that poor Kumar who had proved such a delight to our neighborhood!

I had to brace myself for this interview. I dashed home for a minute to ask my wife to pack up and give me some eatables that she had prepared, and then turned to go to Vasu. I didn't give myself time to develop any resistance. I went around to the yard. Until I turned the corner I had a hope that the jeep might not be there. But there it was. My steps halted for a second at the entrance to Vasu's staircase, where I noticed the plaster on the walls peeling off. Must attend to this, I said to myself, and immediately felt a pang at the thought of how little I had to do with this part of my property. At the foot of the stairs the hyena was still there. No demand for stuffed hyena nowadays, I said to myself. The python was gone, but a monitor lizard, a crocodile, a number of other creatures looking all alike in death cluttered the staircase. I went to the top of the landing, making as much sound as I could. It was about eleven, and I knew Rangi would not be there. I stood on the landing and called, "Vasu, may I come in?" I didn't knock on the door, as I felt it might upset him. Where did I have the time today for this? I hope they'll remember the item—rosewater bottles. I kept brooding as I stood there waiting for Vasu.

The door opened. . . . "What an honor!" he cried sarcastically. I passed in and took my seat on his iron chair, and settled down for a talk with him, although one part of my mind went on repeating, Where have I the time? Rosewater and sandal-paste . . . New Extension and Gandhi Park . . . and so on and so forth.

We had avoided each other since the day I asked for accounts, and had entered into a second phase of quarrel. Last time he himself had come with peace overtures; this time I was initiating them. My heart swelled with the pride of performing a mighty sacrifice on behalf of God and country. If my approach and humbling of myself could save humanity from destruction . . .

I said, "Vasu, I have no time today for anything; as you know, it's a busy day, but I've come here to invite you personally for our function this evening."

He received my words coldly, without even a thanks. He

gave no reply. I looked around; the room was once again cluttered with hides and stuffed creatures and packing sheets and materials. I noticed a small tiger cub in a corner. I tried to win him by saying, "A pretty cub, that!"

He picked it up and brought it closer. "Someone found it right in the center of the road while coming from—"

"Its mother?"

"Will miss her, of course. I was busy with other things, and could take it up only last week."

"You could have kept it alive and brought it up"—discovering more sources of pleasing him.

"Oh, me? No. I've spent a lifetime trying to make you see the difference between a zoo-keeper and a taxidermist." He said it with weariness as if I had been trying to place him among an inferior caste of men. "Anyway, it's easier to rear a dead animal. For one thing, it saves complications with a landlord."

I felt proud that he still recognized me as the lord of this piece of land. Vasu without a live tiger around him was problem enough; I had made the suggestion only to please him. In the hope of pleasing him further I added, "Of course a baby anything is a beauty. I'd have loved to have him around."

"It was a she," he corrected.

"What is the safe age?"

"What do you mean?"

"Up to what age can a tiger be kept as a pet?"

"Until it starts licking the skin off the back of your hand," he said. "Anyway, how should I know? I am not a zoo-keeper."

I wanted to say something nasty about zoo-keepers, that odious tribe of men whom he loathed. "A most peculiar profession. I would not be a zoo-keeper for all the wealth in the world."

He set the tiger cub before me on a stool. I shivered slightly at the thought of anyone taking so young a life. "Doesn't she look cute? I have had more trouble shaping this than a full-grown one. Guess what I am charging for it."

It was really a problem for me. I feared I might antagonize him if I undervalued it. If I mentioned a fantastic figure, he might see through the trick. I thought over the problem a good deal. While my mind was working fast, I stole a glance through the little window over the street. Yes, the fountain would be within the range. From the fountain, down the road, branching off to Lawley Road—he could aim anywhere within the perimeter.

"What are you watching?" he asked suddenly.

"Nothing. I always look at far-off things when I have to do a calculation. . . . I've been thinking over your question. If you charge five thousand rupees, as you told me once—"

"Oh, the problem is unimportant, leave it alone," he said and carried off the cub and put it back, covering it over with a piece of cloth.

I was not to be quenched so easily. I ignored his attitude and said, "About two thousand? The labor of shaping it must have been equally great."

"You are right. It's slightly less. I never charge a round sum. My bill for it would be eighteen hundred and twenty-five, packing extra."

I gave appropriate cries of admiration for his cleverness, and after more talk on the same line we came to the business.

"Why don't you come along with me at three o'clock?"

"To your wonderful function? I have had enough of this tomfoolery."

"Well, you were enthusiastic about it once!"

"That's why I want to keep out. Leave me, enjoy it yourself."

He had still to render us an account. He could not get away from it so easily. But this was not the time to tackle him about it. There was enough time ahead—after tonight, after the elephant was safely returned to Muthu. As a matter of fact I wanted to assure him now that my mission was not accounts. I said, "Everyone is bound to ask why you are not there. You have done so much for us already."

"I have had to spend over two thousand rupees out of my pocket. You have no idea how much of my business I have had to set aside. Time is money. I can't be like some of your friends."

"Let us not talk of all that," I said.

"Who are you to ask me to shut up!" he cried.

We were coming dangerously near another clash. I did not want to lose my head and lose the chance of keeping him with us and saving the elephant. This was all the tactic I could think of. He spurned me again and again as I repeated my invitation, and finally said, "Your whole crowd sickens me! You are a fellow without any sense. Why you are so enthusiastic about a poetaster obsessed with the monosyllable I don't know. And then that local Nehru. What does he think he is? All of you joining and wasting everyone's time and money! If I had had any authority I'd have prohibited celebrations of this kind as a waste of national energy."

I did not want to say that he could keep out if it didn't

suit him. I wanted to stretch out my capacity for patience
to the utmost in the cause of God and country. He was
abusive and angry. I wanted to assure him that I was not
going to mention accounts for a considerable time to come.
So I said, "Vasu, I have come to you as a friend. I thought
it'd be fun to have you around. We could see things together and laugh at things together—you know. Perhaps
you are worried we might ask about those collections—"

"Who? Me, worried!" He laughed devilishly. "A hundred of you will have to worry before you can even catch
me worried," he said, whatever might be his meaning. I
laughed, pretending to enjoy it as a joke. I looked at the
time. I had wasted nearly three-quarters of an hour in
tête-à-tête, and still I had not come to the point. How?
How to come round to the main subject, and ask him for
an assurance that he would not shoot the elephant?

I now took the rice cake and sweets out of my bag and
placed the packet before him. "Ah, I forgot about this,"
I said. "I have brought you something to eat. I found it at
home and I thought you might like it."

"What is it?" he asked. He opened the packet and raised
his brow. "You want to practice kindness on me! All right.
This is my first experience of it from you. All right, all
right, while it lasts." He put a piece in his mouth, chewed
it with a critical expression on his face, and said, "Not bad,
but tell the person who made it to fry the pepper a little
more before putting it in. . . . Anyway, better than nothing." He transferred the whole of it and swallowed it at
one gulp, accepting it as something rightfully due to him.

I was a little upset to see him take it so casually. But
this was no time to dwell on it. I was especially hurt to

think that he couldn't pay a compliment to my wife even for courtesy's sake. He merely said, "If you want to see the best of this stuff, you must taste it at. . . ." some other place, exclusive experience all his own.

"This was prepared by my wife," I said, trying to forestall any nasty statement he might make. But he merely said, "Modern women are no good at this. Modern women are no good for anything when you come to think of it." I did not want him to elaborate the subject as I feared he might say something nasty about my wife. So I tried desperately to change the subject. I suddenly said, "Vasu, I have come to appeal to you not to harm our elephant tonight."

"How can anyone harm an elephant, of all things? Don't you know that even if you drive a bodkin into its skin, it'll only break the point? Anyway, what are you trying to tell me?"

This was challenging. He had risen from the cot, which showed that he was agitated by my question. He tried to look calm, but I found that he was roused. "Who has been gossiping, I wonder." He paced up and down, stood for a moment looking out of the window—as I guessed, at the market fountain.

"Has that bitch been talking to you?"

"Which bitch?" I asked.

"That woman Rangi," he said with heat.

"Who is Rangi?" I asked.

"You pretend you don't know her!" he cried. "Why all this show? I'll wring her neck if I find . . ." He didn't finish the sentence. "Yes, suppose I decide to shoot that elephant. What can you do about it?"

I had no answer for that. I only asked, "What has that poor elephant done to you?"

"Has it occurred to you how much more an elephant is worth dead? You don't have to feed it, in the first place. I can make ten thousand out of the parts of this elephant. Tusks, if my calculation is right, must weigh forty pounds, that's eight hundred rupees. I already have an order for the legs mounted as umbrella stands, and each hair on its tail can be sold for twelve annas for rings and bangles; most women fancy it. Not for us to question their taste. My first business will be to take out the hairs and keep them apart, while the blood is still hot; trunk and the feet with nails—it's a perfect animal that way. All portions of it are valuable. I've already several inquiries from France and Germany and one from Hong Kong. What more does a man want? I could retire for a year on the proceeds of one elephant."

"Why don't you go and shoot one in the forest?"

"Forest! I want to show them that I can shoot anywhere. I want to teach those forest men a lesson."

Strange way of teaching a lesson to foresters. I said weakly, "Shoot a wild one, and no one will blame you."

"This will be wild enough, don't worry."

"What do you mean?"

"You watch out," he said. "You will thank me for my service; that Kumar is mad already; none of you have noticed it. Have you ever observed his eyes? See the red streak in his little eyes; that means at the slightest provocation he will fly off . . ."

"What sort of provocation?" I asked.

"How can I say? Elephants are really crazy animals. Anything, any slight . . ." He did not explain.

I felt worried. What was he planning? How was he going to excite it? "Have you plans to excite it?" I asked point-blank.

He just laughed diabolically. "You want to know every-thing, my boy. Wait, and you will know. Whatever you have to know will be known one day," he said in a biblical manner.

I said, "Whatever horrible plans you may have, remem-ber there will be thousands of persons around—men, women, and children dragging the chariot."

"Let them go home like good citizens before midnight. They can have all the fun until midnight."

"Who are you to say when they should go or come?"

"Now, now, don't try to be nasty. Let them stay or go, that's their business. If the elephant runs wild . . ." He ruminated.

"A few will be trampled and choked in a stampede," I said.

"You are saying things I don't say. I am not concerning myself with it. You have a morbid mind." He said a mo-ment later, "The elephant has been promised me when it's dead. I have it in writing here."

"Who has promised?"

"Why should I tell you everything? As far as I'm con-cerned, you have no business with me at all. How are you concerned with that elephant? It's not yours. I'm not bound to tell you anything. I'm an independent man. You keep it away, locked up, if you like, that's not going to bother me. Why come and talk to me? Get out of here and mind your morning's work."

I had nothing to say. I trembled with excitement and helplessness. I dared not say anything further, lest he should hit me. I pleaded, "Vasu, you are a human being with feelings like any of us. I am sure you are only pretending to be so wild."

He laughed. He seemed delighted at the way he had brought me down. "All right, have your own view of me. I don't mind. You are— Shall I tell you what's the matter with you? You are sentimental. I feel sickened when I see a man talking sentimentally like an old widow. I admire people with a scientific outlook."

"What's scientific about the terrible plans you have?"

"Ah, you see that! You use the word terrible and are carried away by it. You allow your mind to be carried off by your own phrases. There's nothing terrible in shooting. You pull your trigger and out goes the bullet, and at the other end there is an object receiving it. It is just give and take. At one time I was squeamish like you; it was Hussein who broadened my outlook. He used to tell me the way to be broad-minded is to begin to like a thing you don't like. It makes for a very scientific outlook."

"It may be science, but the object at the other end has no reason to be brought down, has that occurred to you?"

"How can you say? What do you do with an animal which goes on a rampage? Should the public not be protected?"

"This is not that kind of animal," I said weakly, feeling idiotic to be trying to change this man's mind; but I wanted to try to the last.

"Unscientific! Unscientific!" he cried.

"What's your premise for this conclusion?"

"Normal behavior of a beast is one thing and abnormal behavior is another. Exactly when a beast will cross the frontier is a matter that's known only to those who have studied the subject. If you had printed my book on wild-life, you'd have found it profitable. I've devoted two chap-ters to animal behavior. But you chose to busy yourself with monosyllables."

I said placatingly, "I'll take it tomorrow and finish it" —carefully avoiding a mention of Heidelberg which was rising to my lips.

"I don't believe your promise," he said. "Did you think I'd wait on your pleasure indefinitely? It's already being printed."

I felt jealous. "Here, in this town? I wonder who could do it."

He laughed out my question and said, "Now, I've given you all the time I can, you'll have to leave me. This is my busy day."

I shuddered at the implication.

The interview with him knocked out all the joy I had felt in this festival. I had looked forward to it for days and weeks, and now I felt like a man working up to a disaster and carrying a vast crowd with me. I'd have willingly stopped the celebrations if it had been practicable. But we had started rolling downhill and there was no way of check-ing the momentum.

It was four o'clock when I managed to reach the temple at Vinayak Street. Men, women, and children thronged the street and the courtyard of the temple. Sen had put up a few bamboo barriers here and there so that the crowd might allow some space for the Mayor and his entourage. He had dressed himself in a dhoti at his waist and had wrapped a red silk upper cloth around his shoulders, and his forehead was blazoned with sacred ash, sandal-paste, and vermilion. He was nearly unrecognizable in his holy make-up. The poet had donned a pink bush-coat for the ceremony, and it hurt my eyes. It reminded me of the labels for K.J.'s drinks. K.J. had spread out his colored water on a wooden platform, and was doing brisk business. Since he had not specified when the supply of free drinks would occur, he was freely plying his trade. The babble of voices was deafening. A few shops had sprung up at the temple gate— paper toys, fried nuts, and figurines in red and green sugar, on little trays.

The back portion of the temple was filled with smoke arising from the enormous cooking going on. A number of the temple priests were busy in the inner sanctum, decorating the God and lighting oil lamps. Kumar was chained to a peg at the end of the temple corridor, under a tree. A crowd of children watched him, and he was briskly reducing to fiber lengths of sugar cane they held out to him. The mahout from Top Slip was perched on his back, painting his forehead in white, red, and green floral patterns, to the huge delight of the children. The mahout was appealing to the children. "Don't make so much noise, give us a chance, give us a chance. Kumar can't hear me if you keep making so much noise." He had scrubbed and cleaned Kumar's tusks so that the ivory gleamed in the sun. He had decorated the tusks with bronze bands and rings; he was very happy that someone had promised the loan of gold head ornaments and brocades for the elephant. The elephant seemed to enjoy it all immensely and was in a fine mood.

My heart sank at the sight of this happy animal. I found Dr. Joshi standing near him, stroking his trunk. In all the rush of work, my promise to fetch him just went out of my head, but he had somehow arrived. I approached him, pushing my way through the crowd of sightseers. I wanted to apologize for my lapse. But the moment he saw me, he said, "Sorry I couldn't wait for you. I had to come to the town on business and have stayed on."

"Oh, that's all right, Doctor, I'm happy to see you. How do you find Kumar?"

He said, "He is in good shape, very good form, I think."

"Will he stand all the crowd and excitement?"

"Surely. What else do you think he is good for? You will find him at his best in such surroundings."

"I was wondering whether he would tolerate fireworks and band."

"Why not? But don't let the sparks of fire fall on him from the torches or the fireworks. Some elephants get a fright when a flare is held too close. Keep an eye on the torch-bearers, and that should be enough."

"Do you think he'll go wild if something happens?"

"Why do you ask?" asked the doctor.

"I've heard some people say that an animal can suddenly charge into a crowd. . . ."

He laughed out my fear. "Don't work up these ideas; people may get into a panic, and that'll be really bad in a crowd like this." We surveyed the jam of humanity. Any rumor might ruin the occasion and create a stampede. The distribution of the offerings was planned to be done at the end of the procession, when we returned to the temple. It meant that most of the crowd would wait for it. One way of reducing the crowd at present might be to distribute the sweet rice as soon as possible. I sought out the chief priest of the temple to ask if it could be managed.

He said immediately, "No. The offering is for the eleven-o'clock service. How could we distribute anything before that?" I didn't know about that. I was obsessed with plans to save the lives of these people who had come out for enjoyment: little girls had dressed themselves in bright skirts, women wore their jewelry and flowers in their hair, and men had donned their best shirts and bush-coats and dhotis and silk. Most of them were going to perish in a stampede tonight as the elephant rushed about madly. My wife and son were somewhere in that crowd. I had no way of reaching them, either. The air was charged with the scent of thousands of jasmine and roses which decorated the chariot.

The Mayor's speech was drowned in the babble in spite of a microphone and loud-speaker. It was purely the journalist's domain, and I kept away from the dais. I saw from far off the pink bush-coat of the poet rising and respectfully presenting the silk-bound copy of the book to the priest. The crowd demonstrated unmistakably that they hadn't assembled there for hearing a speech. The piper and the drummer were providing a thunderous per-formance. The priest was busy placing offerings at the feet of the golden images of Krishna and Radha, and Rangi was dancing. She had draped herself in a faded brocade and wore a lot of tinsel ornaments on her head and around her neck, and she was gesticulating before the golden images. I wanted to speak to her. It was urgent. But it would be improper to be seen engaged in a talk with that woman, and the enormous crowd might boo me. I toyed with the idea of sending an emissary to her, any young urchin, but if such a fellow was bent on mischief, he could expose me and make me the laughingstock of the crowd. That big crowd was looking for an occasion to enjoy anything at anybody's expense.

What did I want to see her for? I couldn't be very clear about it. It seemed vulgar to share a secret with her. If Sastri come to know of it—I don't know, he would have denounced me and left my service. All the same I wanted to attract her attention and do something about it. What? I couldn't say. But I could glimpse her only through gaps between several heads and shoulders. She was agitating her person in such a way as to make it impossible for anyone to catch her eye. All the same I edged closer, pushed my way through the crowd. The incense smoke and camphor and the babble of the priest's recitations over the babble of the crowd suddenly proved too oppressive for me. All night I had sat up working on the forms. And after all this trouble, the whole business seemed to be unimportant. The thought of the pink-coated poet, a fool who could not think of a more sensible piece of dress for himself . . . I found it strangely irritating to think of the poet and all the trouble he had caused me.

The God was beautifully decorated. He wore a rose garland, and a diamond pendant sparkled on his chest. He had been draped in silk and gold lace, and he held a flute in his hand; and his little bride, a golden image draped in blue silk and sparkling with diamonds, was at his side, the shy bride. . . . The piper was blowing his cheeks out, filling the air with "Kalyani Rag," a melody that created a lovely attunement at this hour. The temple was nearly a century old, built by public subscription in those days when my grandfather and a few others had come as pioneers; beyond the temple had been a forest extending up to

the river. Today all the forest was gone; in its place only
a number of ill-built houses, with tiles disarranged by time
and wind, straggling houses, mainly occupied by weavers,
who spread out their weaving frames all along the
street. . . . But the temple, with its tower and golden crest
and carved pillars, continued to receive support.

The story of Krishna and Radha was now being recited
in song form by a group of men, incoherently and cacopho-
nously, while they acted as vocal accompanists for Rangi's
dance, as she swayed and gesticulated. With all the imper-
fections, the effect of the incense and the chants made me
drowsy and elated, and I forgot for a moment all my problems. Vasu was like an irrelevant thought in the midst of
all this. He should have no place in my scheme of things. I
felt relieved at this conclusion. People I had never seen in
my life acted as a padding to my right and left and fore
and aft. I had lived a circumscribed life and had never
thought that our town contained such a variety of humanity
—bearded, clean-shaven, untidy, tidy; women elegant,
ravishing, tub-shaped, and coarse; and the children, thousands of them, dressed, undressed, matted-haired, and so
forth, running, chasing one another between the legs of
adults, screaming with joy and trying to press forward
and grab the fruit offerings kept for the Gods. Half a
dozen adults had set themselves the task of chasing away
the children and compelling them to keep out of the main
hall of the temple. But when they overflowed into the corridor and the veranda, half a dozen others had set themselves a similar task of keeping them out of the assembly
listening to the Chairman's perorations. And they chased
them back into the hall with equal vigor, and the gang of

children came screaming in, enjoying the swing back and forth.

Through all this babble, music was going on. But I had withdrawn from everything and found a temporary peace of mind. The sight of the God, the sound of music, the rhythm of cymbals, and the scent of jasmine and incense induced in me a temporary indifference to all matters. Elephant? Who could kill an elephant? There came to my mind the tale of the elephant Gajendra, the elephant of mythology who stepped into a lake and had his leg caught in the jaws of a mighty crocodile; and the elephant trumpeted helplessly, struggled, and in the end desperately called on Vishnu, who immediately appeared and gave him the strength to come ashore out of the jaws of the crocodile. . . . And so, I told myself, our ancestors have shown us that an elephant has a protected life and that no one can harm it. I felt lighter at heart. When the time came the elephant would find the needed strength. The priest was circling the camphor light before the golden images, and the reflections on the faces made them vibrate with a living quality; this God Krishna was really an incarnation of Vishnu, who had saved Gajendra; he would again come to the rescue of the same animal on whose behalf I was . . .

Unknowingly I let out a terrific cry which drowned the noise of children, music, and everything. "Oh, Vishnu!" I howled. "Save our elephant, and save all the innocent men and women who are going to pull the chariot. You must come to our rescue now."

Unknown to myself, I had let out such a volume of shout that the entire crowd inside and outside the hall stood stunned and all activities stopped. The Chairman's speech was interrupted as my voice overwhelmed the loud-speaker. Rangi stopped dead in her gesticulations. I was soon surrounded by a vast crowd of sympathizers. I felt faint and choked by the congestion.

"Did you shout like that? The Chairman's speech . . ." It was Sen, to whom the only thing that mattered was the Chairman's speech. He was angry and agitated. I heard someone remark, "This man is possessed, listen to him." My shout had brought around me all the friends I had been looking for in the crowd. Muthu the tea-stall keeper was very tender. He said, "Are you feeling well?" I felt not unwell but foolish to have brought on myself so much attention. "Where have you been all along? I've been looking for you." I had now lost the initiative in my affairs. A number of busybodies held my person all over and carried me out to the veranda under the sky and fanned my face. The veterinary doctor felt my pulse and injected a drug into the veins of my arm. The poet had my head on his lap.

"Doctor, don't give me an elephant dose of anything. I have never seen you curing human ills." The crowd that stood over me was enormous—faces everywhere, to my right, left, above, and aside, a glut of breathing, sighing, and noisy humanity, packing every inch of space. The journalist suddenly lost his head and charged madly into the crowd, crying, "If you don't leave him alone, he'll die of lack of air." The incomplete speech of the Chairman seemed to have given an edge to his temper. And people made way.

The Chairman sailed in with a lot of dignity. He stooped over me to ask, "Are you feeling well enough?"

"Absolutely well, nothing is the matter with me. You

may go and continue your speech. Don't stop it on any account, please."

The Chairman looked pleased at the importance given to his speechifying. He cackled like a shy adolescent. The Chairman of the Municipal Council was actually a man who owned a sweetmeat shop and had risen to his present position through sheer hard work. He was supposed to have started life as a servant and ultimately become the owner of the sweetmeat shop. He always wore (even in his sleep, as people said) a white Gandhi cap as an un-wavering member of the Congress Party. A chubby, rosy-cheeked man, who evidently consumed a great deal of his own sweets. Seeing his face so close to mine, I felt re-assured. Here was a man who could save the elephant.

I said, "You must protect the elephant."

"Which elephant?" he asked, rather startled.

I explained. I took my head off the lap of the pink coat and said to the poet, "Take him where the elephant is kept." The poet demurred. The Mayor dodged the suggestion. But I was adamant. The Mayor, being watched by a big circle of crowd, did not want to be seen embroiled in a scene with me, and so left us suddenly. The poet was glad to be out of the spotlight too.

I could now sit up. I realized that I now had an oddly commanding position. People were prepared to do any-thing I suggested. I felt better. At this moment my wife entered the scene, accompanied by my little son. Both of them rushed to me with agonized cries. I didn't like such a dramatic show. So I said to my wife, "What has happened? Why are you behaving like this? I only felt a little choked in there and so came out to sit here."

"You were lying flat on Uncle's lap," said my boy.

"Only because they would not let me rise to my feet." On hearing which my wife burst into tears and went on sobbing.

"Now, now, don't be ridiculous, people will laugh at us for creating a scene and spoiling their day for them. Now go and enjoy yourselves." I was on my feet again and went out of view of the crowd in order to let them carry on normally. I felt rather foolish to have brought so much attention on myself. I left the temple swiftly by a back door and went home through the lanes. My wife and son accompanied me. I felt bad about depriving them of the pleasure they came to enjoy at the temple. My son was openly critical. "Why should we go home so soon? I want to stay and watch the fun." On our way we saw his schoolmaster going toward the temple, and I handed the boy over to him with "Please don't let him join the procession, he must come home for supper."

"I'll bring him back," said the teacher.

We were not gone long when we heard the piper resume his music, and the loud-speaker's mumbo-jumbo over the babble of the crowd, and that made me happy. So life had become normal again at the temple.

Chapter Ten

At home my wife unrolled a mat, spread a soft pillow, and insisted upon my lying down to rest, turning a deaf ear to all my pleading that I was in a perfectly normal condition. She went in to make coffee and nourishment for me. She went on grumbling. "Not eating properly, not sleeping, not resting. God knows why you wear yourself out in this manner!" How could I tell her about Rangi? It would be awkward and impossible. But I could not explain the matter leaving out Rangi. And if my wife should ask, "When and where did Rangi meet you?" I would not be able to reply. I thought it would be best to accept the situation and rest my weary body on the mat and consume whatever was placed before me. Anyway, no one was going to miss me, and nothing in the program was going to be altered because I wasn't there. The whole program was so well organized and started that nothing could be halted. That was the chief trouble now; neither Vasu nor the temple authorities seemed prepared to relax their plans ever so slightly. Each was moving in a fixed orbit as if nothing else mattered or existed.

After the refreshment she had provided me, I fell into a drowse. What had really been the matter with me was lack of food and sleep; now I was having both and benefiting

by them. I enjoyed the luxury of floating off on drifting
cotton wool in the air—the sort of sensation I experienced
immediately I shut my eyelids. My wife sat at my side,
fanning me. She had a lot of anxiety on her mind about me.
I don't know what she had heard. I myself had no notion
what my state had been before I let out the shout about the
elephant. My wife had dressed herself in her heliotrope
silk sari, which she reserved for special occasions; it indicated that she considered the temple function a most important one; it depressed me to see her forgo it. I had implored, "Please go and enjoy yourself at the temple. I can
look after myself quite well. Don't worry about me." She
ignored my advice, replying rather lightheartedly, "I went
there only because you were there," which pleased me. She
added, "Not that I care for these crowds. Babu is crazy
about it, and has taken out all the savings in his money
box for sweets and toys."

"Oh, I should be with him. I could give him such a nice
time," I said remorsefully.

"You will do us all a favor if you keep away from the
crowd," she said. "Now sleep a little."

"Why am I being treated like a baby?" I protested. She
did not answer, and I fell asleep, until I heard soft hammer-
strokes on the walls of cotton wool which had encased me.
But when the hammer-strokes ceased, I heard voices, and
then my wife stood over me. A ray of evening sun thickened
with iridescent specks of dust came in through the ventilator of our dining hall. It used to have a red glass pane
when we were young, and would make me sick when the
evening sun threw a blood-red patch on the wall. Luckily
the red pane had been smashed one mango season, by a
stone thrown by a street urchin who had actually aimed

at the fruits ripening on the trees in our garden, and the pane had never been replaced.

My wife said, "Someone to see you." She did not like any visitor to disturb me. Her tone was hostile. She added, "His name is Muthu. Seems to be from a village."

Immediately I was on my feet. "Ah, Muthu! Muthu! Come in please."

He had his umbrella hooked as usual to his forearm. "I wanted to see you and so came. I told the mistress of the house that I would wait until you were awake. Why did you disturb yourself? Go back and rest. I will wait."

I resisted his suggestion, but he was so firm and insistent that I had no alternative but to go back to my mat. I sheepishly turned back, and he followed me and sat down on the edge of the mat, carefully laying his umbrella on the floor beside his feet. He looked around appreciatively and cried, "What a big house you have! Do you live in the whole of it or have you rented out a portion?"

I lay back on my pillow and hotly repudiated the idea. "I never want to be or ever wanted to be a rent-collector. We have always entertained guests rather than tenants." I put into my sentence all the venom I wanted to inject into the memory of Vasu.

"It all depends," Muthu said. "There is no harm in making a little money out of the space you do not need."

"It depends," I echoed. "My wife will never permit me, even if I wanted it."

"Then you can do nothing about it," he said. "It's best to listen to the advice of one's wife—because sooner or later that's what everyone does. Even the worst bully—I know my own uncle, such a bully for forty years; but at sixty, he became a complete slave to his wife. If people are not slaves before sixty, they become slaves after sixty," he said. He was trying to amuse me—a sick man. It was clear he was trying to steer away from the topic of the procession and the temple affairs. "He waits for her command every moment, and even stands and sits according to her direction," he said and laughed. It really amused me, this picture of the bully fawning on his wife at sixty. I cried to my wife, "Coffee for my friend!" At which he shouted, "Good lady, no, don't trouble yourself, no coffee for me."

"Don't listen to him, but bring the coffee or make it if you haven't got it ready," I cried. He sent back a call, "Good lady, if you must be troubled, let it be just cold water, a glass of water."

"Is it impossible for me to offer you anything?" I cried.

"Yes, yes, I never need anything. I have told you I never take anything outside my home."

"And yet you want everyone to come and ask for tea at the village!" I said complainingly.

"I never force it on anyone," he said.

There was another knock on the door, and presently my wife ran across to open it and came back, followed by Sen. "Another cup of coffee," I cried as she went back to the kitchen. Sen cried, "So good to see you again in this state; the speech went off very well in spite of the interruption. You really gave a shout which could have gone to the heavens, you know."

"Why talk of all that now?" said Muthu.

"Why not?" cried the journalist aggressively. "He is all right. And he was all right. Why should not a man let out a shout if it pleases him? This is a free country in spite of all the silly rules and regulations that our governments are weaving around us."

By the time my wife was ready with two cups of coffee there was a third knock on the door, followed by another one soon—the pink-coated poet came, followed by the veterinary doctor. So there was a full assembly on the mat at my house. My wife had to prepare coffee again and again. She accepted the situation cheerfully; the important thing was to keep me in good humor at home. The veterinary doctor felt my pulse and cried, "You are in perfect condition, you must have had some temporary fatigue or something of the kind, a sudden attack of nerves."

"I have never felt better any time," I said, although the thought kept troubling me that the veterinarian was trespassing unwarrantedly into human fields.

"Haven't you noticed, say, for instance, a dog let out a sudden howl—or an elephant trumpet out for no known cause? It's the same mechanism in all creatures. In our institute we spend a course of six months on comparative anatomy and psychology. Only the stimuli and medicinal doses differ between human beings and animals."

As we were talking the beam of light on the wall had disappeared and a dull twilight was visible above the central courtyard. It seemed absurd, after all the preparations of weeks, that all of us should be gathered tamely on the mat in my hall instead of bustling about in the temple. What a difference in the picture of the situation as I had visualized it at first and as it turned out to be now! So I said with a sigh, "All of us should be there at the temple."

"There is nothing very much to do at the moment," said the journalist. "This is a sort of intermission. The main worship is over now, and the poems have been read and dedicated."

"I missed it," I said ruefully.

The poet said, "You didn't miss much. I felt too nervous, and I don't think anyone understood anything."

"It was quite good," said Sen encouragingly. "Some people came round to ask where they could get copies."

"Probably they expect free copies!"

"Free or otherwise, the world will have to wait until I am ready to print," I said.

Muthu said, "Please give me also a copy."

I said "Yes," although I was not sure if he read anything.

The poet was by nature silent and retiring, and beyond a few sniggerings he said nothing. The journalist had him in complete charge. "Oh, I am sending review copies to thirty newspapers first thing tomorrow, and a special copy to Sahitya Akademi at Delhi. They are wasting funds giving an award to every Tom, Dick, and Harry. For the first time they are going to have a chance to recognize real literature. Our government have no lack of funds, but they don't know how to spend properly, that's what is the matter with them. I am going to show them a way to redeem themselves. I put this into the Chairman's speech pretty strongly, and he just recited it as I wrote it, although he is a Congress man." He laughed at the memory of this trick.

Night fell. Lights were switched on. My wife began her work in the kitchen. I could hear the clinking of vessels. I said, all my responsibilities coming back to my mind one by one, "Did the flower-supply—did the . . ." I fretted about it all until they assured me that everything was going well. And then one by one they came round to asking what really had upset me. I had to tell them about Vasu's plans.

They were incensed. "Who is this upstart to come and disturb us? We will get the police to seize his gun." "We'll throw him out of this town." "I'll knock him down with a hammer, if it comes to that."

I suggested, "Why not change the route?"

"Why should we? We will change nothing for the sake of this man! We will twist his neck so that he faces the other way." "It'll not be possible. The route has been fixed and the license taken for it. It will be impossible to change anything."

"Why not drop the procession altogether?"

"Thousands of persons to be frustrated because of this fool, is it?" "No—never. We'll deal with him. We have been too tolerant."

"Or why not leave the elephant out?"

"Impossible. What's a procession worth without an elephant? You know how much we've spent on the elephant."

"I'll be with Kumar myself, and let's see what happens. He is more sound in mind than any human being in this town."

"No, no, let us disparage no one," said Sen. He swore, and the others agreed. "We'll take the procession route as arranged. Nothing shall be changed."

Muthu became extremely nervous about his elephant. He lowered his voice and said, "I knew something had been going on. It started long ago. Do you know that tailor? He is a friend of Vasu, fancies himself a part-owner of the elephant. And I heard—I don't know—he has already received money from Vasu and has given him a document transferring to him his share of the elephant. I heard also a rumor that it was Vasu who had tried to poison Kumar."

"Aha," said the doctor. "I suspected something like it."

They sallied out in great rage, determined to tackle Vasu in a body. I could not stop them.

They were a determined lot. In their numbers they felt strong. First, led by the journalist, they called on the District Superintendent of Police at his home in Lawley Extension, for which purpose they hired Gaffur's taxi at the fountain and drove to his house. They found that he had just come from a long journey and was hoping to put up a reclining chair and rest on the terrace with a paper in hand. Sen was his friend. He went straight to the terrace and spoke to him.

After listening to their complaint, he said, "How do you know that he is going to create a disturbance? How do you know that he will employ his gun in the manner you suggest? He has an arms license, hasn't he?"

"So any man with an arms license can shoot at anything, is it? Wonderful laws."

The D.S.P. was annoyed at the contemptuous reference to the laws and retorted, "That depends; we cannot simply snatch away a licensed firearm because someone thinks he will shoot."

"So you want to wait until damage is done?"

"We cannot take action unless there is concrete evidence or consequence."

"Can't you do something to prevent possible damage to life and property?"

"That only a magistrate may do, but even he cannot bind anyone over without a proper cause."

The Superintendent was a highly seasoned police officer, seasoned in jargon and technicalities. He refused to accompany them to Vasu's room, but telephoned to the Town Inspector: "Have you made proper arrangements for this evening's procession? Have enough men to handle the crowd along the route; there must be no trouble or complaints anywhere. I've some people here who apprehend a breach of peace. I want you to go with them and tackle a man who is threatening to create a disturbance. Go up with them. Meet them at the market fountain in five minutes." He gave further instructions to the Inspector and bade the delegation to be gone now. By the time they had trooped back to the taxi and driven to the fountain, a police officer in uniform was there to receive them. They jumped out of the taxi, surrounded the police official, and gave an account of the impending trouble. He was a tall, lean man with a lot of belts and cross-belts, a very serious-looking man with lines on his forehead. One look at him and they were satisfied that here was a man who would stand no nonsense from anyone, a grim, determined man.

He simply repeated the doubts that the Superintendent himself had mentioned. "If the man possesses a license, he can keep his weapon where he likes. Who can question him?"

"But can he shoot from the window?"

"Why should he do that? What's your basis for saying it?" They had no answer, and he said, "All right; we'll see what we can do."

The Inspector stayed downstairs. Led by Sen and supported by the veterinary doctor, with the pink-coated poet bringing up the rear, they boldly went up the staircase and knocked on Vasu's door. They were emboldened considerably by the fact that a real live Inspector of Police was down below, waiting to appear at the lightest summons. The door opened, and Vasu's head with its dark halo of hair appeared, set off by the light from his room. "You people want to see me now?"

"Yes," said the journalist. "Rather urgently."

Vasu raised his brows. "Urgent! All of you to see me?" And then he counted, "One, two, three, four persons to call on me! I don't want to see anyone now. So try again to-morrow." With that he turned back and tried to shut the door on the visitors. Since the door opened out, the journalist seized the knob and held back the door. Vasu looked amused. "Do you know, I can just pick all four of you and toss you downstairs, if you really want to know what I can or can't do. When I plainly say I don't care to talk, how can you persist? All right. I will give you each a minute, and one minute grace. Be brief. What is it?" He was not disposed to admit them. He blocked the doorway, and they were ranged on the landing.

The journalist asked point-blank, "We have a report that there is likely to be a disturbance while the procession passes down this road."

"Knowing it, why don't you take the procession around somewhere else?"

"That's not your concern. We will not tolerate any disturbance."

"Oh, iron-willed men! Very good. I agree with you. Don't tolerate any disturbance."

"That elephant belongs to no one but to that Goddess on the hill road. If anyone tries to harm it—" began Muthu, and Vasu said, "Why don't you mind your tea-shop and keep off the flies, but leave these issues to others? Don't try to speak for any elephant."

"We know what you have been trying to do, and don't think we are going to stand any nonsense," the veterinary doctor said. "I have examined Kumar and know him in-side out. He is in a perfect state, more sober than any human being here."

"So what?" asked Vasu.

"If anyone tries to drive him crazy, he'll not succeed, that's what I wish to say."

"Oh, doctor, you may have an American degree, but you know nothing about animals. Do they have elephants in America? Try to get into a government department, count your thirty days and draw your sinecure's allowance. Why do you bother about these matters? Poet, say something in your monosyllables. Why are you silent? Don't become smug and let others fight your cause. Sell me a copy of your verse when it is ready. That's all? Now be off, all of you."

The journalist warned him, "We are not bothered about you. We'll leave you alone. You leave our procession alone. This is a sacred function. People are out there to be with their God—"

"If God is everywhere, why follow Him only in a procession?"

The journalist ignored his remarks and said, "Hundreds of men and women and children with the chariot—"

"What's this special point about women and children? You are all practicing chivalry, are you? If men are to be caught in a stampede, why not women and children also? What's the point in saving women and children alone? What will they do after their men are stamped out? If you are a real philosopher and believe in reincarnation, you should not really mind what happens. If one is destroyed now, one will be reborn within a moment, with a brand-new body. Anyway, do you know why we have so many *melas* in our country? So that the population may be kept within manageable limits. Have you not observed it? *Kumb Mela*, thousands and thousands gather; less than the original numbers go back home—cholera, or smallpox, or they just get trampled upon. How many temple chariots have run over the onlookers in every festival gathering? Have you even paused to think why it's arranged thus?"

Vasu's philosophical discourse could not proceed further, as the Police Inspector came upstairs and showed himself at this moment. He pushed the others aside and accosted Vasu.

The Inspector asked, "You have a gun?"

"I have two," replied Vasu.

"I want to see your license."

Vasu opened a cupboard, produced a brown envelope, and tossed it at the Inspector. The Inspector went through it and asked, "Where are your arms?" Vasu pointed to his rifle on the chair and his revolver on the table. The Inspector went over, picked them up, and examined them. "Are they loaded?" he asked.

"Of course they are loaded. They are not toys."

"Where is your ammunition statement?"

"In that envelope."

"When did you discharge your last shot?"

"Shut up, Inspector, and get out. I don't have to answer your questions. What's your authority for coming and questioning me?"

"Our D.S.P.'s order."

"It's my order that you clear out, with all this bunch of men who have no better business."

The journalist protested against the remark. Muthu jumped up and down in rage. Vasu said, "Inspector, you are trespassing in my house. Where is the warrant, which is necessary for you to enter private premises? Come on, produce a warrant. Otherwise I will complain against you for trespass, and these men will be my witnesses. I'll wire to the Inspector General and the Home Minister. You think you can fool me as you fool all these wretched bullock-cart drivers and cobblers and ragamuffins whom you catch hold of and order about. Whom do you think you are talking to?"

"Be calm, be calm. I came here only as your friend."

"Nonsense, you my friend! I have never seen you."

"I came to ask something of you, that's all."

"What is it? Be brief."

"I just want to suggest, why don't you let me hold your weapons for you in our Market Station? You may take them back tomorrow."

Vasu said, "I see that you are still toying with that gun of mine. Put it down where you took it from. . . . Come on. Don't play with it."

"I'll arrest you for disorderly behavior and lock you up for the night or for any length of time under the Public Safety Act." He took out his whistle and was about to blow on it and call the men who were on patrol on the road below. Before anyone could know what was happening, Vasu plucked the whistle out of the Inspector's mouth and flung it away. It went past the landing and fell with a clatter down below amidst pythons and all the stuffed stuff.

The Inspector was enraged. He raised his arm and tried to slap Vasu's face. Vasu just reared his head back, shielding his face with his hand, and then gave a sweep with the back of his hand and brought it down with a slicing movement on the Inspector's wrist and dislocated it. The Inspector screamed and recoiled as if he had touched fire. He still held the gun in the other hand.

"I told you to put that gun back where you took it from. Will you do it or not?"

"You are trying to order me," cried the Inspector. Tears of pain welled up in his eyes. Vasu held him by the shoulder and propelled him to the cot and gave him a push down, saying, "Take a rest, you poor fish. You should not venture to do things without knowing what's what." And he snatched the gun from his hand and put it away. The police officer wriggled with pain. Vasu kept looking at him for a while and said with cynical laughter, "You have hurt yourself. I did nothing. I never hit anyone. Years ago I made that vow. If I had hit you with my hand—do you want to see what would have happened?" He brought his palm flat down on the iron frame of the cot and cracked it.

The Inspector watched him mutely. Sen asked, "Do you know what the penalty is for assaulting a police officer in uniform?"

"Do you know what the consequences could be for trespass? Anyway, my lawyer will deal with it. Now all of you leave me. I do not want to hit anyone—you now know why. Oh, Inspector, you should not have hurt yourself like that!" He mocked this man in pain.

The veterinarian approached the Inspector and said, "Let's get this dressed immediately. Come along, let us go to the hospital." They were all for leaving. Sen said, "If anything happens to the people or the procession . . ."; Muthu said, "We know what you are trying to do with that elephant. If anything happens . . ."—which only provoked Vasu's mirth. The Inspector got to his feet, glared at Vasu, and said, "I'll get you for this." The poet alone tried to sneak downstairs without a word. Vasu just held him by the scruff, turned him round, and asked, "Where is your patron saint? Send him up next. He is the one who has sent you all on this fool's errand, I know."

While all this was happening—as narrated to me by Sen later—at home my wife was arguing with me to stay put on my mat. I had got a passing notion that I should visit the temple and take charge of the procession. My wife was aghast at the thought. She repeated several times, "The doctor has said you must not . . ."

"What doctor! He is only an animal doctor!" I said. "We can't pay serious attention to what he says."

But she was adamant and pleaded, "Can't you stay in at least one day in a year?" She had prepared a feast for me. She knew all my preferences: potato and onion mash, rice patties fried in oil, chutney ground with green chili, and sauce with brinjal and coconut grating; cucumber sliced, peppered, and salted, and so on and so forth. She was so full of enthusiasm that I had to prevent her with rude remarks from exceeding ten courses. Our house was fragrant with the fryings in the kitchen. All this felicity was meant to be a sort of compensation for me for missing the magnificent flower decorations, music, light, and crowds. My son came home with his schoolteacher and was full of descriptions of what he had seen. He said, "The chariot is made of jasmine buds, and they have fitted small electric bulbs all over it. Father, Father, I bought a sugar cane for the elephant. He snatched it from my hand, and you know how quickly he ate it! I bought him another one, and that left me with only six annas. I bought this whistle." He produced from his pocket a reed whistle and blew through it shrilly. "That mahout has promised to give me a ride on the elephant's back. My friend Ramu says that the elephant is borrowed and that it'll go away tomorrow. Is it a fact, Father? Let us have our own elephant for this temple. The mahout has taught him how to take a garland from a

basket and present it to the God. He is very intelligent,
Father. Father, Father, please let me go and watch the
procession." His mother added from inside, "If our neighbors are going and if you promise to stay in and rest,
I would like to go and see the start of the procession and
come back immediately. The child'll love it. Can't say when
we may have another chance."

"All right, why don't you let me take you both?"

"No, no, I don't want to go," she said. "It's not so important." I enjoyed the status of being more important
than the procession. Such fussing over one came once in a
decade when one fell ill or down a ladder; it was a nice
change from always protecting and guiding others and
running the household.

I lay back on the mat, picked up a picture book, and
tried to read Babu a story—much against his will, as he
wanted only to talk about the elephant and the procession.
He had been talking of nothing else: whom he met, who
fell off the steps leading to the tower of the temple, why
the drummer suddenly ceased in the midst of an enraptured
performance because he found a grasshopper crawling
down his spine—and Babu knew who had perpetrated this
trick because he had assisted him in tracking and trapping
the grasshopper; how he and another friend snatched
from under the chief priest's nose the plantains kept on a
plate for offering to the God, and to this minute no one
could guess what had happened to the fruit. He looked
triumphantly at me in appreciation of his own exploits.
And he narrated how he and his gang had devised a game
of hide and seek betwixt the legs of the devotees assembled
in the hall and how as they stood in prayer with eyes shut,
his friends had crawled between their legs and roused them

by tickling their calf muscles. I realized how he must have
multiplied the tasks of that body of men who had been busy
since morning chasing out the urchins. . . . And how one
of his friends was waiting for a chance to poke a needle
into the side of the elephant. At which I remonstrated,
"Never do that. An elephant will always mark such a fellow
and . . ." I thought I might turn his ideas from these
dangerous phases and picked up one of his picture books
and tried to read him a story. "Once upon a time . . ."
I began, but he was not interested. He suddenly got
up and ran off to the kitchen on the plea that he felt
hungry.

Presently my wife called me in to dinner. She had spread
out a large plantain leaf and had served my food on it as
if I were a rare guest come to the house. She placed a plank
for me to sit on. She watched me with satisfaction as I made
preparations to eat with relish. I suggested, "Why not
also put up a leaf for yourself and let us serve ourselves?"
She turned down my suggestion. She had decided to play
the hostess and serve me ceremoniously. Nothing I suggested was ever going to be accepted today.

I enjoyed my dinner, and kept paying her compliments
on her excellence as a cook. There was a knock on the door.
Babu, who had finished his dinner by now, ran out to open
the door. He came back to say, "A *mami* has come."

"*Mami!*" cried my wife, who was busy serving me. "Must
be our neighbor come to see if I'm ready for the procession.
Tell her to come in and take a seat. I'll see her in a moment."

The boy said coldly, "She is not asking for you. She is
asking for Father."

"What! Who is she?" asked my wife with a sudden
scowl on her face.

I trembled within myself. I muttered with a feeble, feigned surprise, "Asking for me, ha, ha! Must be a mistake!"

My wife set the vessel down and went out of the room, saying under her breath, "Let me see . . ."

The boy tried to follow her. I called him back. "Boy, fetch me that water jug." When he came close to me with the jug I asked in a whisper, "Who is there? What is she like?"

"I don't know. She was also in the temple dancing."

Oh, I knew now. My worst fears were confirmed. All the fine moments of the evening, the taste of exquisite food, everything was turning to gall on my tongue. I knew my wife. Although I had given no occasion actually to test it, I knew that she could be fiercely jealous. Before I could decide in my head what to say and how to say it, she stood before me to ask, "That woman wants to see you. What's your connection with her?"

"Which woman?" I asked with affected innocence. I got up from my dinner, went out to rinse my hands, and, wiping my hands on a towel, came back to the hall. "Bring the betel leaf and nut." I put on a deliberate look of unhurrying indifference, all the time I knew Rangi was waiting at the door. I chewed the betel leaves and went back to the kitchen. My wife had settled down to her dinner, serving herself. She did not look up at me. I said, "Have you any food left, or have I eaten up everything? If there is nothing left, it was your own fault, you should not have excelled yourself in this manner!"

She essayed to smile; this amount of praise, very sincere, of course, had its effect. With lowered head, she was transferring food from the dining leaf to her mouth. Now she looked up to say, "I have asked her to wait in the pas-

sage. I didn't want the neighbors to see her at our door."
She had to lower her voice in order that it might not be
heard by the person concerned.

I whispered back, "You did right, you did right," and
then, "You could have asked her why she has come."

"Why should I? If it's your business, it's your business,
that's all. I am not interested."

I made a sound of being vexed and said, "What a nuisance! Must be something connected with the temple. Can't
rest even for a day." So muttering, I progressed in her
direction. There she was, standing in the passage. She
had taken off her gaudy dance ornaments and costumes
and was dressed in a plain sari; even in the dark passage I
could see the emphatic curves of her body. I stood away
from her, at a safe distance, right at the inner doorway,
and asked rather loudly, "What is the matter?" I did not
want to carry on a whispered dialogue with her.

But she spoke in whispers. "I wanted to know how you
were, Master."

I was touched by her solicitude. "Oh, I'm all right. Nothing was really the matter."

"I saw everything, but could not come over, because I
was on duty before the God."

"Oh!" I said, feeling rather pleased. "Are your duties
finished for the day? What about the procession?"

"It's at nine o'clock. I shall have to get back."

"Oh," I said.

"Won't you go with the procession, sir?" she asked.

My son had been standing around uneasily, but feeling
rather shy in the presence of a dancing woman he went away
and hid himself in the kitchen.

Rangi assumed even a softer and hoarser whisper to say,

"He came to my house in the afternoon when I was at the temple and left a command that I should see him."

I grew apprehensive. "Don't go. Go back to your house and get away to the temple. Be with the crowd."

"He may come to my house again and set fire to it. Only my old mother is there—deaf and blind."

"Why should he set fire to your house?"

"He is wild with me and wants to talk to me!"

"Talk to you! He will probably murder you!" I said.

She brooded over my words. I asked her, "Why don't you tell the police?"

She shook her head. "He won't be afraid of the police. He is not afraid of anything. The police will laugh at me. What can they do? He is not afraid of anything or anybody, that's what he is."

"Don't go to him," I implored her.

My wife had finished her dinner and was passing up and down on various minor errands, casting sly sidelong looks at the two of us in the dark passage. Rangi was sobbing at the prospect before her. "I don't know what he will do to me! He has summoned me. He confided in me. I betrayed his trust. I had to . . . I hope, I hope you have taken precautions."

"Oh, surely," I said with grand confidence and assurance. "We won't let a fellow like that get away with his ideas."

"You don't know him enough. He is afraid of nothing on earth or in heaven or in hell."

"We have our method for dealing with such fellows. We are a match for him," I said.

"He is so strong and obstinate. If he thinks of something, he must do it; no one on earth can change his mind."

This woman seemed to be obsessed with the grandeur and invincibility of the man. I was not going to tolerate it. "Rangi, don't be carried away by the notions you have of that man. He is just an ordinary, common bully; we know how to tackle him."

"Now what shall I do, sir? I have come to you because I don't know what to do. I thought of going there and appeasing him to see if I could get him into a good mood to listen to my words. I have also cooked his favorite *pulav* and have it here." She indicated a hamper of food.

"But you've said yourself that it's impossible to make him change his mind."

She whispered seductively, "I'll try. A woman in my position has her ways."

I don't know what she meant; it sounded mysterious. I said, "He may not let you go back to the procession. Don't go to him. Go home."

"If I don't obey his summons he may set fire to my house, with my blind mother not knowing what is happening."

"I'll arrange for the proper persons to guard your house. Don't let him blackmail you into visiting him. He'll hold you back. He may even tie you up hand and foot. I'll send the proper persons to guard your house," I said grandiosely, without the shred of a notion how I was going to accomplish anything. She brought her palms together in a salute and left me, and vanished into the moonlit street.

I went back to my wife. I found her tidying herself up in the dark anteroom, before a mirror. I said expansively, "You know what's the matter with that woman?"

"How should it interest me?" she asked. I was struck by the cold, indifferent tone in which she spoke. "I don't know who she is, and I don't care." She readjusted her sari and called, "Babu!" He was at her side in a moment. "Coming to the temple?" Yes, of course. He had already gone ahead to the outer door.

I asked her, "Are you going to the temple?"

"Yes," she said monosyllabically.

"But you said you would not go!" I said.

"Now I say I'm going, that's all there is to it," she said. I could see even by the dim light that her ears were red.

"I wanted to speak to you. I thought you might stay here and talk things over." She turned a deaf ear to what I was saying. I followed her, mumbling, "You wanted me to stay at home, now you are going!" I made myself sound pathetic.

"Stay or go, it's all the same to me," she said and was gone down the steps and down the road, with Babu prancing beside her. She had not given me a chance even to shout and pick a quarrel with her.

I didn't like to go in. I sat on the *pyol*, looking in the direction in which she had gone. What was the use? There was a silly little hope that she would repent her brusqueness and come back to make amends. My only other companion for the night was a street dog curled up in the gutter. All the other living creatures of this area had gone to the temple. Not a soul remained at home—except the asthmatic in the sixth house, whom I could hear cough and expectorate. As I sat there and brooded, it gave me time to take stock. The matter with me was that I was not able to say "no" to anyone, and that got me into complications with everyone from a temple prostitute to a taxidermist. I repeated to myself all the stinging rejoinders that I should have hurled at my wife. I should have behaved like one of my ancestors, often mentioned by my grand-aunt, who used to bring home his concubine and have her dinner served by his wife. So when my wife said, "What is your connection with her?" I should instantly have said, "Yes, you are right. I want to seduce Rangi or be seduced by her." If my wife had said, "Of all women!" I'd have replied, "Yes, of course, you are blinded by jealousy. She no doubt chews tobacco and looks coarse, but she has it, it comes through even when she whispers to you. How can any man resist her? I'm sorry for you, but that's how it is. You should take more trouble to keep me in good humor. There is no use losing your temper or sulking or snapping a reply. If I followed the same procedure, you'd not be able to stand it for a second. As a man I have strength, no doubt, to stand all your nonsense. But you should not strain it too much. That's all now, don't do it again."

The moon came over the roof tile of the opposite row of houses, full and brilliant. I could hear the hubbub of voices emanating from the temple half a mile away. It saddened me to be detached from all this activity. I felt like a man isolated by an infection. I had almost, as a sort of revenge on my wife, a plan to appear at the temple precincts and take a hand in the conduct of the procession. Without creating a panic, I would gently navigate the chariot into a different route. Or perhaps if I rushed around a bit and met the D.S.P., I could change the permit for another route. There was not a person in that whole throng who could organize and guide a procession. I swelled with pride. I was the one man who could still achieve results. But I was an outcaste. I felt nervous of going before the crowd again. I was not certain what I would do. Under the pressure of the crowd, if I should let out a cry again—

that'd be the end of me. It might have the desirable effect of making my wife regret her petulance, but it was also likely to see me bundled off to the Madras Mental Hospital by the next train. I remembered a boy, a brilliant fellow in the third form, who strode up and down our Kabir Street for three days, singing all Tyagaraja's compositions night and day continuously, until he had covered most of that inspired saint's works. If he had been left alone for another day he would have completed the repertory; but they seized and bundled him off by the five-o'clock express to Madras; he came back a year later with a shaven head, but sober and quiet. He was a friend of mine in my school-days, and he confessed that he had sung Tyagaraja's compositions only because he was keen on letting the public get an idea of the versatility of that great composer, but now he was afraid even to hum the tunes in his bath. Our Kabir Street citizens had exacting standards of sanity. I didn't want to be seized and put onto the Madras train. . . . Or, even if I didn't create a scene, the crowd would look at me as if I had recovered from a fit of epilepsy. They would not let me go with the procession. All my old anxieties, which had been under a false lull, suddenly rose to the surface.

I took stock of the situation. What exactly was my cause for smugness now? I had done nothing to divert the procession, I had done nothing to disarm or dissuade Vasu; God knew what trick he might have up his sleeve. He might do nothing more than fling a firecracker down from his window or bribe one of the torch-bearers to hold the torch close to the leg of the elephant. All evening we had done nothing but discuss the various methods of maddening an elephant—a needle stuck into a coconut or banana and given it to swallow, an ant dropped in its ear, or a grain of sand in its eyes—it would be the easiest thing to drive an elephant mad, and if people were lucky they might get out of its range or if they weren't a few might be caught and trampled to death, particularly if there was a stampede at that narrow bend on the Market Road, with the broad storm drain on one side and the small mountain of road-metal—meant for the improvement of the road but untouched since 1945—heaped on the other. People would thank anyone who shot the elephant at that moment. That poor elephant, enjoying all the fun today, decorated, happy, and playing with the crowd and children—he must return to the Goddess on the mountain road and graze in the forests of those blue hills and continue to delight the children of all those villages. Muthu hoped that by hiring out the elephant for processions he could earn enough money to build a tower for the temple of the Goddess, which should be visible for fifty miles around. It was impossible to conceive of Kumar's being dissected and stuffed and serving as an umbrella stand or wastebasket in some fashionable home in the Eastern or Western world.

I wanted to do something about it all. My wife had gone out, perhaps expecting me to act as the watchman of the house. Nice notion she had. It'd be good to abandon the house and let her discover that after all she could not presume upon my goodness. Or even a better plan would be to lock the door and take the key away so that when she came back after midnight she might wonder how to get to her bed. It was nearing ten, and the procession should have started now. No one could judge when it would arrive at the fountain. While on the road, the piper might start on a big *alapana,* and until he attained certain flights and heights of a particular melody and returned to earth the procession would not move, even if it took an hour. So by stages and after all the stops it might take hours for the procession to cover the distance between the temple and the fountain.

The procession should have started an hour ago, but there was no sign of the music yet. Only the hubbub of the voices indicated that the crowd was still waiting for it. If it had started, I'd have heard the voices and music moving nearer, and above all my wife would have come back home. However temperamental she might be, I knew she would not go with the procession along with that mass of crowd. She had enough sense to return home in time.

I felt angry at being chained to the house. I would go into the outer fringes of the crowd, unrecognized, and study the situation. I shut the door behind me and stepped down. I went down to the end of the street. I saw two men coming in my direction and I stopped them to ask, "Has the procession started?"

"No, they are waiting for ornaments for the elephant. Someone has gone to fetch them from the Talapur temple, head ornaments of real gold. They are waiting for that."

Ten miles up and ten miles down, and perhaps an hour getting the ornaments out of the temple vaults. No chance of the procession starting before two a.m. What madness! Did it mean that my wife was going to be at the temple till two? With the boy? I was in a measure also relieved; every hour's delay seemed to me an hour's reprieve. I went back home; if the procession was starting late, then there was no purpose in my loitering at the temple gate. At home, I laid myself down on the *pyol*. If I was to be a watchman, I'd better be one thoroughly, not a haphazard one! I didn't want the house to be looted; this was just the chance thieves waited for, when every householder would have gone out to the festival.

Lying on the mat on the *pyol*, as I kept gazing on the moonlit street, I fell asleep. I woke up hours later as I heard drums and pipe music approach nearer—I knew that the procession was on Market Road, parallel to our house. I grew worried about my wife and son, thinking that they were still out. On second thoughts I went inside, and I saw her asleep in her bed, with the child asleep also. I must have been too soundly asleep indeed not to have known when she arrived. She must have come long ago and gone to sleep. She ought to have wakened me; how could she when she preferred to practice all that coldness toward me? In order to mete out the same treatment to her, I went back to my mat on the *pyol*.

I lay tossing on my mat. Far off the piper's music came from the procession. I followed it, visualizing all the stages of its progress. Now it must be passing the elementary school conducted on the top story of the Chairman's sweet-mart, a rickety terrace which would come down any day, but no one could prevent its being there because it was the Chairman's building and was certified to be safe. Some day when it came down it was going to imperil the lives of a hundred schoolchildren and six or eight teachers. But so far it had lived up to the optimistic estimate of the municipal authorities, and most of its ex-pupils were now adults working and earning a living in various walks of life all over India. I preferred to send Babu to another school, however. The drummer made enough noise to shatter the foundations of this precarious building, but it was a matter of courtesy for the procession to stop there, and the piper had saved his breath for his masterpiece—"Bhairavi." He was commencing a most elaborate, intricate rendering of this melody, and that meant the gathering would stand around him, the God would repose in his chariot, the elephant would stand ahead of the procession with the mahout asleep on its back. People would crowd around the piper and behave as if they had no further distance to cover.

It was much better that the procession halted itself there than at the fountain. The time was around midnight now, and it would take at least an hour for the procession to approach the market fountain. I made up my mind to join the procession and mix with the crowd an hour hence, and till then there was no harm in sleeping. "Bhairavi" was as good heard here in a condition of half-sleep as anywhere—and so I allowed myself to be lulled by it, a melody that was my favorite in any case. It brought to my mind my childhood days, when visiting musicians used to come as our guests; there was a room in our house known as the musician's room, for we always had some musician or other staying with us, as my father was very proud of his familiarity with all the musicians in South India and organized their recitals in our town. It had been one of the charges leveled against him by the opposing lawyer: he was supposed to have squandered the family funds in entertaining musicians. Now this room was used as a storing place for old bottles. It was the great joke in those days that when anyone questioned why old bottles were kept so safely, the answer would be that if my uncles sued for them, they might be given their due shares. The room also contained about seventy terse philosophical works, the entire philosophical library collected by my grandfather or someone before him in Sanskrit and Tamil, along with bronze images used for worship. They had been willed to the third uncle but were left in our custody because my uncle was in the railways and never stayed in the same place for more than three months. He was never known to have opened any book in his life after leaving school, but still he occasionally sent us a postcard to inquire if the volumes of philosophy were safe. Whenever my mother got into an argumentative mood, she would arraign my father for being a custodian of other people's property, and demand to know why he should not throw the articles out and get rid of all that responsibility. But my father was fond of his brothers, whatever they might do, and told her not to peep into that room as there was sufficient space in the rest of the house for her to mind.

I must have fallen asleep. When I woke up "Bhairavi" was no longer being played but some other tune, and the music was coming from close quarters across the row of buildings on Market Road. If my judgment was right the procession must now be near the silkware house. The next stop would be the fountain. I was seized with anxiety. The procession was nearing the range of Vasu's window. What reason had I for my smugness? What right had I to presume that Muthu and the rest would have succeeded in restraining Vasu? Suppose they had done nothing, and a torch-bearer scalded the toe of the elephant and drove it mad? Just what Vasu would be waiting for all along. My duty now was clear. I must go and keep the procession away from the fountain and turn it into a side street. There was no use lying here and cogitating, while every minute a vast assembly was moving toward its doom. I should do something about it.

I got up briskly. I could hear my wife stirring, awakened by the pipe and band; she would probably come out to watch from the end of Kabir Street, in which case I did not want to meet her. I walked across, opened the back door of my press, and shut the door behind me. I was going to make a last-minute attempt to stop Vasu. He was not such a bad fellow after all. He would listen to me. He was considerably mellower than he used to be. I looked up at the attic. There was no light in it. Of course he would put out all lights. He was the prince of darkness, and in darkness were his activities to be conducted. Somehow I was seized with a sudden access of wonderful and effective plans. They were not shaped very clearly in my mind yet, but I was positive that I was going to come through it all. If you had asked me to lay a blueprint of my activities before you, I should perhaps have fumbled, but deep within me the plan was ready. I would first steal up to his room and walk softly to his side; he was sure to be watching the window. Why not stun him from behind and save everyone all the worry and trouble of argument? Not practicable, actually. One might talk of finishing off a cobra with a staff of bamboo, but it was always more likely that the cobra would prove smarter. Vasu might after all not be facing the window but actually facing the door. Non-violence would be the safest policy with him. Mahatma Gandhi was right in asking people to carry on their fight with the weapon of non-violence; the chances of getting hurt were less in this process.

I squeezed myself through the little fence between my press and the staircase. He was undoubtedly upstairs. The jeep was outside. It might be a good idea to set its petrol tank on fire. That would keep him busy until the procession passed. He might make a pulp of me if he discovered me in the process, but why not? No one was going to miss me. My wife was actually separated from me now, and there was no one to bemoan the loss. Babu was likely to miss me for a few days, but children adapted themselves to new circumstances with surprising ease. It was pleasing to reflect that my wife would learn a lesson, namely that sulking did not pay and that it did no one any good. If Rangi spoke to me on an important matter, the thing for a rational being to do would be to ask what exactly it was and approach things in a scientific frame of mind. . . . No wonder Vasu was bitter against the whole world for its lack of scientific approach. If people were scientific-minded they would not jump to conclusions when a man spoke to Rangi in a half-dark passage.

I was at the foot of the staircase. The hyena was still there but pushed to the side; it must have been a wasted labor for Vasu—absolutely unsaleable stuff. It was surrounded by a few other odds and ends of dead creatures, nothing outstanding among them, but a miscellany of small game: a wild squirrel, a fox, a jungle dog, and a small cheetah, and so forth; and several reptiles. Vasu seemed to have turned his attention to small industries in keeping with our government's zeal for small industries nowadays. The smell of hide and packing cases overwhelmed me. I went up. I had presumed all along that the door would be open. What if it should be shut? I should knock on it and allow events to develop. I was going to stop him from disturbing the procession; that was certain, but how was a question that I still could not answer. I was prepared to lose my life in the process.

I found the door open. I gave it a gentle push and peeped in. There he was as I had visualized, beside the

window, on a long easy chair. The lights, the Kitson vapor
lamps, and the torches of the procession were already il-
luminating the room, and there were moving shadows on
the walls. The band and the pipe and the shouts of the
men pulling the chariot along could be heard down below.
I could see his silhouette at the window, where he seemed
to have made himself comfortable, with a pillow under his
head. He had stretched his legs on a stool, he had his timepiece on another small table, and his gun lay on the floor
within his reach. I could see so much by the flares flickering along the wall through the narrow window. A few
other silhouettes, the small tiger cub and some other animals, stood out in the semi-darkness. He didn't move. That
was a good sign. He had probably fallen asleep waiting
for the procession to come along. Not all the drumming
(they could at least have had the sense to pass the spot
noiselessly, as a precaution) seemed to make any impression on him. He was obviously a sound sleeper, thank
God.

My decision was swift; I would make a dash for his gun
and seize it. My heart palpitated and my breath came and
went like a bellows as I crawled toward the gun at his side.
If he woke up before I reached it, that would be the end
of me. I had started crawling like one of those panthers of
the Mempi jungle; the distance between me and the gun was
only a dozen feet. I covered half of it, and the other half
seemed interminable. My knees were sore, but I felt that it
was for a good cause that I was skinning them. He was still
asleep. As my fingers reached the cold butt of his gun I
could have swooned with excitement. I had never touched
a gun before and felt scared. I rose to my feet and covered
him with the gun. Below the window the procession was

passing rather quickly, as I thought. I wished I could go
and take a look at it, but he was between me and the window, and if he slept through it that would be the best arrangement possible. But if he woke up, I had the gun
at point-blank range. I would follow the method of cinemas
and command him not to stir until the procession passed.
If he made the slightest movement, I would pull the trigger.
My finger was on it already. Although I had no practice
with guns, I knew if I fiddled with the trigger the shot
was bound to go off. I had the muzzle directly at his head,
keeping it away, just out of his reach, in case he should
try to snatch it from my hand. I would hold him until the
procession passed our road—and then how was our en-
counter to conclude? I couldn't say. I felt rather worried
about it, although I felt triumphant that there had arisen
such a simple solution to our problems. I couldn't keep
my eyes off him, although I felt curious to watch the procession. From my place I could see the upper parts of it;
the top of the chariot, its flower-decked crest and the little
bulbs sparkling on it, the head of the elephant brilliant
with the gold plates from Talapur, and the hunched form
of the mahout. While passing he cast a look through our
window—I thought he had been advised to drive fast. In
a moment he was out of view, and soon the procession itself
was gone. The room was bereft of the reflections on its
walls, and the drums and pipes sounded far away, leaving
a faint aroma of jasmine and roses in their wake. Just at
this moment I was startled by the alarm bell of the timepiece going off. I gave a jump, the gun dropped from my
hand, and I made a dash for the landing and out of
Vasu's reach within a second.

Chapter Eleven

Life resumed its normal pace on the Market Road next morning, although the day started late. It was as if our town were waking up from a fantasy full of color, glitter, crowd, and song. It was difficult to wake to a dull workaday world. The Market Road was covered with litter, banana peels, coconut shells, leaves, and flowers. Municipal sweepers were busy. Sastri came only at nine o'clock and went straight to the type board; he seemed determined to complete K.J.'s labels today. Muthu and the rest had left by an early bus for their respective places. I sat at my desk and placed a pad and pencil in position in order to make a note of payments to be made, cash in hand, and cash promised. My head was still very unclear about the practical aspects of everything.

Our postman, Thanappa, whom we had seen as children —he was old enough to have retired twice over, but was somehow still in service—was my first visitor of the day. I remembered him from days when postmen were given long coils of a red turban and a shining belt, leather bag, and khaki uniform. He had passed from all that to the latest stage of donning a forage cap—a portly old man who not only knew the addresses of all the citizens in the town but also the ups and downs of their fortunes. He was a timeless being. At his favorite corners he generally spread out his letters and bags and packets and sat down to a full discussion of family and social matters; he served as a live link between several families, carrying information from house to house. All this took time, but nobody could hustle him, and we accepted our letters when they came. He was welcome everywhere; his habit when he came to my press was to stand at the doorway and rest his shoulder on the door post and spend at least half an hour exchanging information with me, and only before leaving would he remember to give me the letter or book package. Today he stood at my doorstep and looked serious, blinking through his inch-thick glasses. There was a frown on his face, and he breathed hard with excitement. He held up a letter without a word. I said, "Come in, Thanappa," and asked, "How did you like the procession last night?" He mumbled something and moved in as if he were in a trance. He placed the letter on my desk. "This receipt has to be signed."

I saw it was addressed to Vasu. "This is for him, Thanappa; take it upstairs."

"I went up, but—but—" He wetted his lips with his tongue. "He is dead." He spoke softly and looked scared. "I usually take his mail to his bed," he explained, "though I hate to go into his room. I thought he was sleeping in his chair. I went up to him with the letter. I almost touched him," he said with a shudder. The man looked desperate with the disgust he felt at the memory of that icy contact.

I said, "Thanappa, go and deliver those letters and try to get this thing out of your mind. I mean it, don't speak about it to anyone. I will go up and see for myself and come back."

Thanappa hesitated for a second and decided to follow my advice. He asked, "So this registered letter goes back? Has no one else authorization to sign for him?" He picked up his bag and stepped out.

I went down the steps, around by the side street and through the yard, and stood for a moment at the foot of the stairs with the hyena moldering in a corner, its glassy stare fixing me. I hesitated for a moment in the desperate hope that I might hear the stirrings of feet above. But there was the unmistakable silence of death. I reluctantly took myself up.

There he was on his canvas chair as I had seen him last night, with his arm dangling at his side. I went near and peered closer to see, absurd notion, if he was really dead. For the moment I was not bothered with the mystery of his death but only with the fact. He had accustomed us so much to a still-life view that he seemed logically to be a part and parcel of his own way of life. The alarm clock which had screeched in the dark was now ticking away modestly. Its pale pink face must have watched the process of Vasu's death.

I looked around. The frame of his bed was smashed; that was probably the reason why he could not sleep there but only on the easy chair. Somehow at that moment I took it very casually and never felt bothered about how he might have met his end. I folded my arms across my chest, remembering that I had better not touch anything and leave a fingerprint. Anyway, Thanappa's fingerprints were bound to be there; why add mine to the confusion and complicate the work of the police? My desire to search for Vasu's purse and read the blue letter in it was really great, but I didn't want to touch his purse and provide a simple solution for the police.

I peered closer to see if there was any injury on him. His black halo of hair was rumpled and dry. His eyes were closed. Inert, inert—I could see no trace of any injury on him. Where is all your bragging, and all your pushing and pulling and argument? Are you in heaven or hell? Would he now be looking at the variegated multitude in heaven or hell and ordering them around? I noticed on a low stool the jute bag containing food which I had seen in Rangi's hand on the previous night at my house. I wanted to see if he had eaten it, but the brass vessel was covered tight and I did not like to give it my thumb impression. His clothes lay, as usual, scattered on his cot and on every available space. The lid of his trunk was half open, revealing his familiar clothes, particularly the red-check bush-shirt and the field-gray jacket he affected when he went out on his depredations. I stood over his trunk and kept looking in; if I could have rummaged in it without touching anything I would have done so. I wished I had gloves on. But this was not a part of the world where gloves were known. Not all my precautions to leave things alone could keep me from giving a jump when I saw the green folder peeping from within the folds of his clothes. What an amount of trouble he had given us over it! He had said, "An orangutan has carried it up a tree and gone back to the jungles. If I see it again, I shall ask it to return it to the rightful owner, namely Mr. Nataraj. I know he will oblige us, he is a very reasonable orang—" and laughed at our desperation. All that I could muster to say was, "We didn't know orangutans existed in India." "You want to teach me wildlife?" he had asked aggressively. That was before our last blow-up and break, after which he walked out of my office and I never saw him again until I swallowed my pride and went up to the attic to plead with him for the elephant. The green folder peeped out of a linen bush-coat and a striped Singapore *lungi*.

I brooded for a moment how to extract it without disturbing the arrangement. I went out to the terrace to see if I could find some handy stick with which to grasp it and pull it out. I became desperate; I realized that I must hurry now. The voices of people in the street frightened me. I was afraid that Sastri might suddenly come up and scream for the police. It was essential that I should take charge of that green folder before anyone else saw it here. I fervently hoped that Thanappa had the sense to keep his mouth shut. The alum solution, molds, and various odds and ends of nails were there, but not a cleft stick with which I could pry that green folder out. I thrust my hand under my shirt, worked my fingers through my shirt tail, and gently tugged the folder out of his clothes. A couple of angry mosquitoes buzzed around my ears, but I could not wave them away, as my hands were engaged. Now I had the folder in my hand. This would solve, more than the mystery of his death, the mystery of the funds for our festivities. I could give the poet an account of the monies collected on his behalf, though perhaps not the cash. I hurriedly opened the folder and looked in; the papers were intact, the printed appeal and a list of the donors and the receipt book; but cash? Not much to be seen, except a small bundle of one-rupee currency notes. I tucked it under my arm and was leaving when I caught sight of the tiger cub covered over with a handkerchief on the small table. He had valued it at about two thousand rupees. I seized it with the covering and quietly went down, leaving the door ajar. I passed into the side street; the cub, his masterpiece, was small enough to be hidden under my arms along with the file. A couple of pedestrians were passing by. I walked bravely with my articles, dreading lest someone should be in my office waiting for me. Luckily there was no one. I quickly opened the roll-top, pushed the tiger cub and the file in, and locked it.

My office became an extension of the town police station. The District Superintendent of Police set himself up in the Queen Anne chair. They had found the grille I had put up between the treadle and the staircase irksome, as it made them go round every time by the side street. It was unlocked, and the place was thrown open for the entire city to walk about in. All kinds of persons were passing in and out, going upstairs and coming downstairs. It became so crowded that I found it impossible to do any work in the press, and Sastri had no space to stand in and set his types. The sanctity of the blue curtain was destroyed, gone forever. Anyone could push it aside and go up; I dared not ask who he was; he might be anybody, a plain-clothes police officer, the Coroner's Committee man (there was a body of five to find out and declare the cause of Vasu's death), newspaper correspondents, hangers-on, or the thin-legged policeman sent up for sentry duty on the attic landing to watch that no one tampered with any evidence. Vasu dead proved a greater nuisance than Vasu alive. Anyone who had had anything to do with me for the past six weeks was summoned to my press by the police. Muthu was there, away from his tea-shop; the poet was there; the journalist of course was there, the elephant doctor and the tailor (who was bewailing all along that he had promised clothes for a wedding and should be back at his sewing machine). A police van had gone up and brought all these persons here.

Sastri proved to be the shrewdest of all. The minute he heard of the corpse upstairs he planned his retreat. He hesitated for a moment, smiled to himself, and remarked, "I knew he would come to some such end, these people cannot die normally." He had been preparing to work on fruit-juice labels. He just put the job away, wiped his hands on a rag, and took off his apron; I watched him silently. He went through his process of retreat methodically, pulling off his colors first as it seemed to me. He laid them carefully aside and said, "These things happen only in the expected manner. Only I didn't think it would happen so soon and here. What a worry now! Our press has had such an untarnished reputation all through." He sighed and remained silent as if I were responsible for the bad reputation. Confirming this hint, he said broadly, for the hundredth time within the last few months, "On the very first day he came here you should have turned him out. You didn't."

I asked, "What's your plan now?"

"I am going home and then catching the afternoon train for Karaikudi. I have to attend my wife's niece's marriage. . . ."

"You never told me about it!" I said in surprised anger.

"I am telling you now," said the imperturbable Sastri. "You were so busy the whole of yesterday that I couldn't get a word with you." He pulled out a yellow wedding invitation and showed it to me as evidence.

"When will you be back?" I asked.

"Well, as soon as the marriage is over," he said, preparing to move. "Our train leaves at one o'clock."

"The police may want you here," I said viciously.

"I have nothing to do with Vasu or the police," he said with a clarity of logic rare under the stress of the present circumstances. It was true. This man had resolutely kept away from contacts with Vasu. While all of us were running around him, Sastri alone had maintained a haughty aloofness. No one could ever associate him with Vasu. I had no authority over Sastri now. I could not stop him. He went out by the back door to Kabir Street. At the doorway he paused to say, "Anyway, what's the use of my staying here? There's no room for doing any work here." With that he was off.

As I said, all my friends were there as if we were assembled for a group photo. Rangi—I forgot Rangi—after the night's endless gesticulation and swaying before the God, looked jaded in a dull sari, with unkempt hair. She stood in a corner and would not sit down before so many. The lean man, the Town Inspector, was among those that had to be provided a seat. The D.S.P. from his seat of honor kept glancing around at us. He had demanded a table and I had to request my neighbor of Heidelberg to spare me a table from his office. He was only too willing to do anything. He looked overawed by the whole business, with a murder at such close quarters. He gave me a teak table on which the burly D.S.P. heaped a lot of brown paper, drew it up before the Queen Anne chair, and began to write all that we said. To this day I do not understand why he wanted to hold the inquiry in my office rather than assemble us at the police station. Perhaps they wanted to hold us until the body was removed to the mortuary, which was a small tin shed at a corner of the compound of the District Hospital. Under this hot tin roof there was a long stone table on which Vasu would be laid. I was depressed to think that a man who had twisted iron rods and brought down three-inch panel doors with his fist was going to do nothing more than lie still and wait for the doctor to cut him and examine his insides to find out what had caused his death.

At the mortuary the wise men, five in number, had stood around the stone-topped table, read the report of the pathologist, and declared: "Mr. Vasu of Junagadh died of a concussion received on the frontal bone at the right temple, delivered by a blunt instrument. Although there is no visible external injury to the part, the inner skull covering is severely injured and has resulted in the fatality." In addition to this they had also taken out his stomach contents and sent them to Madras Institute to be examined for poisoning. The wise men reserved their final verdict until they should have the report from Madras. Meanwhile, pending the final disposal of the issue, they ordered the burial of the body according to Hindu rites in order to facilitate exhumation at a later stage if necessary. At this, one of the five assembled demurred. "How can we be sure that the deceased would not have preferred to be cremated?" Since there was no way of ascertaining the wishes of the person concerned, they hesitated for a moment, and the foreman of the five said, as if at a sudden revelation, "We shall have no objection to the final disposal in the form of cremation. The present step is only an interim arrangement until we are able to ascertain with certainty the causes of the death of aforesaid Vasu." Everyone grabbed this sentence as a way out.

Assembled at my press, they desperately tried to investigate the origin of the brass food container found in Vasu's room. They kept looking round and asking, "Can anyone throw light on who brought this vessel? Can anyone say to whom it belongs?" They turned the vessel round in their hands, looking at it closely for any signature of ownership. They failed. I could see Rangi squirming in her corner, twisting and untwisting the end of her sari. She kept throwing glances in my direction and fidgeting; if the police officer had not been so hectically busy writing, bent over his papers, he might easily have declared, "I charge you with being the owner of this brass utensil," and led her off to the police lock-up. When I opened my mouth to say something she almost swooned with suspense. But I merely remarked from my eminent seat on the edge of my desk, "I often noticed his food coming to him in that vessel."

"Where was he getting his food from?" An excellent chance to make the nearest restaurant busy defending its innocence. I thought over the name of any restaurant that I might mention. What about the Royal Hindu Restaurant, that man who used to be my customer once and had walked out after creating a scene over a slight delay in the delivery of his printed stationery? I dismissed it as an unworthy thought, and so I said, "Really, no idea. The deceased must have been getting his food from various quarters." I spoke breezily. The Superintendent looked up, coldly, as if to say, "Don't talk more than necessary." But I was in my own place and no one had any right to ask me to shut up. I added, "It does not seem as if its lid had been opened." The Superintendent made a note of this also, and handed the vessel around for inspection to the committee. They all examined and said, "Yes, the lid does not seem to have been opened." The Superintendent made a note and asked, "Shall we open this to see if it has been touched?" "Yes," "Yes," "Yes," "Yes," "Yes." He took a statement from the five to say that the lid had been opened in their presence.

They watched with anxious concentration as the lid was pried off. It was placed on the table. The smell of stale food hit the ceiling—a strong-smelling, overspiced chicken *pulav*, brown and unattractive and stuffed up to the lid. Everyone peered in, holding his nose. "It was not touched." The verdict was unanimous. "Shall a sample be sent to Madras?" "No." "Shall we throw this food away?" "No." "What should be done with this?" "Keep it till the report from Madras is received. If there is suspected poisoning this food may be analyzed."

The Superintendent wrote this down and took their signatures under it. He passed the container for sealing in his presence, which was accomplished by an orderly waiting at his side, and then the five men appended their initials on the brown paper wrapped around it. The D.S.P. worked like an impersonal machine. He did not want to assume any personal responsibility for any step and he did not want to omit any possible line of investigation, always laying the responsibility on the five wise men chosen for the purpose. If they had said, "Put this Nataraj in a sack and seal him up, we may need him in that state for further investigations," he would have unhesitatingly obeyed them. Sealing up was the order of the day. Vasu's room was sealed, the food container was sealed, and every conceivable article around had been sealed.

The Superintendent's writing went on far into the night; he must have written several thousand words. Each one assembled there had to say when he saw Vasu last, why, and what were that worthy man's last words. While Rangi totally denied having seen him last evening, the others were not in such a lucky position, the whole lot of them having gone there in a body after seeing the Superintendent. They gave a sustained account of what he said to them. It was computed that he must have died at about eleven in the night, and where was I at eleven in the night?—at home sleeping on the *pyol* after seeing my wife off to the temple. My wife was brought in by the back door to corroborate this timing. My son also gave evidence for me. Fortunately no one knew of my last visit to the attic. I bore in mind, like a nail hammered in, our adjournment lawyer's dictum, "Don't say more than you are asked for."

The only satisfaction that I felt here was that our Town Inspector was treated as one of us, made to sit in our group and answer questions before the committee. Normally they should have let him handle the investigation, but the situation was now different; he was also one of us, an aggrieved party. His arm was in a sling and his wrist was encased in a plaster cast, having suffered a slight fracture. He had to clear himself first—a most awkward thing. When his turn came to make a statement, he began bombastically, "I had been ordered to supervise the peace and security arrangements on the Market Road on —— at ——, when I had a call at the control room from our District Superintendent of Police ordering me further to investigate a complaint of threat to the safety of the crowd from one

Mr. Vasu of Junagadh. When I went up to question the said person and take charge of his licensed weapon, he assumed a threatening attitude and actually assaulted the officer on duty, causing a grave injury." He held up the bandaged part of himself as an exhibit. And then, according to him, he went away to take all reasonable precautions for the peaceful conduct of the procession. He had intended to file a complaint as soon as they were free in the morning, and proceed against the said person officially for assaulting an officer on duty. He failed to mention that he had told Vasu before leaving, "I will get you for it."

Muthu and I discussed it later, when the incident was officially closed. If anyone had breathed a word more, it might have complicated the Inspector's version and placed him definitely on the defensive. But everyone was considerate. Still, the Inspector had to prove where he was at the time of Vasu's death, which occurred two hours after his visit. He explained that he had left the security arrangements in the hands of his assistant while he went in the police car to the District Superintendent's residence to report to him, and then to the District Headquarters Hospital to secure medical attention. He could cite both the District Superintendent of Police and the medical officer on duty at the casualty section as witnesses. But still Muthu felt, as he confessed later, "What prevented the man from sending someone to do the job? They might have gone in numbers and overpowered the man. I don't say it is wrong, but they might have done it, and hit his skull with a blunt instrument."

During the following days the air became thick with suspicion. Each confided to the other when the third was

out of earshot. Sen, who walked down the road with me
for a breath of fresh air after the police left us, said,
"That tea-shop man Muthu—I have my own doubts.
People in rural areas are habitually vindictive and might
do anything. How many murders are committed in those
areas! I won't say in this instance it was wrong. Someone
has actually done a public service. I wouldn't blame anyone."

"What should be Muthu's interest in murdering Vasu?"

"Don't forget that the elephant was his and that he was
anxious to save its life at any cost. He could have just
sneaked up. Where was he at eleven o'clock?" He cast his
mind back to find out if Muthu had by any chance slipped
away from the procession. He gave it up, as they had been
too much engrossed in the procession and failed to note
each other's movements.

The poet came up to me three days later, all alone. "I
was with Sen this afternoon in his house in New Extension,
and do you know I noticed in a corner of his room, amidst
old paper, a blunt thing—a long iron bolt which they use
on railway sleepers. He looked embarrassed when I asked
why he had it. Easiest thing for him to have slipped upstairs and gone up from behind. . . . I wouldn't blame
him. He had stood enough insults from that man. I knew
that Sen would do something terrible sooner or later. . . .
I wouldn't blame him."

I knew that when I was not there they were unanimous
in suspecting me. I could almost hear what they would be
saying about me. "Never knew he could go so far, but,
poor fellow, he had stood enough from him, having made
the original blunder of showing him hospitality. Whether
he took him in as a tenant or just as a friend, who can say?

Who will let his house, free of rent, to another nowadays? Whatever it may be, it is none of our business why he gave him his attic; but how that man tortured poor Nataraj! Poor man, his patience was strained. Deft work, eh? What do you say? Smashed his vital nerve in the brain without drawing a drop of blood! Never knew Nataraj could employ his hand so effectively! Hee, hee!"

My wife said the same thing to me that night when I went home. Our friendly relations had resumed since the moment she heard that there was a dead body in the press and that the police had assembled in my office. Since the Rangi episode, the first word uttered between us was my urgent invitation to her to come and say where she had seen me at eleven o'clock on the previous night. She hesitated, wrung her hands in fear and despair. "Oh, why should you have got mixed in all this affair? Couldn't you have minded your own business like a hundred others?" I was very humbled now, and very pleased that at least over Vasu's dead body we were shaking hands again. I had been gnawed by a secret fear that we might never resume friendly relations again and that all was over with us. She rubbed it in now. "That woman, and all sorts of persons, what was your business with them really?"

I had no satisfactory answer for her, so I said, "I have no time to explain all that now, the D.S.P. is waiting, you will have to come and say where I was last night at eleven o'clock."

"How could I know?" she asked. "I will tell him that I didn't see you."

"Yes, say that and see me hanged, and then you will probably be able to collect some handsome insurance on my life."

She screamed and covered her ears; the suggestion of widowhood depressed and upset her.

"You could also say how you deserted me on the *pyol* to guard the house and went out. It will do you good to speak the truth—and if you remember your visit to the temple, you will probably also remember having seen Rangi there, so that you might not be tempted to say that I had gone out with her."

"I didn't see her at the temple," said my wife simply. She had got out of her rotten suspicious mood of yesterday but had not decided to let go of it entirely.

I said, "While we are bantering here, the police—"

"Why should they believe what I say? Would they not think that you have tutored me?"

"Oh, it is only a formality, it is not that they are analyzing evidence of any sort. Don't be silly. They will record whatever you say or I say or anyone says, and that is all that they want—at this stage, so you had better come along." She was very nervous about coming before the Superintendent and she would not hear of the police coming in and recording her statement at home. "After all these years of honest and reputable living," she said, "we don't want the police to be marching in and out. Even in the worst days of partition of property no one dreamt of asking the police to come, and we don't want to do that now." She preferred to walk across the street when the neighbors were not looking and slip into my press by the back door and face the police.

That night I went home at eleven o'clock. Babu had gone to sleep. My wife said, "Hush, speak gently. Babu wouldn't sleep. He was too excited about everything. I managed to send him to sleep by saying that it is all false and so forth. But he is terribly excited about everything, and—and feels proud that you have killed a *rakshasa* single-handed! At least you have Babu to admire you."

"For God's sake don't let him spread that sort of talk. The noose may come round my neck."

She sighed deeply and said, "A lot of people are saying that. After that rent-control case . . ."

"Oh, shut up," I cried impatiently. "What nonsense is this!"

"You may close the mouth of an oven, but how can you close the mouth of a town?" she said, quoting a proverb.

I saw myself as others saw me and felt a revulsion for the picture.

Chapter Twelve

At first I resented the idea of being thought of as a murderer. Gradually it began to look not so improbable. Why not? It had been an evening of strange lapses. I could not remember what I had said or done to bring on all the fuss around me that evening at the temple hall. Later it was quite possible that I had battered someone's skull and remembered nothing of it. Going over my own actions step by step, I remembered that I had gone up the staircase stealthily, opened the door on the landing. So far it was clear. The procession was in the street below. Vasu was lying in a long chair beside the window. I had crawled toward his gun and run out when the alarm clock screamed. Between my entrance and exit I remembered holding the gun at Vasu's head until the lights of the procession vanished. Perhaps while he slept I had rammed the butt of the gun into his skull. Who could say? But what about the time of his death? The corpse doctor had declared that the man must have died at eleven in the night, long before I had sneaked up the attic stairs. After all, the doctor might have hazarded a guess, one more item in a long list of conjectures!

I had clung to a hope that Rangi might have poisoned Vasu and then smashed his head, but the chemical exami-

ner at Madras reported, "No trace of poisoning." With
that the last trace of hope for myself was also gone. While
I sat in my press all alone I caught myself reconstructing
again and again that midnight visit to the attic, trying to
gain a clear picture of the whole scene, but each time I
found it more confounding. When people passing Market
Road looked at me, I averted my head. I knew what they
would be saying: "There he sits. He ought really to be
hanged for murder." My friends of Mempi village never
came near me again. They had had enough trouble with
police and everything for the sin of knowing me and visiting my press. That press! Lord Shiva!! Accursed spot,
keep away from it.

There was not a soul with whom I could discuss the
question. Sen avoided me. The poet was not to be seen.
He took another route to the Municipal School. During
my morning trip to the river and back no one stopped to
have a word with me. The adjournment lawyer and the
rest hurried on when they saw me at a distance. Still one
morning I accosted the adjournment lawyer at the bend of
the street where the barber's house abutted. He pretended
not to see me and tried to pass. "Sir," I cried, stepping in
front of him. He was flurried. "Ah, Nataraj! Didn't
notice—I was thinking of something. . . ."

"I want to ask you—" I began.

"What about? What about?" he asked feverishly. "You
see I am out of touch with criminal practice. You should
really consult—"

"Consult? For what purpose? I have no problems."

"Oh, yes, yes, I know," he cried, fidgeting uneasily.
"I remember that they left an open verdict, nothing was
imputed or proved. After all, who can be sure?"

"Oh, forget it," I said with the casual ease of a seasoned homicide. "It is not that. I am more worried about the collection of dues from my customers. When did you celebrate your daughter's marriage? Months ago! Why don't you pay my charges for printing those invitation cards? What are you waiting for?"

"Oh, yes, by all means," he said, edging away.

"I have no one in the press to help me. Even Sastri has left me. You had better send the cash along instead of waiting for me to send someone to collect it." A touch of aggression was creeping into my speech nowadays. My line of thinking was: So be it. If I have rid the world of Vasu, I have achieved something. If people want to remain squeamish, they are welcome to be so, but let no one expect me to be apologetic for what I have done. I was hardening myself with such reflections, and suffering at the same time. The press was silent. I kept my office open at the usual hours. Visitors were few. I spent my time attempting to read Tolstoi's *War and Peace* (discovered among the seventy terse philosophical volumes in the family lumber room) and diverted myself by following the complex fortunes of Russian nobility on the battlefields of ancient Europe.

I caught sight of the poet one morning beyond the fountain. Before he could detour and take another route to his school I ran forward and blocked his way. I implored him to come into the press and seated him in the Queen Anne.

"What has happened to you all?" I asked.

"They have added eight more hours of work every week for me, with so many teachers absent!"

Ah, innocent poet! What clumsy guile you have cultivated within these few weeks! I asked, "What about Sen?"

"I don't know; he was expecting a call from a Madras paper."

"Don't lie!" I cried, suddenly losing my temper. "Haven't I seen him sneaking in next door to get some work done on Heidelberg? You people are avoiding me. You think I am a murderer."

He remained silent. I checked myself when I noticed the terror in his eyes. He glanced anxiously over his shoulder at the doorway. He noticed the glint of a maniac in my eyes. I wanted to speak to him about the accounts entombed in the green folder, about the monies collected on his behalf and spent away by Vasu, and I wanted to explain to him about the tiger cub I had seized. But all that I could produce was a shout of abuse at the world in general. I realized that I was frightening the poet. I modified my tone to a soft whisper, smiled, and patted his back. I said, "I want to give you a present for all the money collected for your benefit. Something in kind, something salvaged." I fixed him with a look lest he should try to escape, flicked open the roll-top desk, and brought out the stuffed tiger cub. I pulled off the kerchief covering it and held it to him. He looked transfixed.

"Tiger! What for?"

"It is yours—take it," I said. "*He* valued it at two thousand. Something at least . . ."

He reared his head back and gazed on me as if noticing in my eyes for the first time unplumbed depths of lunacy. He pleaded desperately, "No, I don't want it. I don't need it. I do not want anything. Thanks. T. . .h. . .a. . .n. . .k. . .s." He suddenly shot out of Queen Anne, dashed out, and was soon lost in the crowd.

"Poet! Poet!" I cried feebly. In addition to being a murderer, perhaps he thought I had embezzled his funds too and was playing a prank on him now. This was the **greatest act of destruction** that the Man-Eater had performed, destroying my name, my friendships, and my world. This thought was too much for me. Hugging the tiger cub, I burst into tears.

While I was in this state Sastri parted the curtains and entered. "I came by the back door," he explained briefly.

"Ah, Sastri!" I cried in sheer joy. "I thought you would never come back."

He was businesslike, completely turning a blind eye on my emotional condition. "After the marriage at Karaikudi, my wife insisted on going on a pilgrimage to Rameshwaram. And to a dozen other places. A couple of children fell ill on the way. I was fretting all along to get back, but you know how our women are! Sickness or otherwise, my wife insisted on visiting every holy place she had heard of in her life. After all, we were telling ourselves, we get a chance to travel only once in a while. . . ."

"You could have dropped me a postcard."

"True," he said, "but when one is traveling it is impossible to sit down and compose a letter, and the idea gets postponed. . . ." He took out of his pocket a tiny packet containing a pinch of sacred ash and vermilion and held it to me with, "Offerings from all the temples mixed together." I daubed the holy dust on my forehead.

He noticed the tiger cub on my lap and said, "Ah, what a tiny tiger!" as if humoring a child. His silver-rimmed spectacles wobbled, and his face was slightly flushed. I knew he was shuddering at the sight of the stuffed animal; still he pretended to be interested in it and stretched out his hand as if to touch it. He was trying to please me. He said, "Must have been a pretty baby in the forest, but what a monster it becomes when it grows up! . . . Did *he* give it to you?" he asked after a pause.

I couldn't explain that I had stolen it from the dead man. "I meant to give it to the poet," I said, "but he went away, spurned it and went away." I was on the point of breaking down at the thought. "He may not come again."

"It is natural that a poet should feel scared of a tiger. In any case, what could he do with it?"

"He may never come this way again."

"So much the better for us. Anyone who refuses to come here and waste our time must be viewed as our well-wisher. K.J. is our customer, and you may be sure he will always come to us."

"Naturally. Where can he get the magenta even if he wants to leave us?"

"People who have business with us will always come and keep coming."

"Everyone thinks that this is a murderer's press," I said gloomily.

He gently laughed at the notion and said, "They are fools who think so, but sooner or later even they will know the truth."

"Pray, what truth?" I asked.

"Rangi was with him when he died. You know I am on the temple committee," began Sastri, "and she came to see me on business last evening. I had a feeling all along that she was hiding some information. I refused to listen to her problem last evening unless she told me the truth. Much against my principles, I called her inside the house, seated her on a mat, gave her coffee and betel leaves to

chew, and induced her to speak. My wife understood why
I was asking this woman in, and treated her handsomely
on the whole."

"What did Rangi say?" I asked impatiently.

"It seems that evening she carried a hamper of food to
him. He refused to eat the food, being in a rage over many
things. Rangi had perhaps mixed some sleeping drug with
the food, and hoped that he would be in a stupor when the
procession passed under his window. That was her ruse
for saving the elephant that night. But the man would not
touch the food!"

"He might not have felt hungry," I said, remembering
the eatables that I had plied him with earlier that day.

"It might be so, but it embarrassed the woman because
she had duties at the temple that night. She was really
bothered how she was going to get out of the place. When
he understood that the procession might start late, he set
the alarm clock and laid himself in his easy chair. He drew
another chair beside his and commanded the woman to sit
down with a fan in hand and keep off the mosquitoes from
him. He hated mosquitoes, from what the woman tells me.
He cursed the police for their intrusion, which made him
break his cot-frame to show off his prowess, compelling
him now to stretch himself in an easy chair instead of
sleeping in his cot protected by mosquito net. Armed with
the fan, the woman kept away the mosquitoes. He dozed
off. After a little time she dozed off too, having had a
fatiguing day, as you know, and the fanning must have
ceased; during this pause the mosquitoes returned in a
battalion for a fresh attack. Rangi was awakened by the
man yelling, 'Damn these mosquitoes!' She saw him flourish his arms like a madman, fighting them off as they

buzzed about his ears clamoring to suck his blood. Next minute she heard a sharp noise like a thunderclap. The man had evidently trapped a couple of mosquitoes settled on his forehead by bringing down the flat of his palm with all his might on them. The woman switched on the light and saw two mosquitoes plastered on his brow. It was also the end of Vasu," concluded Sastri, and added, "That fist was meant to batter thick panels of teak and iron. . . ."

"He had one virtue, he never hit anyone with his hand, whatever the provocation," I said, remembering his voice.

"Because," said Sastri puckishly, "he had to conserve all that might for his own destruction. Every demon appears in the world with a special boon of indestructibility. Yet the universe has survived all the *rakshasas* that were ever born. Every demon carries within him, unknown to himself, a tiny seed of self-destruction, and goes up in thin air at a most unexpected moment. Otherwise what is to happen to humanity?" He narrated again for my benefit the story of Bhasmasura the unconquerable, who scorched everything he touched and finally reduced himself to ashes by placing his fingers on his own head.

Sastri stood brooding for a moment and turned to go. He held an edge of the curtain, but before vanishing behind it said, "We must deliver K.J.'s labels at least this week. I will set up everything. If you will print the first color . . ."

"When you are gone for lunch it will be drying, and ready for second printing when you return. Yes, Sastri, I am at your service," I said.

FC 75

PRINTED IN U.S.A.